The Star
and the Cross

by

Evelyn Turner

The Star and the Cross

Cover Art by *Angela Anderson*

The Wild Rose Press, Inc.
PO Box 708
Adams Basin, NY 14410-0708
Visit us at www.thewildrosepress.com

Publishing History
First Mainstream Historical Rose Edition, 2017
Print ISBN 978-1-5092-1129-6
Digital ISBN 978-1-5092-1130-2

Published in the United States of America

Nicholas reacted quickly, pulling Katarina down an alleyway and climbing over debris from fallen buildings. A volley of bullets whistled by them, and others in the street ducked for cover. Katarina screamed as another round erupted and Nicholas was hit.

Finally the pain was too much, and he had to stop.

"Katarina, go! I'll keep them from following you." Nicholas's breath was already coming in large gulps.

"No, please, I can't leave you! Lean on me. We can do this." Determined, she ducked her head under his shoulder and slung one of his arms over her own shoulders.

Nicholas spotted the back door of a bakery. "There!" he shouted, and they lurched together toward the door. The sound of Gestapo boots closed in, but the door would not budge. Nicholas gasped in pain as he cocked his pistol and took aim. One of the pursuing Nazis fell. Then from the corner of his eye, Nicholas saw Katarina slump beside him. Instantly blood began seeping through her dress. Now ignoring his own distress, he braced Katarina to keep her from landing on the pavement. He had no choice but to abandon the shooting and seek another alley. Grunting with every step, he dragged Katarina to safety. The sound of guns dissipated behind them. Nicholas collapsed against the stub of what had once been a brick wall and turned Katarina to face him.

Praise for *THE STAR AND THE CROSS*

"Evelyn Turner's relentlessly gripping story of a German Catholic family's heroic and costly resistance to the Nazis and the Holocaust brings a stunning inside-the-nightmare revelation to our knowledge and perceptions of WWII. This rare personal and historic account becomes even more powerful with the knowledge that opposition to the Reich for the fictional Von Rahmels is based on Turner's painstaking research into her own extended family, including the tragedy of her famous prima ballerina mother….Difficult to put down, impossible to forget, *THE STAR AND THE CROSS* offers original, tragic, and inspiring insights into the choices and consequences of one of the world's most desperate battles against extraordinary evil."

~Rod Davis, award-winning journalist, editor, author of novels South, America *and* Corina's Way, *and the nonfiction study* American Voudou

~*~

"*THE STAR AND THE CROSS* is one of the most significant, most deeply telling narratives to emerge from World War II since *The Diary of Anne Frank*. The story's profound power comes from its authenticity. This is fact thinly-disguised as fiction at the behest of a reluctant family member, an essential, never-before-seen glimpse into the horrors and heroics of that conflict."

~Sarah Bird, author of Yokota Officers Club, Above the East China Sea*; 2016 Texas Institute of Letters Lifetime Achievement Award; 2015 Meryl Streep Screenwriting Award*

Dedication

To Captain Loyd Turner,
pilot and my late husband extraordinaire

Acknowledgements

Thanks to Chappell, who first told me to write, as he witnessed where those memories were hidden.

To Pollingers, Neals, Brights, my gratitude for always having my back, and who saw and heard from their visits with me to Berlin; they witnessed the stories.

To Travis, who helped so many times with computer work, and Jim Hamnet with legal work.

Rod Davies and Sarah Byrd gave me the last push to publish, as did Angela Courtin, Media genius and a person of generous heart; Greg, screenwriter for this book; and Angela's dad, Phil. Thanks for encouragement also from Nan Swanson, a great editor, and to The Wild Rose Press, Inc.

Thanks also to DiFonzo's, the best in life, to Shawn and the girls, to my family in Europe, especially my sister in Berlin. Also to Texas friends Brights, Littletons, Hostetler, Walkers, Ada, Fran, Christine, Father Kelly, Gail S, John G, Fran, Robert C, Verna, and my girls Katie, Lauren, Monica, Sarah, and Esther, and my other Sarah, in Utah, also to Robin and to the Hudspeths.

To all twelve million souls and to those who have lived with the memories and sorrow—we shall never forget their stories.

To the aftermath for those who are living.

Prologue

My greatest fear had come to pass. My mother was dead, and I felt like I hardly knew her. She had darted in and out of my life since I was very young, and I never knew what she was running from or what terrors made her scream in the night she hated so much. I festered over why my mother didn't want to be with me the way other mothers wanted to be with their children. She kept my brother with her; why was it so easy to leave me? Why was it so easy to leave any of her children?

My German grandparents took care of me, though as soon as I was old enough they sent me to Catholic boarding school. When I was grown, I visited them in Germany as much as possible. While I knew they loved me, it was not the same as knowing my mother loved me. I like to think she wanted to love me, even if she couldn't. I like to think she tried to be with me, even if she couldn't. I like to think she regretted not being in my life. Now that she had passed, how would I ever know?

I suppose when I was young my grandparents thought they were protecting me. I wish they hadn't. Secrets, lies—such things always surface later. As my mother said many years ago, it's the stars she looked at every night that never changed regardless of where she was, but the cross would be her salvation. Yet I came to the conclusion it was the star that was the cross of our lives.

Maybe it was protection. How can anyone know what they would do in the same circumstances? But when my mother died, it was time for the truth. My grandparents finally told me what my mother had never wanted me to know, what I had never imagined could possibly be true.

After many years of research, this book sat for more years on a shelf, till I married and my husband found it. With his encouragement, we put it in the computer, but then many more years went by before we dared to put it out to the world. I had family who didn't want to talk about what had happened or were still heartbroken over events, whereas I was always trying to understand. It was my husband who told me over and over again, "You did not walk in her shoes." I just hoped, when we found out about her death in 1998, that she took her last breath with peace and not fear.

This is the story that helped me understand. This is the story that helped me forgive.

Chapter 1

Berlin, Germany: May 1943

Father Anthony Von Rahmel glided cautiously but quickly through the streets and alleys of Berlin, his friend Simon Miller at his side. If they were stopped, it would be difficult to explain where they had been, but they needed desperately to get to the relative safety of their homes. They were almost to Simon's. As they approached the end of an alley that led to the Lutheran church he pastored, Simon surged ahead. Only last week Anthony had helped Simon with repairs around his bomb-damaged building, but clearly the rebuilding would have to wait till the end of the war, which they hoped would be soon.

A sleek black car seemed to roar out of nowhere. It screeched to a halt, and two SS officers sprang out and demanded to see Simon's papers.

It would only make matters worse if the SS men knew there were two of them, so Anthony held his breath and pressed into the wall, his heart pounding in the shadows.

"Gentlemen, I am searching for my dog," Simon said casually as he offered his papers. "He ran off during the last air raid, and I'm afraid he will not be able to find his way home."

"What do you do, old man?" demanded one

officer.

"I'm a Lutheran minister," Simon answered. He gestured to the building with a hole in one wall. "This is my church, and I live in the back."

Whether the answer satisfied was irrelevant. One of the Nazis struck Simon in the stomach. As Simon stumbled to his knees, the other officer thrust his papers in his face.

"You may go," the officer barked.

At the wall, Anthony dared to let out his breath. Simon was not badly hurt—he was already on his feet again—and in a few seconds the men would be gone.

"Halt!" Without warning, one of the officers brandished his weapon.

He fired, as Anthony watched in horror. Simon whimpered, grabbing his gut. "Maybe next time he will remember to Heil Hitler," one agent joked.

"What does it matter?" the other responded. "These ministers and priests fight Hitler every inch of the way. We don't need them."

The agents climbed into the car, and the driver backed it up toward Simon, who was barely still alive. Clearly they intended to run over him. Anthony leaped into the street and rushed toward his friend. His hand gripped a weapon of his own. When he fired, his first shot was surprisingly on target, considering his lack of practice in the last few years. He'd given up all weapons when he decided on the priesthood, but during his childhood he'd gone hunting with his father and brothers. Now those earlier times stood him in good stead; blood from one of the agents instantly splattered the window. Anthony fired until his gun was empty and the second agent's mouth twisted in pain. The car went out of control, crashed, and exploded.

That was not Anthony's concern. Simon was. He heaved his friend over his shoulder and stumbled down the street toward Simon's home. Blood flowed freely. By the time Anthony laid Simon down inside the safety of the walls, there was not much to be done. Simon reached for Anthony's frantic hand and struggled to speak.

"Too late. Too late," he whispered.

"Shh. Don't try to talk." Anthony frantically scanned the room for anything he could use to stem the flow of blood.

"It's all right," Simon gasped. "I'm going to meet God." A sob escaped Anthony's mouth. "Simon!"

Simon opened his mouth once more, but all that emerged from his lips was a long, deep rattle. He closed his eyes and was gone.

Anthony buried his friend in the small cemetery behind the Lutheran church. As the last shovel of dirt spread over the grave, Anthony gave in to his personal horror. He had killed. He was a Catholic priest, and he had willingly, purposefully, intentionally killed. Anthony was enough of a theologian to know he should be feeling remorse, guilt, even repentance. But he felt none of that. In the distance, bombs assaulted the city once again. Standing in the dark, Anthony's thoughts wandered back to the start of the path that had led to this moment. He had buried another friend on that day.

****

Warsaw, Poland: September 1, 1939

Father Anthony stepped off the train and peered into the glare of the sun, scanning the scene for his friend, Father Joseph Valochovic. Joseph's ancient black car finally came into focus, with the old priest gripping the wheel. Anthony took easy strides to where it was parked and settled himself in the familiar, dilapidated interior. The two men grinned at each other. Joseph looked frail. He had lost weight since Anthony last saw him, and his hair was sparser and whiter. He seemed somehow shrunken behind the steering wheel. But his eyes still sparkled blue, just as Anthony remembered. Father Joseph started the engine—which sounded reluctant, but complied—and drove the car a few blocks to the rectory. The gorgeous day was too irresistible not to spend part of it outside. The two priests, one Polish and one German, sat side by side on a park bench to watch children play on the grassy slope nearby. Here they could talk about their business while looking quite ordinary, and they could bask in friendship as well as the sun.

Anthony had admired Joseph since his earliest days in the seminary, when as his teacher and counselor Father Joseph had punished him for those small infractions a young man will commit when he is away from home for the first time. They had maintained a close friendship through the years.

"I want you to meet a rabbi while you're here," Joseph said. "Rabbi Thomas." Anthony knew Joseph would have a good reason to ask a Catholic priest to meet a Jewish rabbi, so he waited for elaboration.

"Rabbi Thomas has information about the plans Hitler has for the Jews," Joseph explained. "You need to hear what he has to say."

"But I am German," Anthony protested. "It is my country that has started this hate and blame against the Jews, and Hitler speaks unkindly of Poland, too."

Joseph shrugged. "The rabbi understands that what he has seen in Germany while visiting does not mean that all Germans hate Jews, but it makes him ponder the fate of his people and wonder why they were all being sent to work camps if they could not find passage out of Germany. You must speak to him. I've already told him you were coming today."

A hum in the sky gave them pause, and they instinctively lifted their eyes. The hum soon swelled to a roar, and a German Stuka burst on the horizon. Its gray bulk rapidly filled the sky, and the famous dive bomber raked the ground with artillery. Father Joseph, though older and frail, threw Anthony to the ground and covered him with his own body. Shrieks of the injured and dying tormented Anthony's ears as the ammunition sprayed around them unrelentingly.

Something warm seeped into Anthony's eyes and mouth. A moment later he gagged on the sweet, metallic taste of blood. The sky was silent now, and around him people stirred cautiously. Father Joseph, however, was not moving. Gagging on blood and grief, Anthony gently rolled the old priest off. Joseph's sightless eyes stared at the now empty sky. With tears streaming freely down his face, Anthony gathered his friend in his arms.

The scene around him quickly launched into chaos. Screaming frantic people ran in all directions searching for loved ones and scrambling for shelter. The Stukas were sure to return to the vulnerable scene. Anthony carried Joseph's thin body to the rectory and found shelter in a cellar. As the groan of the Stukas returned, Anthony clutched his friend's body and waited out the next round. He whispered the comforting words of last rites for Father Joseph Valochovic, whose valiant life had come to an end on a spectacular, unsuspecting day.

Anthony did not know how long he huddled in the cellar—long after the skies fell silent again and the city erupted around him. At last he forced himself outside to the garden to bury his friend next to the roses he had loved. Father Joseph's crucifix caught the sunlight as Anthony laid him in the grave. There had been no time for a coffin, but Anthony placed his friend's Bible with him, with a rose marking the passage he had last read.

The roses in Joseph's garden were still colorful in the waning light, randomly untouched by the vicious attack. Over his friend's grave, Father Anthony Von Rahmel vowed to fight Hitler. Somehow, somewhere, he would do something to stop this unholy terror.

Warsaw was bedlam. Anthony had lost a dear friend, but he was still a priest. As much as he might want to leave that desolate place and tend to his own grief, he knew he must stay to help the wounded and bury the dead. Taking stock of his own condition, Anthony was shocked to see a long bloody gash that ran the length of his forearm.

Rummaging in the rectory kitchen, he found some good brandy for cleansing the wound and a dishtowel for bandaging it. He smiled to himself. "What a waste." Before he poured, He took a long sip of the brandy and let the warm feeling coast down his throat and warm his stomach before he poured more over his arm. As he wrapped the wound tightly in the towel, he said a silent prayer for strength. Then he ventured back to the streets to see what he could do to help.

For several days, Anthony labored night and day burying the dead and treating the wounded. Never had he given so many last rites in such a short time. Everywhere he looked he saw the tear-stained faces of parents holding children—some dead, some alive. Anthony felt he could do little to comfort them, but he tried. War hung in the air, with the Germans advancing on one side and the Russians from another. Fighter pilots flew daily over the city with their armaments blazing. German ground troops arrived and began their version of atrocities. Anthony's own wound stubbornly refused to heal, and each day he felt his strength slipping away. Swelling and redness told him an infection was settling in, despite his efforts to keep it clean and bandaged. Perhaps if he had withdrawn from the work in the streets and taken cover in the rectory, the wound could have begun to heal. But the need was too great, and time was too limited.

If Anthony was going to get back to Berlin, he would have to leave Warsaw before there was no way out, but there remained the matter of Rabbi Thomas. Father Joseph had been determined that Anthony should meet the rabbi, so Anthony was hesitant to leave without finding him. As he worked in the streets, Anthony gently probed for the whereabouts of Rabbi Thomas.

The effort paid off. Laboring to move broken rock from the street one day, another man joined him. Strangers working side by side was not unusual. After an hour or so, though, the man softly said, "I am Thomas."

Anthony nodded almost imperceptibly. "Tell me where we can talk."

Under the cover of darkness, they met. Anthony prayed that the information Rabbi Thomas shared was only a tangle of rumors. Could Hitler really be planning this terror for the Jews? Would his own countrymen really stand by and let it happen? It was time to go home, to meet with his own contacts. It was time to do something. As Anthony made his way through the debris of the city one last time, he knew his life would never be the same.

The next day he managed to board a train for Germany. Heading for Munich to see his parents and siblings, Anthony leaned his head against the dirty window of the train and looked up at the brilliant blue sky. He detested the smug look on the German soldier's face as he checked and rechecked Anthony's papers. The soldier questioned him repeatedly about why he had been in Poland. Swallowing his fury, Anthony simply explained he had gone to visit a friend from his seminary days. He didn't want to answer this pimple-faced kid trying to be tough, but out of the corner of his eye he saw another German soldier with his finger on the trigger of his rifle.

At last the soldier moved on. Anthony looked out and cringed as the train passed refugees walking, carrying all the belongings they could hold. Blood seeped from his gashed arm, a steady reminder of what he had just been through.

It took three grueling days of interminable delays to get to Munich.

Anthony hadn't been in Munich for some time. His own parish was in Berlin, and the demands of his schedule as a priest there left him little time to visit Munich, the land of his childhood.

The Von Rahmel family was one of Germany's wealthy Catholic families with a heritage that stretched back to the Hapsburg dynasty. They owned homes in Berlin and Munich, as well as factories and apartment buildings in both cities. Anthony's parents habitually traveled to Berlin each July to visit him and to check on their factories, staying in their summer home in Grunewald during their visit. They had missed this year, though, instead prevailing on Anthony to check on the factories and the tenants in the family-owned apartment buildings.

Anthony knew his parents and sister were in Munich, and quite possibly his three brothers as well. Hans, Heinz, and Edwin spent as much time there as they could. Dietrich, a boyhood friend, was also considered part of the family. His father had come to work for the Von Rahmels when Dietrich was five years old, and the family had enfolded the little boy as one of their own, especially after his father died.

In the distance, Anthony saw his father riding his favorite stallion in the arena. Jona Von Rahmel was a quiet man and happiest when he was with his horses. Even though he had inherited wealth and no financial worries, he worked in his profession as a veterinarian, traveling to the local farms and zoo to provide assistance with a variety of animals.

Anthony caught Katarina's eye first. His sister was going out to join their father as Anthony shuffled up the drive. She ran toward him, catching him just as he fell to his knees in exhaustion. Even through his pain, Anthony loved seeing his sister. At seventeen, Katarina was a stunning beauty, with violet eyes and long silver-blonde hair. She had grown up pampered and spoiled by all her brothers, but especially by Anthony, the oldest.

He well remembered the night of her birth. As his dog, Misha, whimpered and pawed at him, Anthony had heard the footsteps running down the hall and known immediately that something was going on. His Aunt Helena was giving birth. What he had not known at the time, when he was sixteen, was that Helena was determined not to share her husband with this child. Only later did Anthony learn that Helena had been begging her sister—Anthony's mother—for weeks to take the child. When Katarina arrived, and Lisa Von Rahmel at last understood that her sister was serious enough to give the child away to someone else if she did not take her, she had given in. Lisa and Jona, parents of four boys, welcomed a tiny little girl into their family. Helena's husband, Richard, was away on business in America. With grief and heartache, he would receive the news that his child had been born dead.

That first night, as the baby lay in her cradle, Anthony had crept into her room and taken her in his arms. So small, so fragile, he thought as he felt the smoothness of the baby's skin and smelled her newborn sweetness. He promised he would take care of her all her life.

As Katarina grew and Anthony entered adulthood, he told his parents on many occasions they should tell Katarina the truth about her birth mother. Lisa and Jona could never bring themselves to do it, but the inevitable happened only a few weeks before Anthony's trip to Poland. Sorting through boxes in the attic of the family's home, Katarina found a box of old papers. Letters. Two birth certificates. Adoption papers. She had understood instantly. Her brothers were not her brothers at all, but her cousins. Her parents were her aunt and uncle. Aunt Helena and Uncle Richard were her parents.

Katarina had begged to travel to Berlin and talk with Anthony about this life-shattering information, but he had been on the verge of his trip to Poland and had to put her off. Now they sat together on the steps outside the family's home, with no words between them. Certainly Katarina longed to probe the questions of her birth with Anthony, but just as clearly he needed immediate help. Closing his eyes in exhaustion, Anthony felt his sister stretch her sweater around his broad shoulders.

Hans was the first to reach them. Between Hans and Katarina, they managed to get Anthony inside and up the stairs to his old bedroom. By this time, the entire family had gathered, none of them willing to leave until they knew how seriously Anthony was injured. Lisa Von Rahmel took charge, briskly ordering the housekeeper to call for the doctor and telling Katarina to have the cook bring hot water and towels.

When the doctor arrived, everyone still lurked around Anthony's bed. He was awake, but not strong enough to tell them where he had been and what had happened. The doctor nearly had to force the family to leave the room. Lisa and Katarina refused to go. After a thorough examination, he declared that Anthony's only wound was the gash in his arm, which needed to be properly cleaned out and stitched. Anthony had collapsed from blood loss and exhaustion. The doctor's instructions were for everyone to let Anthony sleep for several days—longer, if that's what it took.

For four days, Anthony drifted in and out of

consciousness. In his dreams he saw the horrors of Warsaw and heard the ringing voice of Rabbi Thomas insisting that his information was true. Katarina never left his side, and often when he awoke another family member would be holding vigil as well. In his haze, Anthony resolved to tell his family what he knew as soon as he could manage to do more than grunt.

When he was at last able to leave the bed, Anthony herded his family to the wine cellar. He refused to answer their relentless questions until they were gathered in a place where no one would overhear them. Gravely, he began his explanation.

"The German invasion came so suddenly that children playing in the park were slaughtered before my eyes. Father Joseph is dead. I helped bury whole families. When the German troops arrived, they butchered people in the streets. I am here today to tell you that I met with a member of the Polish Underground who has proof that the Jews are being collected and sent to central locations. The synagogues are being burned—often with people still inside."

Anthony paused to survey the shocked looks on the faces of his family before he continued. "At the rectory there, I met a ragtag group, the beginnings of a Polish resistance. They were there to tell me to get out and away. They had witnessed, in another town, a hundred priests taken out into the square and shot. The church has been a target for Hitler from the beginning, and I know I've been watched ever since I refused to place his flag with the swastika in the middle of the cross in my church. I did hang it outside, or I would probably not be here now. The Vatican has asked me to consider returning to Rome to stay, but I can't do that and leave you all here."

Jona muttered, "I have heard rumors, but I had no idea it was so bad."

"We have seen this coming for several years," Anthony went on. "We've been through it here—seeing the synagogues closed, the Jewish shops closed, the Jews forced to wear yellow stars for identification. Now they've taken it to Poland. I was shocked to see Polish people pointing out Jews to the Germans! To save themselves, some are turning on their friends and neighbors. Hitler is determined to destroy an entire race of people."

The unspoken questions hung in the room: Is Poland only the beginning? How many other countries will Hitler invade with his campaign of hate? How many people will die before this is over? In one corner, Edwin had his arm tightly around Rita, his Jewish wife. What would happen to Rita?

Anthony continued. "I've watched what is happening for too long in silence. As a priest, as a man, I can no longer stand by and do nothing while Hitler carries out his extermination. I will help any Jew who wants to leave Germany. I will hide them, provide food, do whatever is necessary to help them survive. But I cannot do it alone. I have helped in small ways with other clergy, but it is not enough. It will be dangerous, and we have to be very careful. But we must decide what we can do, and do it."

Everyone began talking at once. They didn't know what they could do, but they wanted to help. Anthony choked back the pride swelling in his chest.

"I have to go back to Berlin," he said. "My parish will be wondering what happened to me. But I will be back."

****

Individuals in the Underground in Berlin warned Anthony that his family should keep a low profile and not arouse suspicion with the authorities. They had been under scrutiny since 1933 when Anthony first began to question the rise of Hitler. A low profile? His family was well known throughout Germany, and Katarina, in addition to being a stunning beauty, had risen through the ranks of her dance company to be a prima ballerina, headlined at performances on a steady basis. A low profile? This was not possible. But Anthony was determined to take action.

Two weeks later, Anthony returned to Munich. As he came into town, he impulsively decided to drop by the opera house to see Katarina before going home. He loved to see his sister dance. She moved as if nothing bound her, a free spirit, a wisp of smoke wafting over the stage. Even after years of watching rehearsals and countless performances, Anthony still felt the breath sucked out of him when he watched Katarina dance. Standing on the sidelines, he watched her rehearsing, lost in movement and focused on her art. When she finally spotted him, she leaped off the stage.

"Anthony! You're back!" She threw her arms around his neck and kissed his cheek. "Come say hello to Anna."

Katarina tugged him onto the stage to greet her best friend. Their teacher, the Meister, as they called Herr Jamoursky, admonished the dancers for their "clumsy attempts at dancing." The Meister, who had come from Russia to teach dancing, was the only teacher Katarina had ever known, and he demanded exact performances.

She hoped some day she would come into the world of Eugenia Eduardouwce, the most famous dancer ever, in Katarina's estimation.

Every female in the company noticed Anthony the minute he entered the stage. His good looks were a bane to his calling to the church. Most of the women stared, wishing he were anyone but a priest. None of the Von Rahmel boys lacked for female attention, but it was Anthony who even as a child presented a strength and confidence that caused people to turn and take notice. With his wavy dark blond hair, glinting blue eyes, and tall stature, he was far too good-looking for the holy figure he presented. The black clothing he wore in his profession seemed only to accentuate his classic features.

After a few polite greetings, Anthony said, "Katarina, come with me to the café so we can talk."

Katarina rolled her eyes. "Is this going to be a lecture?"

He gave her one of his engaging smiles. "When I went to Poland, I left before we could clear the air about Aunt Helena."

Katarina sobered. "All right, just let me go and get changed." She called to her friend. "Anna, keep Anthony company. I don't want Helga near him."

Katarina never had a kind word to say about her understudy, and Anthony's intuition told him Katarina was right. Helga was malicious and heartless. She had briefly dated Edwin before he married Rita. Edwin had always loved Rita, but their families kept them from marrying because of the difference in their religions. Edwin finally decided to marry against his family's wishes. While the Von Rahmel family soon accepted

Rita, Helga never got over what she deemed betrayal. Katarina was right not to trust her.

****

The quick walk to their favorite café was invigorating. Once there, however, they were dismayed to see the predominance of men in military uniforms. Anthony cringed as he saw heads turn and officers staring at Katarina. Every time she walked into a room, she drew admiring looks. Her dancing was well known throughout Germany, and even if it weren't, her youthful beauty would have made it impossible for her to escape notice.

Still, Anthony wished his sister could be insulated from the gawking Nazi officers.

They found a table in a corner, made small talk, and placed an order, all the while hoping the crowd would thin out. Finally it seemed safe to speak their hearts.

"Katarina," Anthony began, "I'm sorry for what you have gone through these last few weeks. Aunt Helena feels terrible and wants to make peace with you. If you can forgive the rest of us, why can you not forgive her?"

His sister's blonde head remained lowered as she refused to look him in the eye. When he started to speak again, she raised one hand to stop him. "Anthony, I need time. Aunt Helena gave me to Mother to raise simply because she didn't want a child in her life. She didn't want to share me with Uncle Richard. We all know how much Uncle Richard loved me all those years, right up until his death. How fair was that to him? Surely it was only a matter of time before I found those papers in the attic."

"Aunt Helena has her own issues," Anthony said gently. "She was the youngest, raised by a nanny while Mother and Aunt Martha married and moved away. She's always had trouble believing people would not abandon her. She was afraid Uncle Richard..."

"You can't really finish that sentence, can you, Anthony?" Katarina now gazed coolly into her brother's eyes. "Is there really any excuse for abandoning a child?"

"Katarina, you don't know what it's like to be in her shoes!"

Katarina shook her head. "When he died, Uncle Richard looked at me and said, 'I should have known.' I didn't know what he meant at the time. Now I do. I should have known, too. We have the same violet eyes, Anthony. As he was dying, he knew I was his daughter."

Anthony shifted in his chair uncomfortably. "Katarina, we were going to tell you many times. We all loved you so much and looked on you as our little princess. Hans, Edwin, Heinz, and I—we marveled at you. How could we hurt you with the truth?"

Katarina took his hands in hers. "Anthony, I promise I'll think about it and try not to be bitter."

As a new group of Nazi uniforms began to fill the café, Katarina and Anthony left. They strolled arm in arm back to the apartment Katarina shared with her friend Anna. Outside the building, Anthony kissed her cheek.

"Aren't you coming up?" she asked.

"Not tonight. I need to go talk to Mother and Father."

They watched a group of brown shirts pass them.

Anthony waited until the soldiers rounded the corner before continuing. "I know the family didn't want to believe what happened in Poland. Hans and Heinz still wonder if they are going against their own country."

"Talk to them," Katarina urged, her voice barely above a whisper. "We have to do something."

Chapter 2

Rome: April 1940

In 1940 the world was still stunned by Germany's assault on Poland. For most Europeans, the last six months had been a nightmare, as the rest of the world watched and waited to see what Hitler would do next.

Peter Ashley, cousin of the Von Rahmel siblings, was the son of Lisa's sister Martha and Lord Ashley of England. Even though they grew up in different countries, the cousins had been close through the years. Peter and Anthony had a lifetime of fond memories. As best friends, they had shared secrets no one else would ever know. For many years the two had taken time each spring to visit each other. In the spring of 1940, they planned a week in Rome. Travel was increasingly hazardous with their countries at war with each other, but they needed this face-to-face contact to understand what was happening in both their countries.

Anthony loved walking the streets of Rome. Even as a child he had been in awe of the Vatican and all it represented. On his way to the café where he was to meet Peter, Anthony thought, This is where I want to be. Before I leave Rome, I must find out where the Church stands in regard to the actions of Germany. I need to know what is expected of me as a priest in a country where people are beaten and killed daily. Why is the church not coming after Hitler's invasion and the way they are treating the Jews? They are our own people, and God's creation, and their blood is the same as ours. The weight of the last few months was heavy on his shoulders. His pace quickened as he approached the café, and he tried to pretend no one was around him. He wanted his eyes to see only the familiar sights, the sacred places, the city as it was before the world turned upside down.

Inside the café, Anthony found a secluded corner and sat at a table. A waiter appeared for a brief exchange. It was only moments before his cousin entered. With his light brown hair, slim-built five-foot-ten frame, and drop-dead good looks, Peter was unmistakable. His smile and sense of humor seemed to float along with him. Peter had always assured Anthony that his humorous side had come from his Scotch and English side of the family, not the Germans.

Peter had not been enthused when Anthony announced he planned to study for the priesthood. He complained that he was losing his best friend, that nothing would ever be the same between them. But the years had proven him wrong. Anthony and Peter were still best friends. However, as they embraced in a Roman café, they knew that this visit was about more than just wanting to see each other.

"Peter, it's so good to see you," Anthony said. "I took the liberty of ordering wine. Let's order dinner, and then we can catch up on the news."

Right away Anthony saw the questions in Peter's eyes. The cousins were much too close for Peter not to know that Anthony needed to talk to him about something serious.

Anthony continued, "Father shared the news from Aunt Martha's letter. She said you're in the service of England now, but she didn't say what you're doing."

As if reading each other's thoughts, Peter and Anthony leaned forward simultaneously; the fine lines on Peter's face creased deeper. He spoke in a whisper as he watched Anthony rub the wet ring the wine had left on the table. Peter spoke in French, one of several languages they had both learned at the insistence of their mothers. It served them well now.

"Anthony, it's going to become more and more difficult for us to meet. I work in the intelligence division of the Queen's service, and I can assure you that things are going from bad to worse." A faint bead of sweat formed on his brow. "My friend, you must be very careful of what you say and do."

The meal came. Peter was silent through dinner, listening to Anthony boast about his sister's dancing and how she floated across the stage like a swan. After the waiter cleared away the dishes, they sat and sipped brandy.

Peter's voice was low. "I have sources in Germany, and if you are willing, I can let them know how to reach you."

Anthony caught his breath. What was Peter offering? "Peter, I'm horrified by what I've seen. I can promise you that I will be there when needed. My brothers have all been forced into military service. Hans is in Panzers, learning everything there is to know about armored vehicles. Heinz is flying with the Luftwaffe, and Edwin works at the local headquarters in Berlin. Hans and Heinz are already in combat, but they trust me and do not ask questions they know I can't answer."

"What about Edwin?" Peter asked.

"He and I are trying to convince Rita that she and her family must leave Germany, but she won't listen. I'm not sure someone won't find out about the false papers; there is always someone who will seek out information. It's frustrating knowing the dangers and wondering how soon disaster will fall on my own family."

"Anthony, come back to England with me, or make arrangements to stay here in Rome. I have contacts. You can help the effort without being in immediate danger."

Anthony smiled weakly. "I made a promise to Father Joseph, and I can't go back on it. I need to be in Germany."

Peter continued sipping his brandy while Anthony told what had happened in Poland months ago. Peter was not shocked by anything Anthony told him. In his position in the intelligence world, he had read reports coming out of Poland. The candles on the table were burning low when they finally said their goodbyes. Peter had a sinking feeling in his stomach. He thought the whole family needed to leave Germany. They had homes in Switzerland—why would they stay? He knew Anthony would find out information to benefit them in the cause against Hitler, but at what price?

****

The pace of the war escalated. More and more German troops stomped through the streets of Europe. In Berlin, Anthony was slowly preparing to use his church as a hiding place for Jews until he could find a way for them to leave Germany. The building had rooms the congregation didn't use that could easily be hidden with false walls and antique ecclesiastical furniture. Edwin was trying to move his wife's family out of Germany, but still Rita would not leave her husband. And without Rita, Edwin could not convince her parents to leave, either.

Anthony visited Munich as often as possible. He worried for his parents and for Katarina, who continued to dance in the public eye. On one visit he arrived at the opera house just in time to watch a man in a Gestapo uniform kiss Katarina's hand. His heart clenched, an apprehensive feeling in the pit of his stomach. The notorious political police arm of the Nazi party had unlimited powers of arrest, and spies everywhere. What were they doing with his sister? Breathless, Anthony watched as the Gestapo officer thrust his right arm forward in the Nazi salute. "Heil Hitler!" The dancers and the Meister awkwardly returned the salute. As the stranger passed him in the shadows, Anthony saw his piercing, sharp blue Aryan eyes. He had the perfect German nose and square jaw.

Shaking off the feeling of evil crawling through him, Anthony quickly made his way to Katarina's dressing room. There, he paced like a tiger, waiting for Katarina to finish her practice session.

Helga, Katarina's mediocre but arrogant understudy, walked in. "To what do we owe this visit from the holy man?" she sneered.

"I came to see my sister," Anthony answered calmly.

"It's sickening. Your brother could have had me, and just look at what he ended up with. A Jew wife. Not a good move, was it, priest?"

Anthony took a deep breath as he raised his brow

in surprise. He looked at Helga, knowing she was one of many who had been brainwashed by the Nazi propaganda. Her eyes were cold. When Edwin had dated her, she had been attractive in a simple way, small, with short blonde hair that framed her face and deep brown eyes. It was the curve of her mouth that had hardened and now embodied the bitterness of her soul.

Unexpectedly, Helga threw her arms around Anthony's neck. Her robe gapped open, revealing her smooth nakedness. Before Anthony could react, she whispered in his ear, with lewd suggestions of the many ways he could make love to her. Anthony gently but firmly pushed her away.

"Helga, why would you want to do this? Close your robe. I've seen it all before."

Her face snarled in anger. "You think you're better than I am. I don't like you or your family, and I'll bring you all down."

Anthony's voice strained as he grabbed her arm. "You stay away from my family. Edwin cared about you at one time, but he is in love with his wife. No one in my family has ever done anything to you to warrant such spite."

She yanked her arm away from him. "Don't tell me what to do. Your brother left me for a Jew, and I will make it my mission to destroy him and his family. I know exactly who to talk to. In fact, your sister is having dinner with him tonight. Won't he be interested in what I have to tell him? The first to go will be Edwin's beloved Jew wife, but the rest of you will be close behind. You can go to hell with your precious Jews!" Helga stormed out of the room, leaving Anthony to catch his breath.

A few minutes later, Anthony heard Anna's voice pleading with Katarina not to go out with the Gestapo agent. They were both surprised to see Anthony when they came through the door.

"Anthony!" Katarina exclaimed. "You're white as a ghost."

"What did the Gestapo agent want?" he demanded.

"Anthony, it's nothing. Colonel Frederick Spitz has been here a few times to arrange some performances. We are to dance for Hitler. The company is moving to Berlin, and we have other engagements around Europe. I know how uncomfortable everyone is when he's here, so I agreed to have dinner with him just to get him to go away."

"Dinner? You mean a date?"

"Not exactly. It's at some embassy." Katarina changed the subject. "Didn't you mention you wanted to talk to the American ambassador? I saw in the newspaper that he is here in Munich and will be at the embassy dinner tonight."

Anna glanced at the clock and sucked in her breath. "I've got to go, Katarina. I'm late myself." Anna slid her feet into street shoes and was out the door.

Katarina continued with her light tone. "I'll bet she's meeting Hans. He's on leave, you know. He has finally seen Anna as something more than my little ballerina friend. They're quite smitten with each other. I think they're even sleeping together."

"Katarina!" The rebuke in Anthony's tone was sharp.

"Come on, Anthony. Is there no room for someone to be happy these days? Anna and Hans are happy together. In the middle of all this misery and what's happening to our family, let's be happy for them."

Anthony's eyes narrowed. "What do you mean? What's happening to our family?"

Katarina's head snapped up. "So you haven't been home yet?"

"No, why?"

"Then you haven't heard."

"Heard what?"

Tears filled Katarina's eyes. "We've been told to leave our estate. The Nazis want it for their own use. Father and Mother are devastated. They won't even let Father take any of his books or the horses. We can only take our clothing and a few pieces of china."

Anthony was stunned.

"They said that it is for the good of Germany," Katarina continued. "Since we have homes in Berlin and Switzerland, we are not being put out on the street. Most of the household left this morning with Helena to open the house and summerhouse in Berlin. I'll follow soon with the company. It's not that we have a choice. We were just told we needed to move our Dance Company to Berlin. That was how I first started to speak with Frederick when he gave the order."

"It seems that all roads for this family lead to Berlin," Anthony said, sighing. He did not want his family in Berlin. His father's factories there had already been confiscated by the Nazis and were being used "for the good of Germany." Anthony's own activities in the Underground were growing. He hated the thought that what he was doing might put his parents in peril.

Katarina dressed warmly and placed an extra scarf around her brother's neck. When they went out, the night air was cold for the month of March. They didn't speak for a couple of blocks.

Finally, Katarina said, "Anthony, talk to me."

Anthony sighed. "Father loves his land, his horses, and his books. He has collections that have been passed down for generations. I can't recall a day in my life that he was not riding or reading—or both. And now they have to leave all of that, and for what? Berlin is not safe. We have to convince Mother and Father that they need to leave for Switzerland as soon as possible."

Katarina put her hand in his coat pocket as they continued to walk. "I'll be in Berlin with you. Edwin is already there. We will help Father and Mother through this. You know they will not leave Germany easily." She paused, studying his face. "Let me give the American ambassador your message at the embassy tonight. It's a perfect time. Perhaps my night out with Colonel Spitz has a reason. Write a letter and tell the ambassador what you know. I promise no one will see me passing it to him."

Anthony shook his head. "Putting it in writing is far too dangerous."

"Let me help you, Anthony."

He considered his sister; she was serious. But she was so young! "Promise me that after this dinner party you won't see this Frederick Spitz again."

Katarina responded with a sullen look. "I can't promise that, Anthony. He is a very difficult person to refuse, and I don't want to complicate things for the company. Besides, he may not be all that bad. Just because he's Gestapo doesn't make him like the others."

Anthony stared at his sister. "You can't be serious! He is the poster boy for the Hitler program. You must be aware he can be lethal. Don't be so naïve."

"Anthony, stop! Must you worry so much?"

Anthony had the distinct impression Katarina was holding something from him. Was it possible she had a genuine interest in this man? The thought made him shudder.

They came around the corner nearest to her apartment just in time to see her neighbors, the Silvermans, being shoved into a van. The youngest son broke away and ran. He had gone only a few steps when shots splintered the crystal night. The young man collapsed, his blood quickly coloring the sidewalk. His mother screamed in anguish and tried to climb over her family, only to be pushed back by another soldier. An agent turned the young boy over and shot him again. Katarina instinctively lurched toward the boy, but Anthony pulled her back out of sight.

Finally the van pulled away. Katarina wept on Anthony's shoulder as they clung to each other. As a priest, Anthony wanted desperately to go to the boy on the sidewalk and give him last rites. As a brother, he knew he must take care of his sister. With heavy heart, he prayed for the boy and steered Katarina toward her apartment. The vultures would soon be out; all the Silvermans' belongings would be placed on the street, or their apartments looted, or another family moved into them as if nothing happened.

Inside, they saw Anna curled up in a chair, bundled in an old blanket, shaking uncontrollably.

"You saw!" Katarina exclaimed as she ran to Anna.

"He was just a boy! Why would they kill him?"

Katarina stroked Anna's hair. "Anna, we don't have answers to these questions. But the walls are thin.

Watch your voice."

Anna nodded between sobs.

Katarina looked around. "Where is Hans? I thought he would be here."

Anna took a deep breath. "I saw Hans after I left practice. He wants Anthony to meet him at their favorite hotel tonight." A smile broke through her sobs. "Hans asked me to marry him." She proudly showed Katarina and Anthony a beautiful sapphire ring with diamonds set in a perfect circle. It was a family ring they both recognized.

A cloud crossed Anna's face. "What's the matter?" Katarina asked.

"It feels like a cold, clammy hand has gripped my throat, and I can't breathe. I don't believe I will see a wedding day."

"Oh, hush, Anna! This is a time for joy. Right, Anthony?"

Anthony's eyes were again drawn to the street, where blood ran into the gutter. Sick at heart, he forced himself to turn and smile at Anna. He sat across from her and took her hands in his. "Anna, don't let fear take away your happiness. This is a joyous moment and only good thoughts should come to you. Hans obviously loves you very much."

"Come, Anna," Katarina said. "Lie down for a while and rest." Katarina led her friend to the bedroom.

Anthony wrote an address on paper. When Katarina returned to the room, he said, "Just get the ambassador alone and ask him to meet me at this address. No one will suspect a paper with a simple address, but if you think anyone is watching, throw it away and don't go anywhere near the ambassador."

Katarina took the paper. "Please don't worry about me. Go and see Father, and drive with him to Berlin. I tried to talk him and Mother into escaping to the cabin in Switzerland, but he would not. He did manage to have Joseph move the horses over. He is heartbroken to leave behind his precious books, though. He needs your support."

Anthony left the apartment. The wind whipped at him as he walked the streets of Munich, becoming increasingly convinced it had been a mistake to involve his sister.

****

Katarina was nervous as she dressed for her date with Colonel Spitz at the Italian embassy. Though she frequently attended such functions as a prominent dancer, tonight she had a mission. The paper Anthony had given her was hidden deep in her small purse, folded six times to make it small.

A knock at the door told her Frederick Spitz had arrived. Katarina smiled as she opened the door and saw him take pleasure in what he saw. She wore a striking black silk dress with silver lace and small butterflies woven into the lace. Her hair was pulled back and held in place by a large black bow, enhancing her violet eyes, long black lashes, and perfect widow's peak. She knew she looked her best.

The moment they arrived at the embassy, all attention was riveted on Katarina.

Many had seen her perform, and most of those present knew of her family and their holdings. Her dance card filled up quickly with men anxious to meet her, and after dinner she saw little of Colonel Spitz. The moment came when she was able to dance with the

American ambassador.

"Fräulein Von Rahmel, I've heard your brother came to see me a few months ago in Berlin. I'm sorry I missed him. Please tell him to try me again."

Katarina hadn't realized how nervous she was until she heard the quiver in her own voice. The music swelled and gave her the cover she needed. "My brother would like to meet with you before you leave for America. He has information for you. I'm slipping into your palm the address of a church where he is waiting. Please go to see him." Without missing a step, the ambassador nodded politely. Katarina hoped that was agreement, for Anthony's sake.

As the dance ended, she was startled to hear Colonel Spitz's voice. "Do I get the chance to dance with you?"

With a deep sigh of relief at her mission accomplished, she spent the rest of the evening wishing it were over. The ambassador made such a discreet exit that even Katarina did not notice when he left. Spitz behaved like a perfect gentleman and wished her goodnight when he took her home. Katarina was startled when he said he would see her again. It was not an invitation or a request, but a statement.

He turned and left before she could answer.

Chapter 3

Berlin: 1943

Katarina Von Rahmel danced and blossomed into independence. Father Anthony Von Rahmel said Mass and prayed.

And around them the war raged. The conflict that began with German aggression toward its neighbors consumed more and more of the world's energy. The Nazis invaded France, Luxembourg, Belgium, the Netherlands, Norway, and one after another the nations surrendered in the hope of keeping their people alive. Hitler's troops overtook the nations of Eastern Europe, aimed at Russia, and invaded Greece and Yugoslavia. Italy reared its head in a quest for power. The Japanese bombed Pearl Harbor, startling the U.S. into overt action at last. English parents sent their children to the countryside to escape the German bombs raining on England's cities.

As 1943 opened, anyone looking at the Von Rahmel family from the outside would have seen calm. The truth was the family encountered turmoil at every turn. To Anthony it seemed a lifetime ago that he had promised his friends to help however he could. His promise meant that he lived daily with the knowledge that a wrong word, a thoughtless gesture, could result in discovery of his underground activities. On the exterior, he was the priest of a Berlin parish, saying Mass several times a week, baptizing babies, presiding at weddings, burying the dead. At the core, though, his life was focused on helping people escape from Germany. So far he had only been able to help move a limited number of doctors and scientists from Munich and Berlin. Anthony's hands clenched and his teeth gnashed each time he saw another van full of Jews on their way to God only knew where. Every day he beseeched the Almighty God to bring an end to the war.

The end of 1942 had brought a round of atrocities that touched the Von Rahmels. A second cousin to Anthony's mother had spoken out when he witnessed the beating of a Jew. The next morning, his parents found him hanging from a street lamp. The message was clear. The incident made Anthony more determined than ever to be aggressive in the new year.

If he had more help, he could do more; Anthony was sure of that. His brother Edwin was his closest collaborator. Edwin was still in the military, but his work was in communications now, and he had the resources to manufacture convincing papers for any occasion. His help had been invaluable.

Everyone lived in fear of document inspections and knew Gestapo agents could confiscate papers at any time, and without the proper papers, individuals had not even the weakest line of defense should they be confronted by authorities. Rarely was anyone who disappeared ever seen again. They had tried to intimidate Anthony once by picking him up to interrogate along with many other Germans, their ages from five to a hundred, for no reason, just because they could. Another time, they had briefly questioned all the brothers, Anthony, Heinz, Hans, and Edwin, but they had remained faithful to both family and country, though not to the Nazi system.

As a priest, Anthony could still travel at night, despite the curfew. He frequently moved through the city to a convent garden, where he found instructions left by persons unknown hidden behind a brick. While he never knew who sent the instructions, they knew him, and they knew the code words Anthony and Peter had established.

And then there was Katarina. Anthony constantly feared for her safety. Only a handful of people knew that the ballet company was hiding people trying to escape Germany. With Edwin's help, Anthony provided them with paperwork, and the company provided them with cover as workers supporting the company as it traveled. They were always asked to perform for the generals and the upper echelon of places they invaded. When the company came close to the borders of Norway, Denmark or Switzerland, certain individuals simply slipped away and disappeared. Because of the seemingly menial nature of their work, no one paid much attention to the staff that came and went with the company. In truth, these individuals were highly educated people whose ethnicity or outspoken personalities put them at risk.

As much as Anthony did, he always wished he could do more. A priest seen in one place too many times would bring suspicion, so at times he had to curtail his activities and focus on his parish. For weeks at a time, he remained within the parameters of his parish and did nothing that might be construed as suspicious. At other times, he ventured further. His clerical status still allowed him to cross borders with relative ease, and he had seen Peter several times in Rome as well as Paris. Peter provided names of individuals—mostly professors and scientists—who needed to leave Germany.

Late one evening, Anthony was returning to his rectory when a shadowy form emerged from the darkness and stood in front of him. Anthony's heart quickened briefly. The man was not in uniform, but it could still be a trap. Anthony said nothing.

Then the code word came. It was safe. In silence the man gestured for Anthony to follow him to a nearby mostly deserted restaurant. They worked their way back to the darkest corner, where another man was waiting. Both strangers appeared to be in their mid-thirties, with clear green eyes and light brown hair and gentle smiles. Here was the help Anthony had waited so long to find. He half held his breath, not completely sure he wanted to believe they were who they claimed to be.

"I am Grigory," said the man who had stopped Anthony in the street. "This is my brother Nicholas." His speech bore a distinct Russian accent.

Anthony assessed the brothers. Grigory was small and wiry, while Nicholas was a bear in stature.

"Perhaps we could speak French," Grigory suggested. "Your cousin said you are fluent."

Grigory seemed to be the one running things.

Anthony nodded agreement.

Grigory leaned forward to speak in a hush. "Do not worry about the French. We have papers if we are stopped, saying that we are bringing art from France for Hitler and others to keep. We know Rabbi Thomas and your cousin Peter. It's a small world, our circle of fighters. Right now we need someone on the inside, and we need a safe house. Rabbi Thomas said you might be able to help. We are Russian Jews, and no one knows we are in Berlin. Nicholas lost his wife and two children in Poland. He has business friends in England, and that is how we met Peter."

Anthony's eyes shifted to Nicholas. The loss of his family explained the silent sadness in his eyes.

Grigory continued. "We must find out where Hitler is sending the Jews. We do not believe they are going to work camps. Once people are shipped away, no one ever hears from them again. There are more than just slave camps; there is something more sinister going on. We also need to find what they are developing for warfare, to give to the British. They have workers in all sorts of caves and factories where there is development of new bombs, aircrafts, and more. If we can't get this to the British, then the whole world could end up speaking German."

Anthony nodded his understanding. "I have heard rumors," he said.

"Rumors that Hitler is exterminating Jews by the thousands! But we have not been able to confirm the stories. We must find out the truth and let the rest of the world know what is happening."

Anthony's heart pounded. This was a turning point—something much bigger than smuggling a few individuals out of the country. "What information do you have to work with?"

"V2 rocket experiments, troop movements. I've been sending what I learn to the British. I've been with the French for the last six months recruiting help. The Resistance is growing all over Europe."

"My brothers are in the German military," Anthony said.

Grigory nodded. "I know. I realize that may be a conflict of interest for you."

Anthony's head snapped up. "No! It's not. I don't want to put them in danger, obviously, but I assure you they are not serving the Führer because they want to." He looked from Grigory to Nicholas. "What do you want me to do?"

"We understand you are involved with the Rosengranz Circle."

Anthony nodded. Even for someone involved in underground operations, his cousin Peter was amazingly well connected. He had put Anthony in touch with a Lutheran minister, and through Pastor Simon Miller, Anthony had become involved with the Rosengranz Circle—military men, labor leaders, professionals, and many others with a passion to resist the Nazi regime and stop the destruction of Germany. Everything they did, however, happened in secrecy and code and near isolation. If the Gestapo found a weak link in the chain, disaster would come to all.

"There are many powerful people in that circle," Anthony said, "but the information they send out of Germany is not always trusted."

"We're doing our best to verify everything," Grigory said. "Many of us have been traveling to Rome or Paris passing information back and forth. That's where we need your help. As a priest, you can use the Vatican as a shield and get information out that we can't. We don't know how long Hitler will get along with the Vatican, but for now we believe you are safe."

"No one can make promises in this business,"

Anthony observed.

Grigory nodded. "The time may come when you have to leave quickly. So be ready. We think your family should leave now."

Anthony saw a flicker of anxiety in Nicholas's eyes and turned his head ever so slightly to see what Nicholas saw. A Gestapo agent had entered the restaurant. His demeanor suggested he was looking for someone in particular. Grigory and Nicholas slid their chairs further into the dark corner, pulling Anthony with them.

"This is what we are reduced to, Father," Grigory whispered in French. "We are full of fear."

They slowly sipped their drinks in silence, waiting for the officer to leave, the air thick with smoke and the smell of stale beer. Anthony's drink was fire in his throat as he watched every movement of the Gestapo agent. When the officer left without causing a scene, they let out a collective sigh of relief.

"Father, we are aware of what you and your sister are doing," Grigory said. "Peter told us about your last visit to Rome, and that you are frustrated in not being able to do more. If we work together, we believe you can do a great deal."

Anthony sat quietly looking at the two men and wondering if this was a trap despite the code they had exchanged earlier.

"Father," Grigory continued, "if you do not believe who we are, Peter told us to tell you he will convert you before you die."

Anthony gave a great sigh of relief as he smiled. Only Peter knew this ongoing joke between them. Still, what Grigory and Nicholas were asking him to do was more than he had done during the past few years. Did he have the courage? Could he live up to their expectations?

Nicholas was wringing his hands in a nervous gesture that contradicted the calmness of his voice. "Your sister is performing for Hitler again and attending a reception afterward. We need you to ask her to take some pictures for us. There are blueprints of areas where the military stores some of their gasoline. We need to know where the storage areas are. Our informant told us exactly where the blueprints are on the second floor, but he cannot get to them. Can you convince your sister to slip out of the dinner and take some pictures? We will come by in two days and provide you with details and a special camera."

Anthony hardly knew what to say. Katarina had been helpful the last couple of years, but this sounded far more dangerous than anything she had ever done. She was barely twenty-one years old, after all. Could he really ask this of her?

"We know it's a big responsibility," Grigory said. "It's not easy to ask someone you love to do this, but she is in the best position to succeed."

Anthony could hear the voice of his headstrong sister in his head. If she were ever to learn that he had shielded her from this mission, he would never hear the end of it. "I will speak to Katarina and let her make the decision. I expect that she will say yes, but I need to hear that from her."

****

Berlin: March 1943

Katarina took a slow breath and let it out. It was wearying to live in three worlds.

She was the dutiful daughter to her parents, the prima ballerina of whom they were so proud. Then there was the world of Anthony—hidden Jews, secret missions, stories they would never tell their parents. And the most private world of all was inhabited by Frederick Spitz. For more than two years she had gone to parties and official dinners with Frederick. At first, it seemed like a harmless way to keep the peace around the ballet company. Frederick arranged some performances for military and government occasions, and Katarina was the lead ballerina. It was only natural that they should have contact and see each other at parties. Her family would never approve, especially Anthony, but Katarina was sure she was in no danger.

Frederick Spitz was a handsome man, a skilled dancer, gentlemanly in every way.

Every time he smiled and his blue eyes crinkled, her heart softened a bit more. By the time he asked her to have dinner alone with him in a restaurant—no official party—Katarina had convinced herself that the uniform did not define the man. After all, her own brothers served in the German military. Did that mean they agreed with Hitler?

Certainly not. Why should it not be possible that Frederick was in the Gestapo for reasons he was not free to explain? He could be stubborn, there was no doubt about that, but Katarina had never witnessed the kind of violent explosions Gestapo agents were known for. Frederick was attentive to her every wish when they went out together. He told her stories of his childhood and visited his mother regularly. If the circumstances of their meeting had been different, the Von Rahmels would have thought their daughter had found herself a great match.

Frederick was Katarina's secret. However, she was not sure how much longer she could keep it. He was nearly ten years older than she was, but Katarina was old enough now for Frederick to make his intentions clear, and she now believed a marriage proposal would not be long in coming. The heart-stopping truth was that she wanted to accept. As the war swirled around them, somehow she and Frederick would be able to live in this private world they were creating together.

Katarina fidgeted with a hairbrush in her dressing room as she contemplated what Anthony had asked her to do. She was not sure she could disappear from the dinner function long enough to accomplish the task without arousing Frederick's suspicions.

And despite her growing affection for Frederick, she couldn't take the risk of his discovering what she was really up to.

It had been an exhausting week: so many mistakes on stage, keeping secrets about Frederick, an increase in air raids, friends picked up for questioning and not returning.

Each time the ballet company's belongings were searched, Katarina's heart nearly stopped. If her activities were revealed, so many people would be destroyed.

And in the last few days, Frederick had pressed her harder than usual with questions about Anthony's frequent trips to Rome. He didn't seem satisfied with the simple answer that obviously a Roman Catholic priest living in Europe would have reason to visit Rome. What was he doing? Who was he seeing? Frederick wanted to know. Katarina played dumb—and sometimes she truly did not know. Batting her violet eyes at him was proving less and less effective at distracting Frederick from his line of questioning. She prayed she was not putting her brother in danger by continuing to see Frederick. Making a choice between Anthony and Frederick—she didn't even want to think how that would rip her apart.

She heard Frederick's voice in the hall, talking to Helga. That was one bright spot: Helga had resigned from the company yesterday. No one was surprised; she had missed countless rehearsals and performances lately. Clearly her heart was not in the ballet. But Helga had watched Katarina closely, almost to the point of stalking, so Katarina was more than glad that she would soon be gone. The change also meant that her friend Anna would become her understudy. Perhaps this promotion would cheer Anna up. She seemed so unhappy lately. Anna had convinced herself she would never see Hans again. Because of Hans's military service and the demands of the war, they saw each other infrequently and had never had the chance to marry. Katarina cut off talk about the danger her brother was in, however. She didn't want to hear Anna's fears about Hans; that would make them too real. "It's bad luck to talk about it," she would tell Anna.

Katarina turned to answer Frederick's rap on her door. She offered her cheek for a kiss of greeting and smiled. "What are you doing here?" It was the middle of the afternoon; she hadn't expected to see Frederick before the evening's performance.

"I just wanted to see you," Frederick answered. "You're the bright spot in my day."

Katarina blushed. No one else said things like that to her.

"Are you ready for tonight's performance?" Frederick asked.

"Of course. I know how important it is."

"Katarina, when you dance for the Führer tonight, you must do your very best. Dancing for the Führer is a great privilege, and after the performance you will sit with me at dinner instead of with the other dancers."

Katarina rubbed her forehead, not quite sure how to respond. He seemed to be in complete control. How could she do what Anthony asked if she were under Frederick's thumb? Finally she found words. "It's a dance performance. I am a professional. Of course I will do my best. You don't have to tell me what to do."

Frederick kissed her on the neck. "I'm sorry, Katarina. I don't mean to sound like I'm ordering you around. I have never felt this way about a woman before."

He smiled and his eyes crinkled and her heart melted. "I'd better get back to rehearsal," she said, stroking his cheek. "I'll see you after the performance tonight."

After he left the room, Katarina moved to the window, where she could see him leave the building, as well. Then she hurriedly put on some street clothes. She was due to meet Anthony at the rectory for final instructions. At the rectory, she rapped on the door quickly and immediately opened it. Flabbergasted, she saw Heinz standing there beside Anthony. With a big smile, she ran toward him. How long had it been since she had seen Heinz? Too long. Her smile soon faded when she saw the fury on Anthony's face.

"What happened here?" Katarina asked. "Look at the two of you. I've never seen such anger between you."

Heinz gathered Katarina in his arms and hugged her heartily. "It's nothing for you to worry about. Anthony is upset because I have been assigned to fly missions over England."

"Missions?" Katarina asked. "You mean, to drop bombs?"

"I don't like it either," Heinz answered, "but it's my job. I can't pick and choose the missions. If I refuse, I will be sent to jail or executed on the spot. Where will that leave the family?"

Anthony groaned. "Heinz, please don't involve Katarina."

Heinz nearly growled. "I think it's a bit late to tell me not to involve Katarina, after what you've asked her to do. I told you a long time ago that I would never question what you are doing, and I would even help as long as it didn't compromise my position as a pilot, but there's no need to involve Katarina."

"Stop it!" Katarina cried. "I've heard enough. Stop this insane foolishness. I am a big girl. I make my own decisions."

Heinz put up a hand in surrender. "I'm sorry. I had no right. We're all in this together."

****

Anthony stood in the window watching Heinz walk down the street until he could no longer see him. He cut such a fine figure in his Luftwaffe uniform. Anthony was startled to realize two men were following Heinz—Gestapo! Why Heinz? He was one of Germany's top ten pilots and had just received the Iron Cross. Anthony resolved to warn Heinz as soon as possible.

For the moment, he had to turn back to Katarina, and with much reluctance gave her the small camera designed to look like a tube of lipstick. She had not hesitated two days ago when he asked for her help. How he wished she had said no. But now there was no turning back. They had already gone over what she needed to do several times, but he again gave her instructions. If she could not get away at the dinner without arousing suspicion, she was not to take any action. She must be able to slip away unnoticed or not at all. Katarina left with the promise that she would be extraordinarily careful.

Her performance that night was flawless. Not until she was sitting at dinner did she feel sick. She had to force herself to breathe normally. Of all nights, why did Frederick choose this one to ask her to marry him? She could still feel his lips on her as he whispered in her ear, "You are the most exquisite woman I have ever known." He'd had to uncurl her fingers to slide a ring on her hand. He credited the tension in her body to nervousness about dancing for Hitler, and she gave him no reason to think otherwise. But his proposal had not come at a moment when she could enjoy it.

Now she sat beside Frederick at the dinner table, trying not to look at Anna or the Meister. By now they had both seen the ring glinting off her finger, and she saw the alarm in their faces. They did not approve any more than her family would approve. If only she could get them alone and explain.

But what would she say?

Her family would just have to realize that not everyone in the Gestapo was an evil person. They didn't know Frederick the way she did.

Katarina pushed the peas around on her plate, wishing this night could be joyful.

And she still had to think about the pictures for Anthony.

"Excuse me, Frederick," she said, "I need to use the ladies room. I'll be right back."

Her legs felt like rubber as she rose, determined to concentrate on the mission.

She found the room easily and was thankful to see a bathroom on the same floor. If anyone caught her, she would explain she was looking for the bathroom. With a prayerful breath, she slowly opened the door. Her eyes soon adjusted to the darkness, lightened only by the glow of a full moon through the window.

Oh, please, let me find the file! It seemed like hours before she spotted the file cabinet in the far corner. The moon gave out enough light, and she soon found the papers to photograph. She lined them up on the floor and began to snap pictures. By the time she finished, sweat rolled down her back. She was closing the file cabinet, having replaced the files, when her eye caught a folder marked "Camps." When she opened the file for a quick peek, she nearly gagged at the pictures. Quickly, she took more photographs.

Her stomach heaving, she cautiously opened the door to leave. By now she really did need to find a bathroom. The contents of the last file had made her extremely nauseated. She barely made it two doors down to the bathroom before she became violently ill. When she finally stopped throwing up, she rinsed out her mouth, adjusted her dress, and opened the door to the hallway. When she heard her name called, she jerked around and went pale as a ghost.

"What has taken you so long, Katarina? And why come to this floor for a bathroom?" Frederick wanted answers.

Before she could answer, bile again rose in her throat. She motioned to Frederick she was returning to the bathroom, certain that he would be able to hear the sounds of her vomiting through the door. When she finally emerged looking even more pale, she responded to the question still on his face. "I wanted privacy. I did not care to have everyone hear me so sick in the other lavatory. I'm sorry if you were concerned."

Frederick wiped the beads of sweat from her forehead. "Mein liebchen, I did not realize you were so sick. Let me see that you are taken home. You do not need to stay."

She nodded, relieved he believed her.

Anna stood at the door to the banquet hall with the Meister. Spotting Katarina, Anna ran to her. "Katarina, what's wrong? You look so sick."

Frederick spoke. "Anna, please take Katarina home immediately. Unfortunately, I must stay to hear the speeches." With that, Frederick returned to the banquet hall.

The Meister brought their coats, and Katarina gratefully accepted his arm for support. She and Anthony had tried to convince him the time had come for him to leave Germany. Edwin was even working on his papers. But still he refused to go. Katarina was mindful Gestapo could come for him at any moment, even if he was essential to Germany's premier ballet company.

The car Frederick had arranged dropped them in

front of Katarina and Anna's apartment building, and they dutifully went inside. However, as soon as the car was out of sight, Katarina whispered to the others, "We must get to Anthony."

They walked the few blocks in silence, staying close to the walls of the buildings. When they reached the church where Anthony waited, it was a foregone conclusion they would not leave until morning. Anthony was waiting in darkness behind his desk. As soon as Katarina cracked his office door, he ushered her in and turned on a low light. But this time Katarina was sobbing.

"It's horrible! I found the papers you wanted, but I found something else that made me sick. I would not have believed Germany could be doing these things if I had not seen the photos with my own eyes. I took pictures. They are killing Jews. They are murdering them in horrible ways."

The others sat motionless, stunned.

"Here. Develop the film and see for yourself."

As Katarina handed the camera to Anthony, he flinched. "I don't recall such a ring in the family," he said coolly.

Katarina suddenly felt like a child again. Her lips quivered as she looked to her friends for support. They shifted uncomfortably in their chairs, saying nothing. Knowing she was on her own, Katarina stared her brother down and calmly stated, "Frederick asked me to marry him."

Anthony's fury was instantaneous, though he said nothing. Katarina stood her ground.

"I'm sorry, Anthony. Please try to understand and give Frederick a chance. I've known him more than two years now. In the last few months, things have taken a more serious turn."

"Katarina, this is a farce!" Anthony stormed. "What on earth would possess you to accept this proposal of marriage, especially at this time? Why not wait until this terrible war is over and you see what kind of man Frederick really is?"

"He's charming, he's handsome, and he loves me," she said quickly.

"And do you love him? Do you love a Gestapo agent?"

She repeated what she had said to both Heinz and Anthony a few hours ago. "I'm a big girl. I make my own decisions."

Anthony shook his head slowly and walked over to the window. "You must be very tired. Get comfortable until morning. You will all be safe here until the morning. I must leave to deliver this film."

****

In the darkness, Anthony was armed with his standard cover story, should he be stopped. He was needed to visit the sick for last rites. He had a valid address of friends who would back him up and say that their elderly mother had asked for the priest.

He arrived at the convent garden, removed the brick in the wall, and placed the camera in the hollow space. Damn, he thought. He had hoped to find paperwork for the Meister and Rita behind the brick. But he felt only empty space.

Chapter 4

Berlin: July 1943

Frederick did not want to wait a long time to marry. He had visited the Von Rahmel home only once since their engagement. The tension was so thick Katarina couldn't wait for the encounter to end. Frederick had openly stared at Rita, to the point that she had excused herself and left the room. Katarina's nerves had been on edge constantly since her engagement. Why was it so difficult for everyone to understand how she felt about Frederick? Despite her parents' reluctance, Katarina determined to enjoy the wedding preparations.

Today, however, Katarina walked on clouds as she strolled down the street after the final fitting for her wedding gown, being made over from the one her mother had worn many years before. In only a week, she would become Mrs. Frederick Spitz, and she wanted to relish the moment. She would not think about what was going on around her. She would not think about Hitler's goons confiscating private homes and businesses. She would not think about what was happening in her own family's home in Munich, now occupied by Nazis. She would not think about the people targeted in the university, or the fact that Anthony was forever looking for food for those who could no longer safely enter stores. This week she would be happy. This week the war would not touch her. This week she was a woman in love with a man.

How she hoped that Anna was feeling better. They both bemoaned the fact that Anna was not with her friend for the last fitting, but Anna had been too ill to leave the apartment for two days. Surely she would be better in time for the wedding. Although Anna did not find Frederick endearing, and she grieved the fact that she had not been able to have her own wedding, she was being a good friend during these weeks.

Katarina was less than two blocks from home when the air raid siren sounded. Her first instinct was to run toward home and find Anna, but she knew she had to stop. The attack could come at any second. She ducked into a doorway that offered slight shelter and tried to think of the safest place to go. The bomb shelter was a block back, closer to where she stood than the apartment was. Reluctantly, Katarina retraced her steps and headed for the shelter. It was already crowded when she got there, but she squeezed in and carved out a corner of privacy where she could block out the screaming siren and concentrate on her thoughts.

Mentally she did an inventory of where her family members would be at this moment. Her parents and Rita would have sought shelter immediately. Anthony had drilled into them that air raids were nothing to take lightly. Anthony himself had only recently returned from another trip to Rome. Many times he had remarked that the Vatican was a gift. He used his travels there for his own safety as well as to take advantage of the printing presses from time to time. Even the religious frocks he smuggled out of the

Vatican were gifts because they allowed Peter and his friends to move around Rome unnoticed.

If Anthony was disappointed with the position of the Church and the Pope, he did not openly discuss it. He understood that the Church faced a difficult choice. If the Church condemned Hitler, he could invade the defenseless Vatican, and there would be no one left to help the priests who were trying to make a difference. Yet neither could Church officials be known to endorse anything renegade priests like Anthony might do. Right or wrong, history would tell.

Heinz, she knew, was disillusioned. The last time he was in Berlin, he told them he had tried to convince his commanders they needed more recruitment and equipment for training pilots. Heinz felt Hitler had no real respect for the military, ignoring its needs and putting most of his efforts into the concentration camps. Heinz was also furious that the Gestapo had questioned him about his relationship with a French woman. They had wanted every detail of the relationship, using the excuse that with so many French resistance groups they must be sure she was not with one of them. Heinz had seen through the façade. Using this excuse to question him, they had tried to intimidate him into betraying Anthony.

Katarina was so engrossed in her thoughts about Anthony and Heinz that she did not immediately realize the air raid was over. Most of the others had left the shelter. One of the last to leave, she finally emerged onto the street—and was appalled. Such destruction! More buildings than usual had been destroyed. Not just damaged, but destroyed. Amid wails of horror, people were digging frantically through the rubble, looking for their loved ones. Katarina heard the sirens of fire trucks in the distance. With a sudden sense of foreboding, Katarina began running toward her apartment building. She turned the corner and looked at the pile of concrete that had been the building where she and Anna lived.

"Anna!"

Her downstairs neighbor was standing among the rubble, watching rescue workers help survivors dig for their families.

"Frau Stein," Katarina sobbed, "have you seen Anna? Did she go to a shelter with you?"

Frau Stein just stood there crying. Katarina was shaking as she climbed over the debris, calling for Anna. She had just begun digging when her hand touched the red scarf, one she had given Anna years ago after a trip to Paris. Anna had been so proud of the gift. She always wore the scarf when she was sick, swearing it had healing powers. Now Katarina heaved bricks and pipes aside, ignoring the pain in her hands as debris tore into her flesh.

Anna looked as if she were sleeping, her face peaceful, serene.

Katarina dug harder, till she managed to pull Anna's body out. Sobbing, she rocked her friend with no awareness of passing time. When she felt a hand on her shoulder, she knew without looking that it was Anthony.

With cold eyes, Katarina took in her brother. "Where is your God when we need him?"

Anthony simply turned to Anna to administer last rites. He then instructed the rescue workers to take her body to his church. Katarina was numb and mercifully slipped into darkness.

When she woke, she was in a bed at Anthony's rectory, and her parents were nearby. It was two days before she was ready to speak to anyone.

"I'm sorry, Anthony," she said simply. "I should not have spoken as I did. But I do not understand this God of yours."

Anthony had dealt with doubters before. "Katarina, he is your God as well as mine. Do not forsake him."

Katarina searched her brother's face with a question on her lips, but decided it was better not to ask it. God had taken Anthony from her family a long time ago, and as her faith dwindled, his only grew stronger.

"I realize Anna is in a far better place," she said. "I'm not sure where that place is, but it has to be better than this hell. When Anna said she would not see Hans again, we all worried for his death. How ironic that she was predicting her own." Her voice caught. "How will we tell Hans?"

"I've already sent a message," Anthony said hoarsely. "I gave him a few details and told him Anna was buried in the Friedrichsdorf cemetery."

Katarina let out her breath. "I missed her funeral," she said flatly.

"I'm sorry, Katarina. You seemed so ill. Her family was ready to have a service, and we did not know when you would be ready."

"You'll have to show me where the grave is."

Anthony nodded. "When you're ready."

Katarina hesitated, then asked, "Has Frederick been by?"

Anthony swallowed once before responding. "Yes, he was here. He seems anxious to proceed with the wedding on schedule."

Katarina's eyes widened. "But that's in five days! I'm a wreck."

"You'll have to work it out with him, but he does seem to have his mind made up."

"Yes, he would, I suppose."

"He also asked a lot of questions about Aunt Martha and Peter. He had a sudden curiosity about our English relatives. I have to say, Katarina, his line of questioning made me quite uncomfortable."

"Stop! I'm going to marry him. He has a right to be interested in my family."

"If only that were it. I'm certain he has other motives."

Katarina turned her head and refused to listen further.

Frederick's words still rang in Anthony's ears. Dispensing with any social politeness, he had said, "Priest, you will perform the marriage ceremony. I couldn't care less about a church wedding. God is for the stupid. But I know it is important to Katarina."

In his full dress uniform, Frederick had walked slowly around Anthony's office, looking at books on the shelves and papers on the desk. "Priest, your family is well spoken of. One brother is a top ten Luftwaffe pilot, another a leading tank commander with General Rommel. I am told Edwin is doing an impeccable job with the communications assignment."

Frederick paused, and Anthony met his gaze. "We are a proud family," Anthony said. "We work hard."

"There is the matter of Edwin's wife. Helga insists she is Jewish, but we can't seem to find any paperwork on her that says anything but Catholic. Even her birth certificate shows Catholic. Helga swears she grew up in the same town with all of you. Childhood sweethearts, they were. We seem to be at odds here."

Frederick raised his eyebrows in question, but Anthony gave no sign of response. "Well, as I said before," Frederick continued, "a perfect family. You are the brother that the sun rises and sets for, in your sister's eyes. Everyone says you are the perfect priest. Surely you know that the time will come when anything to do with your church and your God will disappear. Now I am marrying the princess of your family, and you have nothing to say? You have voiced no objection. You have not even wanted to have a drink with me. I find that strange."

Anthony stared right into hell in this man's eyes. "Katarina is a big girl. She makes her own decisions." Anthony kept his voice on an even keel but hoped Frederick would hear the warning, nevertheless. "We care only for her happiness. She says she loves you. If she wants you in her life, then so be it."

Frederick hammered his fist on the desk. "I don't believe you, priest!" And he had walked out of the room.

Anthony left Katarina settled in their parents' home, and from there went straight to the main train station. The timing was right to move a few people out of Germany. He had picked up visas and passports from the convent garden that morning before first light. Now he would wait near a beverage stand in a busy train station to pass them on. Austria had closed off since falling rapidly to Hitler, but Denmark and Greece were still viable ways out of the country. Each time he moved people, it seemed to be harder.

When was the world going to see the reality of

what was happening? This question nagged at Anthony every day. The Nazi party had grown from seventeen thousand members in 1926 to over a million. There seemed to be no end to the late night arrests, with wagons picking up entire families. Murder on the streets had escalated as Hitler stomped his way around Europe. Yet the United States had turned away a boatload of Jews, sending them back to their fate. What hope was there?

This country was not the Germany Anthony loved. He would rather see it completely destroyed than have this madness continue.

Chapter 5

Berlin: July 1943

With a pit in his stomach, Father Anthony Von Rahmel bound his sister to Frederick Spitz in sacred matrimony. This was not the wedding any of them would have pictured for Katarina. Despite the prestige of the Von Rahmel family, Frederick insisted on a small ceremony, and Katarina had not argued. The bride's hands, still scraped up from digging through rubble, were hidden under white gloves. As he spoke his vows, the groom barely looked at the bride, instead glaring at the presiding priest, the new brother-in-law he already detested. The feeling was mutual. Anthony felt only revulsion for this man to whom Katarina had just promised her life and future. He wanted the wedding over and the evil man out of his church. The tears his family shed that day were not tears of happiness, but of despair.

Frederick was not the only Gestapo agent present. Men in the congregation watched every move he made, their eyes darting around. Anthony and Edwin had decided long ago that Rita would not attend the wedding. The plain fact was she had to stay out of sight and out of contact with anyone connected with the Gestapo.

Also missing from the wedding was the family's

longtime friend Dietrich. He had flatly refused to serve in the military as the Von Rahmel sons did, instead managing to go underground completely. The last Anthony had heard, Dietrich was in Poland with Grigory and Nicholas, looking for exploded pieces of rockets the Germans had tested. English intelligence wanted as much information and as many rocket pieces as they could retrieve. Since Dietrich spoke fluent Polish, he was invaluable to the operations there.

Aunt Helena attended the wedding but stayed at the back of the church with a considerable number of empty pews between her and the rest of the congregation. In addition to her emotional estrangement from Katarina, Helena had endured her own encounters with the Gestapo as they snuck around her home asking questions about neighbors who seemed to have left everything behind in an instant. Using her wit and charm, she deflected their interest from her own house, where, in a small secret place, she regularly housed refugees Anthony was moving out of the country.

With the brief ceremony over, Anthony pronounced them man and wife. Frederick kissed Katarina possessively, making Anthony's stomach lurch.

Katarina's wedding night was a nightmare. Even though Frederick knew she was a virgin, he was brutal as he took her. With no foreplay, no thought of her feelings, he simply spread her legs and pushed himself inside her. After he had satisfied himself, he rolled off her and turned his back. Feeling bruised and battered, Katarina lay beside her new husband wishing she were anywhere else. Finally she slept from sheer exhaustion. Her last thoughts before dropping off were that surely tomorrow would be better.

To her dismay, Frederick's lovemaking only got worse as the days passed. There was no tenderness, no love, no thought given to her comfort. He forced her to perform acts that shocked her, and made it a point to tell her every night how terrible she was in bed. Katarina learned to think of other things whenever Frederick wanted sex, to go to a place within herself where it didn't matter what he did.

As the weeks passed and her marriage became more and more strained, Katarina was forced to realize she could not make Frederick happy. Besides the verbal and physical abuse, he grilled her continuously about her activities and her family. What had they done that day? Who did she visit? Where was she during the air raid? How many hours had she practiced dancing? The barrage of questions never stopped, and he no longer even pretended to be interested because the Von Rahmels were now his family.

Frederick no longer smiled and crinkled his eyes at Katarina. He had become pure Gestapo.

When Frederick suddenly stopped coming home at night, Katarina was thankful for the peace and quiet.

Frederick had set up an engagement in Munich for the ballet company to perform before the highest-ranking military officers. With the daily bombings all over Germany, Katarina was hesitant to travel. The train system was a target for the Resistance, and it was filled with soldiers serving as guards. She knew that Anthony had been with Grigory and Nicholas when they placed explosives on the tracks to blow up a train with food going to German troops. At the root of it all, Katarina resented that while the German people were struggling to survive, these military officers demanded to be entertained. Her dancing had become a well rehearsed performance rather than an expression of the joy in her soul.

With Frederick's constant harassment and the stress of returning to Munich, Katarina could barely perform in her home city. She felt physically ill whenever she thought of the family's estate only a few miles away, taken over by Nazis. Her father's prized horses were gone; most of his books had been burned. Her father did not know that Katarina had smuggled out his two favorite books when the family left the estate, one by Schiller, the other by Browning. They would be her gift to him when the war was finally over.

Katarina shook with fear as Gestapo agents stormed into dressing rooms and searched everyone's belongings. They ripped apart dance costumes and threw luggage at the walls. She tried to explain that she was married to Colonel Spitz of the SS, but the agents only glared at her and continued their rampage. In the meantime, the performance was beginning on schedule. Just as Katarina was ready to make her stage entrance, the Gestapo led two of the company's male dancers out. She heard an agent say, "Transfer these homosexuals to one of the concentration camps." All the dancers trembled, but none dared say a word. Anyone who objected would be led away as well. The Meister wiped tears from his eyes.

Once again home in Berlin, Katarina told Frederick of the vicious search. She hoped that deep inside him would be an ounce of indignation that his wife should be treated this way. Instead, he shouted at her, "How dare you question what the Nazi party does?

Homosexuals are the enemy, like the Jews. They must be put away." He shoved her against the wall and raised his hand in a fist. But he did not strike her. Instead, he left and did not come home for two days.

Katarina resolved to talk to Anthony. He'd been right. They'd all been right.

Frederick's purpose in marrying her became more obvious each day. She had waited as long as she could before admitting it. Frederick had never loved her; he merely wanted to keep close tabs on her family, and his frustration was growing daily with the lack of information forthcoming. She had to find a way out. But until then, she had to appear normal, following her normal routines. If he came home, she attended to his every wish, she slept with him, she served his meals. But, each day, she wished he would not come home. So far he had not physically imprisoned her. She was, after all, a prima ballerina who must be free to rehearse and perform. One morning, she prepared to leave him a note to say she would be out most of the day.

Her pen was dry. Pulling open a desk drawer, she rummaged for another one.

That's when she saw the paper.

There needs to be more elimination of Jews. Too many are still alive. There are too many homosexuals in the performing arts. Must get rid of them for the good of the Third Reich.

Stunned at her discovery, Katarina slid the paper gently aside and looked at the one beneath it.

We must find and punish everyone helping the Jews.

Fear clutched her heart. She would be late for rehearsal, but the Meister would just have to understand. Katarina could not stop now. The main drawers of the desk were locked, but Katarina had seen where Frederick kept the key. A few minutes later, she had the drawers unlocked and was looking at a folder labeled "Deportation of Jews."

Underground activity in Berlin, France, Italy. Who is in the Rosengranz Circle, if it really exists? Are they military? Labor leaders? Clergy? Who is responsible for the suspected plot against Hitler? SS wants them found and hanged.

Names of people who had been caught, tortured, and executed leapt off the page. With shaking hands, Katarina opened another folder, labeled "Von Rahmels."

There on paper was her family history dating back five hundred years. All their pre-war financial holdings were neatly listed, and next to each name of a member of her family was a description. Heinz and Hans had glowing reports of their service record and loyalty, followed by a notation: May be difficult to go after such an upstanding family.

Next to Helena's name was watch, and next to Anthony's Jew lover. In fine print beside Edwin and Rita's names was Need to find out more about her heritage. Family says she's Catholic and has baptism papers to prove it.

Katarina saw her own name with a star next to it. Waste of time to marry her.

Have not gotten any information on what the priest is doing. Can't penetrate this family. Loyalty to family and God is greater than love for Germany.

To her shock, in the family file Katarina saw the Meister's name. Needs to be arrested.

Forcing herself to breathe steadily, Katarina closed the drawer and made sure it was properly locked. She returned the key to the hiding place.

How long had Frederick been keeping files on her family? It seemed to her the Meister could be arrested at any moment. In a flash of lucidity, Katarina knew she had to go to the opera house immediately. She would see Anthony, but first she would hide the Meister.

Katarina couldn't make her legs move fast enough. Just before she turned the final corner and would have the rehearsal hall in sight, a hand clasped over her mouth. She felt a man's breath on her neck.

"Be still."

Edwin! Katarina wriggled around to see her brother. They both peeked around the corner in time to see SS men leading the Meister out of the building. He fell as they reached the street. The soldiers kicked him as he lay on the sidewalk, deliberately stepping on his glasses as he reached for them.

Katarina struggled against Edwin's hold. She could not stand there and let them do this! But Edwin's grip was one of iron as he pulled her back down the street. He did not speak until they had put a four-block distance between them and the soldiers.

"Listen to me," Edwin said. "It was a trap. I only found out this morning they were arresting him today. The information came across my desk in such a way it was obvious the Gestapo wanted to see if I would warn him. If I had, they would know where the leak was in their headquarters. They tried to set me up. We could not warn him without jeopardizing the whole operation."

Edwin leaned forward, his hands on his knees,

trying to catch his breath. "Katarina, go home. Don't tell anyone you saw me today. I don't want to hurt you, but I'm sure it was your husband who told my superiors of his suspicions."

"I'm leaving him," she blurted out.

He searched her eyes for the rest of the truth.

"Edwin, I have to tell you about the folders I saw today in Frederick's desk." Katarina quickly recounted what she had seen.

"Go home," Edwin instructed. "I will find Anthony. He is meeting with Grigory tonight. We have to make some changes. It's time the whole family leaves Germany. I've been an idiot not to have the papers ready before now."

"Don't blame yourself, Edwin."

"Katarina, you must think of something to tell Frederick to explain why you were not at practice today. He will know of the Meister's arrest and will want to know your reaction to what you saw. He's going to try to trick you."

Katarina kissed her brother and walked away with heavy steps.

The truth was she did not feel well, and she would not be lying when she told Frederick she had been too sick to go to practice. Her walk slowed as she passed rubble from the recent bombing. She watched people in their tattered clothes, wondering how many of them could still believe in their Führer.

Her main concern now was whether her family could safely get away from their homeland. Would Anthony even agree to leave? If Edwin was being closely watched, could he still get the paperwork they needed?

She stopped, exhausted, and leaned against a building. The air raid siren went off just then, but she could not move. She didn't care. She just wanted silence, a barrier to the outside world and all its terrors. She didn't see the people around her scurrying for shelter, didn't hear them urging her to hurry.

What had she done to make this man she married hate her? Crying openly in the street as her back slid down the side of the building, she vowed she would never again let a man use her. She covered her head with her arms, lost in her world of silence. For the rest of her life she would use this response to close out the real world when it became too difficult.

Chapter 6

Berlin: March 1944

"We have to get her out of Frederick's house." Edwin stood at the window of the rectory, scanning the street out of habit.

"I agree," Anthony answered. "He only married her to get to us. He's just trying to figure out his next move."

"We have to make sure he doesn't get the chance to make a next move."

"Especially not against Katarina." Anthony sighed. "Yesterday the police questioned Father and Aunt Helena again. I'm sure it's Frederick's doing."

"I haven't dared forge any papers lately," Edwin said. "I know in my bones he would find out if I did, and I can't take the chance. There's too much at risk for the family."

"I will get Katarina out of there today," Anthony promised. "She hasn't been feeling well the last few weeks. Her stomach has been giving her a lot of trouble."

"Considering the stress she lives under, how could she feel well?"

"Just in case, she's seeing Dr. Bernard today."

****

With her hands pressed into her eyes, Katarina

chastened herself for not having thought this through carefully enough. She had written Frederick a note saying she was leaving him. Thinking she would be gone before he could get home, she had asked a neighbor boy to deliver the note to Frederick's office. But the boy went sooner than she meant him to, and she took too long to pack. She should have finished packing first, or not sent the note. What was she thinking? She owed him nothing. But it was too late to undo her actions. Frederick's fury had thundered through the door as she snapped her suitcase shut. Now he was screaming at her. She wasn't sure if he was most angry about the fact that she wanted to leave or that she had told him she was four months pregnant.

"If I'd wanted a child, I would have impregnated someone worthy!" he raged. "You know we are making a pure race. Officers all over Europe are impregnating women for the Third Reich. You are not pure. You and your brother love the imperfect, and I would never want a child with you."

Katarina shook with fear as Frederick slammed his fist down on the desk.

"You stupid bitch!" he screamed. "Do you think I care about this baby? Do you think I want this child? Have it aborted for all I care."

He towered over her so closely she could see the madness in his eyes as he began laughing hysterically.

"Maybe I should change my mind. We need good little soldiers. Maybe this child should come with me. I will make it a true follower."

Rage of her own swallowed Katarina's fear. "Never will you have my baby!" she cried.

He raised his hand to strike her.

As she screamed, a patch of black wool swooped past her and grabbed Frederick's arm. Anthony!

Anthony twisted Frederick's arm with strength that surprised them both. He held it firmly behind Frederick's back until he heard the officer catch his breath in pain. With his jaw set solidly, Anthony murmured into Frederick's ear, "If you ever touch her or come near her again, as God is my witness, I will kill you with my own hands."

Anthony looked up and caught Katarina's eyes. She picked up her suitcase and moved toward the door. Anthony was right behind her.

They moved quickly down the steps to the street, where to Katarina's surprise and relief, Edwin waited in a car. Anthony threw Katarina's suitcase into the back seat and pushed her in behind it. The car was already moving when he jumped into the front seat.

Edwin glanced at them both.

"I'm fine," Katarina said, in response to his unspoken question. "He didn't hurt me. Thank God Anthony showed up when he did."

Edwin blew out his breath in relief. "Anthony, I have news for you. Grigory and Nicholas are in the cellar at the rectory waiting for you. They've been to Poland and the Hartz Mountains here in Germany to see the slave labor with their own eyes. They're hiding two scientists in Weimar that we need to get out quickly."

"Bomb scientists?" Anthony asked.

Edwin nodded. "They know too much to stay here safely. We have to get them to England or America."

"I can't imagine more destruction than we have now," Anthony said, "but the scientists I've talked to seem to think this bomb could destroy the world."

"It may seem far-fetched, but Grigory and Nicholas believe them. We already have visas and passports we can use. Peter is waiting for them in France. If we can get them that far, Peter will take care of the rest."

Katarina laid her head back on the seat, reliving the scene she had just escaped. How could her judgment have been so clouded for so long? And now a baby was on the way.

They arrived at the Von Rahmel home without further incident. Jona and Lisa opened their arms to their daughter without judgment, for which Katarina was grateful.

"Edwin, you should get back to work," Anthony said. "I can walk back to the rectory."

"No, I'll drive you. I still have a few privileges with this job."

They drove for a few minutes before Edwin broke the silence. "Anthony, why didn't you tell me you were in Paris last month?"

"Ah, so you found out." Anthony sighed. "There was nothing to be gained by dragging you into it."

"My God, Anthony, why did you put yourself in that position? You met with Peter in an open restaurant. I thought we were past those days."

Anthony laughed, suddenly thinking back to that night. "At the time it was frightening, but it's of no significance now. Peter asked Grigory and me to meet him. We didn't know much about the restaurant Peter picked. It was full of German officers. Grigory and I went in and sat down at the most obscure table we could find. We didn't say a word for ten minutes, just got very busy looking at the menu. Suddenly we looked up to see Peter walk in, dressed in all his glory in a

German admiral's uniform. He actually stopped and spoke to several officers as if he knew them!"

"I've always known he's crazy," Edwin muttered.

"Well, it worked. No one paid any attention to us, and we had a nice meal."

"What did Peter want?"

"He's afraid the Rosenkranz Circle may be discovered soon, and we should all be prepared to leave the country at a moment's notice."

"I've got to find a way to get you some papers."

"Don't worry about me. It's Heinz I'm worried about. Peter says the Gestapo are questioning him often. Apparently Heinz is getting serious with this French woman he's taken up with."

"I hope he's being careful," Edwin said. "What about Dietrich? What do you know of his whereabouts?"

"Actually, Dietrich has been in Berlin for the last week," Anthony admitted. "Peter needs him here, but he didn't say why. I'm not even sure why Grigory and Nicholas are here."

"Peter's working on something."

"He said something about gathering soil samples on the beaches of Normandy, but he wouldn't tell me why."

"It's probably better if you don't know."

Anthony nodded. "He tells me the funny parts, though. On the last night there, German guards swept through the beach. Peter saw a large German shepherd trotting toward him. He put his hands over his head, certain that the dog would tear into him. Instead, the dog sniffed his face, then hiked his leg and pissed in Peter's face. Peter says it's a sure sign the German dogs hate the British."

Edwin laughed. "I can just see Peter. We'll certainly have stories to tell when this war is over. What else happened in Paris?"

Anthony hesitated, then said, "Peter offered us some explosives and weapons he has hidden in the forest outside Paris. That was the real point of the trip, it turned out."

"Weapons? What will you do with weapons?"

"I have no intention of holding one in my hand, Edwin. I am a priest. But Grigory and Nicholas…"

Edwin stopped the car two blocks from the rectory, a cautious habit they had developed a long time ago. The less Edwin was seen with Anthony, the better.

****

Anthony made his way through the dark rectory to the basement bookcase filled with old Bibles and religious books rescued from bombed churches. The hook he sought was so small he had to dig with his fingers to twist it before the shelves slid back. He greeted Dietrich, Grigory, and Nicholas with genuine happiness, but he was a bit surprised to see Abraham there as well. Rita, Edwin's wife, did not know her brother was still in Berlin. Anthony had found him one morning standing in front of the church, and from that moment he had been part of the Underground. He moved around Berlin with his handheld radio, transmitting essential information.

The somber group got down to business.

****

The following morning, after early Mass, Anthony entered his study to find Frederick sitting behind the desk with his feet propped on it. Every drawer in the room was open and papers scattered on the floor. Several other Gestapo agents were still rummaging through books and papers.

Frederick stood up and crossed to the full-length mirror, where he adjusted his uniform. His eyes locked with Anthony's as he returned to his seat at the desk.

"Priest, your brother's wife is Jewish, and it is about time we start facing some facts about the Von Rahmel family. The Führer no longer cares how well your brothers are performing for their country. It cannot be a country until we rid it of all undesirables, and we do not want any Jewish blood running through the great Von Rahmel family, now do we?"

Anthony looked at Frederick coolly, saying nothing.

Fredrick slammed a book down on the desk. "Priest, I have had just about enough of your sanctity. Do you really think that because your sister is having my child any of you matter to me? Trust me. It is only a matter of time."

Anthony never even flinched as Frederick stormed across the room and brushed past him, motioning for the others to follow.

Breathing evenly, Anthony made sure Frederick's car had left, then went to the basement and pushed the hook on the bookcase. In the cellar, Abraham and Edwin waited.

"Abraham, I want you to send a message to Grigory and Peter to meet me in Rome as soon as possible." He turned to his brother. "Edwin, memorize these codes and names. Abraham and Katarina already know them." He handed a slip of paper to Edwin.

Anthony opened a cabinet and removed one of the

weapons Grigory had provided. When he started loading bullets into it, Edwin and Abraham looked at him in shock.

"Anthony!" Edwin said. "You are a priest."

"I know." Anthony double-checked the bullets.

"Can you do this?"

"I will if I have to."

Chapter 7

Rome: April 1944

Relations between the Vatican and Nazi Germany were a thin string ready to snap. Always on guard, no one from the Vatican would publicly denounce the Nazis. In fact, it was rumored that the Pope had made a deal with the party to avoid invasion.

Under these warped circumstances, Rome remained a safe place for Father Anthony Von Rahmel. At times a few other priests—without the Pope's knowledge—helped him move people out of Germany, and Rome was secure territory for surreptitious conversations between vespers and morning prayers—or sometimes in broad daylight in the Vatican gardens.

Anthony suspected the Vatican knew what he was doing but had closed its eyes.

A cardinal had once approached him as he knelt in prayer and murmured that he was considered a renegade priest and ought to show proper obedience to the Church. Before Anthony could form a respectful response, the cardinal had rustled away. No one overtly questioned his coming and going or why he was in Rome as often as he was when he had a parish to run in Berlin, and so far the Nazis had not accosted him in transit to and from the holy city.

As safe as Rome was for Anthony, he worried

about Peter's presence there. However, he knew they had to meet. The word was out that the Nazis had a clear description of Peter and that he was to be apprehended at all cost. Anthony's family endured questioning on a regular basis about their cousin's whereabouts, but Peter had conscientiously made sure that for the most part the Von Rahmel family could answer honestly that they did not know where he was.

Peter appeared in Rome dressed as a French cardinal, with all the appropriate documents to prove his legitimacy. Anthony was praying in a chapel at St. Peter's Cathedral when Peter slid in next to him. He acknowledged his cousin almost imperceptibly as he finished his prayers. Later, they walked in the gardens outside the basilica.

Anthony was the first to speak. "Peter, I'm not sure the family can take any more risks. Edwin no longer knows which troop movements are for real and which are traps. He's more and more hesitant to send you anything, because he can't be sure the information is accurate."

"I understand your frustration. When the Rosengranz Circle transmits information about the military, about ninety percent of the time the British ignore it."

"You've missed so many opportunities because your superiors didn't believe the transmissions. Why should anyone believe there are Germans who want to end this war?" Anthony's tone sounded bitter even to himself.

"Anthony, now is not the time to give up!" Peter smiled. "Don't forget I was the face under that dog's raised leg. That should count for something."

Anthony laughed at the memory of the story about Peter. Then he sighed heavily. "It's more than that. It's Frederick. He'll stop at nothing to destroy us. We moved Katarina back home. She is pregnant, and her husband doesn't care. Her ballet company is in shambles since he had the Meister arrested. We depended on them for so many things, and now we don't dare ask for anything."

Looking as if the weight of the world was on his shoulders, Anthony sagged into a park bench. Peter sat beside him and spoke softly.

"Anthony, you are not alone. People all over France and Holland know about your group. We're trying our best to work from inside the Resistance group in every situation. I have agents everywhere, people even you would not suspect."

"The risk is becoming too much, Peter. I don't care so much for myself, but what about the family?"

"Stay low for awhile and let us see what we can do for you. Dietrich, Grigory and Nicholas are staying in Berlin for the time being. They have their eyes on you, and they will always know how to reach me." Peter reached for Anthony's shoulder. "Trust me. I will not let you or the family down. A lot of people are alive because of you and Katarina."

"I just don't know if we can keep going. Katarina is having a baby, after all. There's another life to think about."

"We have an agent in Berlin working right under the generals' noses. We haven't heard from him for awhile, but Grigory is trying to find out what the problem is. This is bound to break open soon."

Anthony shrugged off his cousin. "I wish you

hadn't told me that. I don't want to know anything more! It's hard enough as it is. On top of everything, I have a lunatic Gestapo agent for a brother-in-law, and he's hell-bent on destroying our family."

A cardinal waved a hand in greeting across the lawn. Anthony waved back and nudged Peter to do the same. The cardinal was striding toward them.

"What do I say if he speaks to me?" Peter asked, an uncharacteristic anxiety in his voice.

Anthony chuckled. "He's an Italian and doesn't speak French. So just speak French and let me take care of the rest."

"This is your revenge on me for all the times I skipped Mass, isn't it?"

Anthony chuckled.

The cardinal passed by them with only a smile. Anthony lowered his head in deference and gave a greeting in Italian.

Once the cardinal had passed, Anthony stood up and stretched his long body. "I need to walk some more. Besides, we can talk more freely if we're moving."

When they came to a secluded area, Peter reached under his false cardinal robes and removed a weapon. As Peter checked the clip, Anthony raised his eyebrow.

"Peter, there is no one here to fear."

"True enough. But when I leave these gates and enter the streets of Rome, that changes. I can't pass as a French cardinal forever."

"Well, put that thing away while you're inside the gates."

"You're in a cocoon here," Peter said. "But the minute you leave the grounds of the Vatican, it all changes."

"Nothing surprises me any more," Anthony said. "My own aunt in England could be bombed by my own brother just trying to keep his nose clean so that no one discovers what I'm up to. When you leave here today, I will wonder if I will ever see you in Germany again."

"Don't worry about me, Anthony. Germany will lose the war, and I will return. Germany will change in the eyes of the world, and it can only be for the good."

"The world may never trust Germany again, Peter. That's reality."

"One step at a time, Anthony."

"I have seen Germans beat Jews to death, and drown them in the rivers."

"Anthony, now is not the time to torture yourself."

But Anthony would not be deterred. "The Nazis forced Jews to use their sacred prayer bands, their *tefillin*, as cleaning rags to scrub the streets. That's like asking me to use my crucifix as a shovel."

"Anthony, please, don't do this!"

"Hitler wants the world to conform to his insanity, and most of my country has stood by and watched it happen. They look at this man's distorted vision as their own vision for a better world. How can this be?"

Anthony searched his cousin's face for answers. "The rest of the world is no better. Do they think that because it is not happening in their countries, it doesn't matter? Where is America, Peter?" Anthony demanded. "Why are they turning away the Jews who are only trying to survive? Children, Peter! Children! Why are the Allies not doing more?"

Peter pulled his cousin to his chest and held him there.

Chapter 8

Berlin: May 1944

It took Anthony only ten minutes to throw on clothes and get out the door. Heinz was home for a few days, and he had come to the rectory with word that Edwin wanted to see them both.

Heinz had married the French woman the Gestapo was so suspicious about, and she was having his child. When he told his family the news, he exacted a promise that they would take care of Elvia and the child if anything happened to him.

As war losses grew heavier each day, Heinz was training young pilots as fast as the system could recruit them. Outward appearance and official records continued to suggest Heinz Von Rahmel was a loyal German serving his country to the best of his ability. Nevertheless, he endured many restless nights of Gestapo interrogation about his family. During one session, they had actually accused the Von Rahmels of leaking information on the Siemens Electrical Works' involvement in aircraft manufacturing.

Heinz suspected that the orders for the heavy questioning had come directly from Frederick, and Anthony had to agree.

When Anthony and Heinz arrived at the cemetery where they would meet Edwin, they found him pacing the cellar of the maintenance garage. Tucked away in an obscure corner of the cemetery and covered in ivy, it was nearly invisible and served as a safe alternative to meeting in the cellar at Anthony's rectory. It was fairly easy for people to stroll through the cemetery, perhaps pause at a particular grave, then move on and end up near the maintenance garage.

Grigory was already there. Edwin handed a canister to Grigory and began to speak, mostly to Anthony.

"This is an unholy mess. A British agent has been working at Templehof all this time. I didn't know about him, but he sure as hell knew who I was. Anthony, who else knows? What will they find out when they question him?"

"Do you mean they've arrested him?" Anthony asked.

"God, we are all down the river!" Edwin said. "The Brit had vital film showing where the V2 rockets are being built in the Hartz Mountains. How could he have known to hand it to me as I was walking out the building? He bumped up against me, and the next thing I knew I saw him surrounded. It was clear what was happening."

Heinz took a deep breath.

"I just kept walking. I felt something in my pocket but didn't know what it was then. I had to wait till I was sure it was safe to look."

"Do you know where they took him?"

"To the Chamber Building for interrogation, I'm sure. Since he slipped me the film, they will not find anything on him. But that doesn't mean they can't make him talk."

Edwin was running his hand through his hair. He scanned the panicked faces around him. "God, what are we going to do?"

Anthony took control. "Heinz, what do you know about this interrogation room?"

"Only that it's on the top floor and there are no bars on the windows."

"We have to get him out."

"It's a long shot. We could all be killed."

"I'm deadly serious," Anthony responded. "Heinz, go back to the church and have Abraham get word to Dietrich. You must provide passage for him on an aircraft to a safe place in France."

"Jesus, Anthony, you're crazy! Just how do you expect me to perform this minor miracle?"

Anthony glared at his brother. "Don't take the Lord's name in vain."

Heinz let out an exasperated sigh.

****

They came back together several hours later. Grigory and Nicholas brought along Uwe Fischer, a Lutheran pastor Anthony had collaborated with over the years. Even though Anthony was surprised to see Uwe, he welcomed the extra help. The group went over the fragments of information piece by piece, deciding the best course of action and knowing every minute counted. They could not afford to give the ruthless Gestapo time to interrogate at length. If this particular agent broke, they would all be in immediate danger.

****

They were in position on the roof of the Chamber Building, all except Uwe, who waited on the street outside the building, ready to create a diversion if necessary. With ropes tied around him, they prepared to lower Dietrich to the unbarred window.

Edwin gave instructions. "The guards stay at the far end of the hall. You have ten minutes to get him out before the changing of the guard on the floor. Then we have twenty minutes before anyone passes below us. They go from one end of the street to the other."

Anthony looked at his watch and said, "Go."

Soundlessly they lowered Dietrich, who stealthily pried the window open and slid soundlessly into the room. The agent was slumped unconscious in the chair where he was tied. Flashing a knife, Dietrich cut the ropes, then put a finger to his lips to silence the awakening agent. He froze momentarily when he heard voices outside the door, but they passed and drifted farther down the hall. Dietrich lifted the agent on his shoulder and with great difficulty managed to get them both out the window. The roof team began to pull on the ropes. The agent stirred again, opening his one good eye, and promptly passed out again.

The plan was working. In a matter of minutes, the whole crew had moved several rooftops over. When they heard shouts coming from the Chamber Building, they knew the agent's absence had been discovered, and they scrambled off the rooftop and into a dark stairway.

Grigory turned to Anthony with a hoarse whisper. "I'm not sure you and Uwe can get him to Helena's on your own. Do you want me to stay with you?"

Anthony shook his head. "That will only attract attention. We will manage. We just have to get off the street as fast as we can." It didn't help that the rescued agent was too unstable to stand on his own feet. Clearly the man's collarbone and several ribs were broken; his face looked like a rotting pumpkin weeks after picking. Nicholas was trying to calm the disoriented man, who did not seem to realize he was being rescued.

Grigory said, "There is a car waiting at the corner. Don't be startled by the Nazi driver. He's one of us. He'll take you to Helena's."

The ten-minute walk to the corner seemed like hours. Uwe and Anthony kept the agent between them, walking like a drunken trio. Uwe even sang a few bawdy lines for effect. Anthony was glad he was not in priestly garb. As they approached, the driver jumped out of the car and opened a door. They eased the injured man in as quickly as possible and lurched in after him. Anthony pulled the door closed as the driver hit the accelerator.

Helena was waiting at the door when they arrived, and Anthony commended the man to her care, knowing he might never learn what happened after that.

As Uwe and Anthony returned to the street, looking as normal as possible now, Anthony felt the cold metal of the weapon stuck in his belt. Grigory had insisted he carry a gun before they left the cemetery, and Anthony had taken it reluctantly, all the while praying he would never need to use it.

****

It did not take Frederick long to step up his rampage of revenge. Anthony had slept only two hours when Edwin turned up at the rectory to shake him awake. Edwin looked as if death itself had come to him.

"Anthony! They took Rita!"

Anthony was instantly awake. He sat up in bed and pushed back the blankets. "Katarina was crying when I

86

got to the house last night," Edwin explained.

"Frederick himself had come. He pushed his way past her and demanded to know where I was."

"Did he hurt her?" Anthony was out of bed now and fumbling for clothing.

Edwin nodded. "When she wouldn't tell him anything, he split her lip. He told her he's taking the baby for the Third Reich as soon as it's born."

"She must be beside herself."

"She's hysterical, not only because of the baby, but because Frederick charged through the house until he found Rita. He carried her out himself."

"Edwin, I'm so sorry. I don't know what to say."

"This is not a time for words, Anthony. This is a time for action."

Visions of Simon bleeding in the street flashed before Anthony. Simon gasping his last breath. Simon lying in a shallow garden grave.

"Anthony!"

He had to focus on Rita.

"Heinz managed to get a Luftwaffe uniform," Edwin said, "and I processed the paperwork for the agent. I took it over to Helena's. I was so busy saving the life of an agent I don't know that I didn't get back in time to protect my own wife."

"Edwin, don't. You can't beat yourself up. You did what you thought you had to do."

"Mother and Father were away overnight. The bastard waited until he knew only Rita and Katarina were home, and of course Katarina couldn't fight him off."

"We'll figure something out, Edwin."

"Helga is behind this, I just know it. I have to

speak to her."

"Edwin, don't waste the energy. We have to concentrate on finding out where they took Rita."

Edwin dropped into a chair and put his head in his hands. "It's as if all information about her is out of my reach."

"We won't give up," Anthony promised him.

"I'm going to find Helga," Edwin said, getting up again suddenly. "She knows something, I'm sure of it."

As soon as Edwin closed the door behind him, Anthony threw a glass paperweight against the wall, then pounded the nightstand with his fist.

****

Finding Rita had a price tag.

Edwin knocked on Helga's door and she opened it, looking as if she expected him. She wore a translucent nightgown that clung to her freshly powdered body. Edwin pushed past her, disgusted. As he inspected the room, he saw a decanter of wine and two glasses.

He turned to admonish her. "Helga, this is a futile attempt. I told you long ago that we were through."

"Oh, Edwin, there is always room for compromise." Helga cooed seductively as she slithered into a chair. "You know I have something you want."

Edwin moved closer to her. "Helga, isn't this a little melodramatic, even for you?"

Opening her legs, Helga lifted her gown to reveal her nakedness. "You won't think so if I don't tell you where they sent your Jew wife. Make love to me now, and I'll give you the information. If you don't, by the time you find her, every officer in the camp will have had his way with her."

Edwin lunged toward her, and before she could

escape his grasp he had his hands around her throat. "Tell me where she is, you stupid whore. That's all you will ever be, a pathetic whore for Hitler. I will kill you." He squeezed harder.

She managed to croak, "Ravensbrück."

Edwin let go of her throat, appalled, as he backed away from her. "My God, Helga, how could you have sent her to Ravensbrück? What sort of monster are you?"

Ravensbrück was nothing but a concentration camp where the women were used, then killed when the camp guards had enough of them. The reports he had read said inmates there were mostly from Poland but included Jehovah's Witnesses and resistance fighters, also. It was only about 60 miles outside of Berlin, along Lake Schwedt.

As Edwin headed for the door, he heard the click of a gun cocking behind him.

At the same instant, the door crashed in, and Edwin heard two shots. He whirled around and saw Helga lying on the floor, blood oozing from her chest and her eyes as lifeless and cold in death as they had been in life.

"Good God, Dietrich, how did you and Grigory know I was here?"

"Anthony, of course."

"Now, look, Edwin," Grigory said, "when we get to the street, you have to walk in the middle of people and try to blend in. We will be right behind you. I promise you we will find Rita. Meet us at the cemetery later."

****

Anthony read the note Edwin had left him at the

cemetery cellar. He wasn't waiting for a group plan; instead he had launched out on his own to find his wife. Anthony shut his eyes and breathed a prayer. When he opened them, he surveyed his collaborators.

"We have to catch him," he said. "He's going to do something rash. Grigory, what can you do?"

Chapter 9

Ravensbrück: May 1944

For the first time in years, Rita said her Jewish prayers. And for the first time in her life she discovered how fiercely she could hate.

As she was herded onto the train with hundreds of other innocent people, she felt eyes boring into her back. She turned around, and there glaring at her were Helga and Frederick. They had made sure she left Berlin immediately to keep Edwin from finding her.

Knowing she had nothing to lose, Rita had broken out of line and, with all her strength, slapped Helga across the face. Frederick held Helga back from retaliating, reminding her glibly that Frau Von Rahmel's days were numbered.

When the train arrived at Ravensbrück, Rita was stripped naked and paraded in front of the camp officers. As if she were a bowl of ripe fruit, they fondled her in areas where no one but Edwin had ever touched her. Two of the officers chose her as the "Jewish whore." Her head was shaved, and she was color-coded as a Jew. She had already seen various other colors marking prisoners and assumed each color represented a different reason for imprisonment.

Edwin would find her. Rita knew that. She vowed to survive until he came.

****

Edwin determined to leave Berlin with only his uniform on his back. Grigory caught him leaving the city, but Edwin resisted any advice, instead demanding to know the locations of the safe houses in the fifty-six miles between Berlin and Ravensbrück. Grigory begged him not to do this alone. Nicholas and Dietrich would meet him at an address Grigory gave to Edwin. Nicholas and Dietrich had broken into camps before; it would be much safer.

"I'm not waiting. Your plan will take too long to organize."

Grigory paced the sidewalk, rubbing his neck. "Look, you're going to have the Gestapo and everyone else looking for you when you do not return to work. I've been doing this long enough to know how quickly someone can be detected. What good will you be to your wife if you are shot?"

But Edwin insisted. He just wanted the locations of the safe houses. "At least get out of that uniform," Grigory pleaded.

Edwin shook his head. "At least for now, I think I can leave Berlin more easily in uniform."

And he had gone.

Grigory had worked a miracle, however. When Edwin reached the safe house outside of Ravensbrück, Dietrich and Nicholas were already there, with a plan to get Rita out and keep both Edwin and Rita hidden until it was safe to move them out of the country.

Time was their worst enemy. It was only a matter of time before Edwin's superiors would launch an all-out search for him, and it wouldn't take long for them to figure out where he had gone. And rumors indicated the camp had stepped up brutality, essentially executing women at whim.

The three men stood silently in the middle of the room as a middle-aged woman slipped in. She never spoke as she placed cheese, black bread, and tea on the table. She left just as silently as she had entered. Watching her leave, Edwin's eyes questioned.

"You can trust her," Nicholas assured him. "We have been using this house for three years. She doesn't ask questions and doesn't want to know what's going on. Her husband was part of our group until he was discovered in Holland and killed. She would like nothing more than vengeance."

Nicholas moved the bed and began to pry off a baseboard. He pulled papers from the wall and placed them on the table. "These are blueprints for the compound. You must present your papers here." Nicholas pointed to a building as he handed Edwin and Dietrich false identification documents. "You will be able to move around freely with these papers, but you will have to meet the camp commander. If you get a chance to shoot him, do it."

"I'll be your driver," Dietrich said.

The papers looked authentic. "How did you get these papers so quickly?" Edwin asked.

Nicholas laughed. "There are plenty of German officers to kill. You just have to be at the right place at the right time. Just tell them you were sent from Berlin and that you are there to make sure they are meeting their quota of SS uniforms the prisoners are supposed to be making."

Edwin sagged into a ragged overstuffed chair. "Do you think we can get her out tomorrow?"

Dietrich let out a long breath. "If we can't, we'll devise a plan to go back the next day. I'm sure just seeing the layout for ourselves will give us more options. We'll need some luck to find her quickly." It would take a week before the opportunity came to leave. The first place the Gestapo would look for him was the camp, so they lay low till they knew there was the perfect window.

"Can't we do something to speed things along?"

"The camp has a book with the women listed," Nicholas explained. "If they let you look at it, you might find something. Some of the electric fences around certain areas of the camp are not turned on. You might get lucky."

Nicholas shrugged into his coat and picked up a bag. "Aren't you going with us?" Edwin asked.

Nicholas shook his head. "More than two people in the car would cause suspicion. I can do more good back in Berlin than waiting for you here. We've alerted other safe houses of your eventual arrival." He paused somberly. "Edwin, you know you cannot go back to Berlin, right?"

Edwin nodded, thinking of the family he might never see again.

****

In the morning, dressed in German uniforms and looking like an SS Hauptsturmführer and his driver on routine duty, Edwin and Dietrich entered the compound. With his stomach in his throat, Edwin left Dietrich with the car—correct procedure for his assumed role, after all—and entered the main building on his own. Edwin focused on keeping his hands from shaking and prayed his voice would sound smooth.

Nearly two hours later, he returned to the car. Dietrich jumped and performed his duty, opening the rear door for his officer.

"You were gone a long time," Dietrich muttered as he returned to his position behind the wheel.

"The commander wanted to tell me all about how well they run the camp—and the benefits of working here. They share the women, then kill them when a new group comes in. May they all rot in hell!"

"Did you find out anything about Rita?"

"The commander showed me his records freely. I believe I know where Rita is."

"Do you know how long they plan to keep her alive?"

"I told him that this is merely a routine inspection of the compound. The belligerent pig said they do not share their women with outsiders, but if I see one I like, he might make an exception. I will tell him I want Rita."

Dietrich nodded. "Good. Then if we can't get her out today, that will keep her safe until tomorrow."

"If I have to, I'll tell him I did not finish the inspection today."

They drove around for twenty minutes and were sickened by what they saw. The women were living skeletons with lifeless eyes. They passed women being beaten with no mercy for no apparent reason. He almost vomited when he saw the dogs attack on command, thinking of their own dogs, who only knew to wag tails and slobber all over the humans they knew. A wire fence kept the women herded and confined.

Edwin searched the face of every woman he saw behind every fence.

"Dietrich, stop the car!" he shouted suddenly. "My God, it's Rita. What have they done to her?"

Every inch of her small frame seemed to be bruised, and her beautiful hair was gone. Edwin couldn't miss the distinctive blue eyes, even now standing out against her sickly pale face. Her feet were swollen, and it was clear at least one toe was broken. How could they have done so much damage to her in just a week?

Dietrich lurched to grab Edwin as he climbed out of the car, but he was too late. All of Edwin's good sense left him at the sight of his wife. He sprang from the car and began to close the distance between him and Rita. In response, Rita limped toward him.

A guard shouted for Rita to stop, but she didn't. Edwin was already pulling out his weapon, as was Dietrich. Shots rang out just as Edwin's fingers touched Rita's through the fence. They spoke simultaneously: "I love you."

Then Edwin went down.

On the other side of the fence, Rita collapsed. Their blood mingled in the dirt.

****

Dietrich had never run so hard and fast, zig-zagging to avoid the bullets flying around him. Edwin was barely alive as Dietrich managed to drag him away from the fence.

Edwin protested. "Leave me. I must stay with her."

Dietrich couldn't leave Edwin in the compound. The authorities would figure out who he was all too quickly, and then the inquisition would begin to find anyone who had helped him. Too many people's lives were at stake, including the other Von Rahmels.

Dietrich shoved Edwin into the front seat and ran around to get behind the wheel. He pushed the gas pedal to the floor instantly, all the while trying to recall from the camp plans where the fewest number of guards were stationed. He found an opening and drove the car through the wooden fence ahead of him, thankful that the guards on duty seemed to be poor marksmen. Even so, bullets riddled the car, and one found his shoulder. He kept hearing Anthony's voice in his mind, praying, "Lord, protect me; Lord, cover me with angels' wings; keep me faithful; surround me with protection."

Ignoring his own pain, Dietrich looked over at Edwin, this man who was a brother to him. Edwin had been the first Von Rahmel brother to put his arms around six-year-old Dietrich when his father died. Edwin was the one who had demanded his parents let Dietrich sleep in his room until the little boy was no longer scared.

As Dietrich raced toward safety, Edwin's life left him.

****

The priest at the safehouse asked no questions. After they buried Edwin in the forest, the priest offered Dietrich whisky. He could drink it, or he could pour it over the wound while the priest probed for the bullet. Dietrich opted to drink the whisky.

When Dietrich was well enough to return to Berlin a few days later, he went directly to Anthony's church. It looked as if the church had sustained some major damage from the nightly bombing in his absence. As he kicked at bricks that had once been a wall, the church sexton said Father Anthony had gone to his parents' home.

Dietrich's steps were long and difficult as he made his way to the Von Rahmel home. When he stepped inside, Katarina was holding a stuffed bear that Edwin had given her for the baby. Jona was reading his Bible, while Lisa repaired some old socks; new ones were almost impossible to come by. Anthony stood and stared out the window, as he did so much of the time.

When Dietrich cleared his throat, all eyes turned to him. "I'm sorry," he said. "We tried."

Anthony kept looking out the window, his heart for the first time filling with hate for others as he silently prayed for such thoughts to leave.

Chapter 10

Berlin: July 1944

The Von Rahmels learned to live with their sorrow and the new fears that plagued their lives daily. Anthony was close to obtaining the necessary paperwork for his family to escape to Switzerland, and even though from all appearances Frederick had slowed his harassment, the Von Rahmels had no way of knowing the worst was yet to come.

Katarina was now seven months pregnant and finding it increasingly difficult to walk. As the baby grew larger, so did her swelling feet.

Edwin's superiors had apparently accepted the theory that he had perished in a bombing attack and now lay under the tons of rubble piled along the streets of Berlin. The bombings were nearly continuous. As soon as the Americans stopped, the British began. It was pointless to try to rebuild anything, or even to clear the rubble away. Rita's parents were confronted by the Gestapo. For many years they had lived with a false sense of protection by convincing everyone they were Catholic and displaying the papers to prove it. They even attended Mass regularly. But the time came when the Gestapo did not care what papers they carried. Seeing the van pull up in front of their home, Rita's parents had pushed her brother Abraham out a bedroom window. He could do nothing to save them now; but he might still help someone else.

Abraham burst into the cellar at the cemetery. Grigory, Nicholas, and Anthony looked up, surprised.

"Something terrible is coming down," Abraham said, gasping for breath. "Gestapo agents are at my parents' home asking questions about the Von Rahmels."

"Calm down and catch your breath," Grigory said.

Abraham managed to get out the simple facts of what he knew.

Grigory's voice stirred in anger. "Damn! Our information was wrong. Frederick was not supposed to move on the rest of the family until tomorrow or the next day. We had hoped for some lead time."

Anthony was shocked. "You knew it was this imminent?"

"We had hoped for a little more lead time," Grigory said again. He turned to Anthony. "You can't go back now. You were supposed to take papers to your parents later today. We'll have to do it now. I told Abraham to find my parents and Rita and move them to Helena's. She can hide them."

"I have to go to the rectory," Anthony said. "I have documents hidden in my books. We can't take the risk they will be discovered after I'm gone."

Grigory sighed. "Okay. We'll go there, but make it fast."

One by one they gathered their weapons, each knowing what they had to be prepared to do.

Their car rounded the corner at the rectory. Anthony slid out of the car determined to move in and out of his office in stealth. Though the sun had set, he did not reach for a light switch. Instead, he felt behind the door for the vestment he left hanging there routinely. If he wore it now, its bulk would provide better cover for the documents he took from the books. For six minutes he heard nothing but his own breath as he retrieved the incriminating papers and dressed in the vestment. He had almost decided to breathe a sigh of relief as he opened the door to go out to the street and rejoin the others.

Gunfire erupted.

Anthony dropped to the sidewalk with the distinct conviction that the bullets were meant for him. Beyond him, a car motor gunned. Anthony looked up to see Grigory screeching toward him. A door swung open, and Nicholas's strong arms yanked Anthony into the back seat.

"What happened?" Anthony asked. Everything had flashed past him too quickly to sort it out.

"You've been a target for a long time," Grigory said. "They thought they finally had you."

Fright surged through Anthony's chest. "Grigory, we have to get to Katarina. She's home alone right now."

They were within a block of the Von Rahmel home when they saw Frederick's sleek black officer's car parked in front, with a van right behind it. Frederick stood on the sidewalk looking consummately triumphant. Katarina was being herded into the van, holding her stomach, her face wrenched in pain. Turning to Frederick, she spit in his face. He responded by slapping her so hard she stumbled backward. She would have fallen to the sidewalk if one of the Gestapo agents had not mercifully caught her. In another moment, the van had pulled away with Katarina inside it. Frederick pompously folded himself into the back seat of his car and signaled his driver with a routine gesture.

Anthony laid his head against the car window. "We will find her," Grigory promised.

Anthony slowly turned his head toward his trusted friend. "I want him dead. I will not go to my grave while that man draws breath. I want him to die in torment."

Grigory started the car. It was unsafe to linger any longer. "Anthony, we will find her," Grigory reiterated. "They've only just taken her. Our sources will tell us soon where she is going."

"My parents…"

"Dietrich will get your parents out of Berlin by nightfall," Grigory said.

****

As soon as darkness fell, three shrouded men approached Frederick's apartment. "Anthony, let us do this," Grigory pleaded. "You're a priest. Don't soil your hands with this."

Father Anthony Von Rahmel shook his head. "Even God wants this evil man thrown into the pit of hell. I'm only doing what we should have done a long time ago." He saw the cocked expressions on the faces of Grigory and Nicholas. "It's all a matter of survival, isn't it?"

A quick search of the papers on Frederick's desk turned up an order to send Katarina to Dachau. Having found what they wanted, the men quickly placed explosives under the mattress in the bedroom, with a detonator set to go off immediately if any weight was placed on the bed. Outside at the car once more, Anthony faded into a crevice across the street. "You go," he said. "I want to see with my own eyes."

"He might not come home for days," Grigory reminded him.

"I will wait."

Wordlessly Grigory and Nicholas agreed to wait as well, at least for a few hours.

Grigory motioned that Anthony should get in the car, then moved the vehicle further down the block.

When Frederick came home close to midnight, he had a young woman on his arm, and he was laughing. Anthony leaned forward to watch. What kind of monster could seek pleasure after the destruction of innocent lives?

They watched as a candle was lit in Frederick's window and saw the silhouette of the young woman's shapely body as she undressed. Minutes later, an explosion spurted flames out of the apartment.

Anthony turned to his friends. "We can go now."

****

Dietrich was already at the safe house waiting for them. "Your parents are well on their way," he told Anthony. "They had no problems getting out of Berlin and will soon be safe."

"And my sister?"

"Katarina was taken to Mobbitt Prison, but I don't believe she was there very long. The orders were probably to get her to a concentration camp as soon as possible."

"Dachau," Anthony murmured. Dietrich nodded. "We believe so."

Grigory asked the question Anthony had been

expecting for days. "Anthony, can we help you get to Switzerland? Or perhaps find you an assignment in Rome? Your Italian is very good, after all."

"I am going to find my sister and get her out of hell," was Anthony's intractable response.

"I had to at least ask." Grigory rubbed his hands together expectantly. "Okay, then, let's get moving. We have work to do."

Chapter 11

Mobbitt Prison: July 1944

Frederick's orders insisted Katarina should be moved swiftly to Dachau. First, however, at Mobbitt Prison, the guards did their best to be sure she feared for her life. They struck her repeatedly and forced her to kneel. At one point, when she wavered in her obedience, a guard's heavy boot struck her back and knocked her over. Yet still she glared at them, burning the details of their faces into her memory.

By six o'clock the next morning, Katarina found herself standing with hundreds of other prisoners at the train station. Moments before, a young lieutenant had hurriedly pressed papers into her hand with the whispered admonition that they might save her life. Katarina could see immediately that the papers were not in proper order, but they provided some kind of identification.

Tears streamed down her cheeks as she surveyed the hulk of a train belching black smoke against an innocent sky. Most of the people around her had no clue what horror lay ahead of them, but Katarina knew the great danger she and her baby faced. If she had not been so heavily pregnant and with such swollen feet, perhaps she could have gotten out of the house when she saw Frederick's car approaching. If she'd had possession of her dancer's body, she might even have broken away on the front steps and lithely disappeared into the neighborhood. She knew so many hiding places from her imaginative childhood. But the weight in her belly, the thickness of her feet, and the pain in her joints had made her a sitting-duck target.

Suddenly a soldier advanced through the mob, knocking people out of his way with a wooden club. Katarina was directly in his path. She winced and lurched toward the train. To her surprise, a hand emerged from the train and someone pulled her up, out of the soldier's path.

Katarina's eyes gradually adjusted to the dim lighting inside the train car. Far too many people were pressed inside it to allow any daylight to reach the rear corner to which she retreated. Her toe knocked against something, and she saw a bucket—a makeshift toilet, she knew, which would be completely insufficient for the population of the car.

For the first time, she looked at the face of the man who had heaved her out of the soldier's path. He was an older man, with deep lines around his eyes that suggested a lifelong habit of smiling. He soon gave her the only smile she had seen since in days.

In terror for her safety, Katarina settled into the most horrific hell she could imagine. The baby's movement within her womb reminded her constantly that she must stay alive. This child was worth living for. Katarina discovered that the elderly gentleman who had befriended her had been separated from his wife and grandchildren. Apparently determined to look out for someone, he had chosen Katarina. When she was tired, he offered his lap for her head. He stood in front of her when she could no longer ignore the growing pressure on her bladder and was forced to use the bucket, as many before her had already done. He waved his papers before her face to move the air when the stench became overbearing. When morsels of bread were thrown randomly into the train car at various stops, he shared with her what little he gathered.

Around her, Katarina heard people murmuring about the Americans. Weeks had passed since the Americans assaulted the shores of Normandy, so surely the war was near its end. Whether this was true or not, no one could confirm, but they clung to the hope that it might be true, that even Hitler would begin to see that he could not win the war he had started.

Throughout this journey of hell, the kind gentleman whom Katarina came to know as Mr. Weissman told her stories of his life. He had been a pharmacist and had owned his own drugstore. Proudly he named his nine grandchildren, for whom he had been caring while his son and daughter and their spouses were all in America. They had gone to visit his brother two years ago, and he had insisted they should stay in safety and leave the nine children in the grandparents' care. But he had never imagined he would end up on a train with no clue what had become of his wife and the grandchildren.

Periodically he ceased his storytelling long enough to softly sing the songs of his synagogue. When he did so, and Katarina saw his unflagging hope, her appreciation for Anthony's passion grew, and she understood Aunt Helena's commitment to keep hidden those who needed hiding. This man who was helping a stranger was the embodiment of why Anthony and

Helena fought as hard as they did to prove the error of Hitler's ways.

The heat on the train would have been unbearable under more humane circumstances, but the inhabitants of the car had no choice but to bear it. Lack of water was making everyone drop their inhibitions. Katarina rubbed her large belly and begged the baby to hold on. They would soon have help. Anthony would come for her. As long as he was alive, he would not abandon her to a concentration camp. Of this Katarina was certain.

Katarina had only glanced at the papers pressed into her hands. Now she tried to read through the sweat dripping off her face. The papers read that she was to go to a prison close to Dachau, but not to the concentration camp itself. The papers bore her name, a brief history of who she was and to whom she was married—along with gross fabrication of her crimes. The documents said she had been arrested for handing out propaganda and taking important documents from the post office that were addressed to her husband. She only hoped the mysterious lieutenant was right, and that these papers would be enough to save her life even if they were full of lies.

****

Dachau Concentration Camp: July 1944

The train slowed its lumbering speed and the brakes screeched as it rolled to a stop. Katarina roused herself, expecting that this was merely another long stop. Perhaps more rock-hard rolls would hurtle through a cracked door. However, the doors swung open to their widest breadth, and a voice screamed orders for everyone to climb out of the train. Many fell as German soldiers brutally pulled and pushed them. Katarina clung to Herr Weissman's hand, accepting his steadying force.

Terrorized by the brutality of the soldiers, the prisoners did as they were told and lined up beside the train. Then hell was unleashed. Guards took children from mothers who, in the face of the weapons around them, dared only the feeblest protests. The elderly were separated into two lines, one for men and one for women. A soldier marched over to Herr Weissman and Katarina and, with a hard blow with the butt of his rife, broke the lock of their hands. The soldier ordered Herr Weissman to join the other older men.

Ignoring the pain searing her wrist, Katarina reached for her friend's hand again and stared defiantly in the soldier's eyes.

"You cannot hold onto him," the soldier said. "He must go with the others." Katarina reached into her pocket and silently gave her papers to the soldiers, desperately hoping they would mean something to this soldier. He glanced at them, then signaled a colonel, who came over and studied them. Katarina knew her fate was being determined in this instant. Would the papers save her life—and perhaps Herr Weissman's?

The officer read the papers closely, then studied Katarina. She fixed her violet eyes on his, refusing to look away. Suddenly he bellowed to a soldier, "Take my position on line three. I need to escort this one personally."

Katarina didn't move, searching deep inside herself for the courage to withstand this moment. Nodding toward her friend, she said, "Please let Herr Weissman come with me. He has helped me through this entire journey."

The colonel gazed at her blandly, then turned to Herr Weissman. "What is your profession?"

"I'm a pharmacist, a chemist."

"Let me see your papers."

He read the papers quickly, then leaned toward Katarina. With his hot breath in her ear, he said, "I will do you this favor. And when the time is right, Fräulein Von Rahmel, you will return the favor."

Horrified, Katarina quickly agreed.

He scanned at the papers again, a puzzled look on his face. "Which is the correct name, Von Rahmel or Spitz? It looks like someone was in a hurry to fill this out, and both names are on it, with question marks." He looked at her long and hard before giving a shrug when she didn't answer immediately.

Setting aside the paperwork, the colonel escorted Katarina and Herr Weissman through a door, then gave instructions to a soldier to take Herr Weissman to the laboratory. Katarina reached for her friend and placed her arms around his neck.

"Herr Weissman, this is all I can do. You must survive. I pray you will find your way back to your wife and family."

Tears puddled in Herr Weissman's soft brown eyes. "You, too, must survive—for your baby. You did not come this far for nothing. Perhaps this little one will change the world for the better."

At that moment, Herr Weissman was roughly torn from her. Katarina realized for the first time since this nightmare had begun that she was completely alone and stifled a sob.

The colonel turned to Katarina. "Fräulein Von Rahmel, it seems a mistake has been made. You were to be sent to the prison next door. For what you did, the punishment is to be shot. However, your chances of survival are much better here. With the women arriving here for the first time, you would be sent to one of the sub-camps once you are processed."

"How comforting," she whispered.

He looked at her curiously. "So why don't we take our chances and keep you here? I'm not sure how this happened, but we can just pretend you're at the prison, can we not?"

Katarina stared at him, unsure of an advantageous answer.

"It's just one hell for another, Fräulein," the colonel said. "I know your husband." He seemed to wait for a response, but she gave him none.

"Now, Fräulein, we have to process you like any other who comes into the camp. Your papers may call you Von Rahmel, once a respected name in Germany, but everyone here will know you as the wife of Colonel Spitz. That is punishment enough. We will not cut off your hair, and that will make you stand out."

"Please don't do this," she whispered. "The others will not understand."

"You are correct," the officer answered. "They resent anyone who receives special favor, and that itself is punishment." Unexpectedly, he became familiar. "Katarina, my name is Colonel Gold. I will help you survive as best I can. Your baby will be born for the Third Reich, and we must keep the bloodline pure. Your husband should have waited and taken the baby. And in exchange..."

Katarina swallowed the vomit that rose involuntarily.

He paused to consider his next words. "I cannot control everything. You must use your own wits, and I will help in small measure."

She knew from the way he spoke he was just as evil as the rest of them and had no regard for any of the prisoners or their lives. He would treat her no differently than he would any one of the other prisoners. She summoned everything she had to give the officer a smile that would light up a street lamp. All the while, she tasted bile in her throat.

Katarina was sent to the showers along with the other women and, like them, stripped of her clothes and given ill-fitting camp clothing to wear. Her new shoes had belonged to some poor soul who was long gone. She had to stuff paper in them to keep them from falling off when she walked. Her assigned bunk was much too high for her to climb into in her state of advanced pregnancy, but there were no other options. The other women did not dare defy the guard, Frau Messer, by suggesting a rearrangement. As she struggled to pull herself up, a blow from behind nearly took her breath away. She turned in pain to see a woman's face that would burn into her memory for the rest of her life.

Frau Messer took great pleasure in inflicting pain.

"Climb up there, you stupid bitch," Messer said. "That is where you will sleep until the end of your days." She turned to the other women. "Look at all your pitiful bald heads, and look at her." The guard grabbed a fistful of blonde hair. "What is this? Why does she still have her hair?"

No one looked at Katarina's hair, however. Their eyes were fixed on her pregnant mound. Some had been there so long they could barely move, much less muster energy to hate this doomed woman already cursed by her beauty.

Katarina began the month of September cleaning the ovens where human beings had been placed one by one, in single file. Weeks of repeating this task had not steeled her against its egregious horror. Every day she hung her head, gagging at the reality of what she was cleaning up. Why children? she asked herself over and over as she scraped their ashes out to make room for the gassed bodies that would soon be carried in so the process could begin all over again.

She had a moment of happiness one day when she saw Herr Weissman being escorted to a lab to work. They had kept him alive! But she could hear the screams from the lab and thought with horror about what they might be forcing Herr Weissman to do there.

Soon enough after her arrival, Katarina found out that even her smallest infractions resulted in beatings from Frau Messer. Only once had she been beaten in the face before word came from Colonel Gold that Frau Messer must not touch Katarina's face. Each day Katarina lost weight, even as her baby grew. Many of the other prisoners shared their scraps of food with her, their own maternal instincts rooting for a healthy baby. The baby turned and kicked almost continuously, a gesture of victory against the odds.

Finally, though, one day overcome with fatigue while cleaning the ovens, Katarina fell to the floor and began to cry. She was damp to the bone from the day's freezing rain, and rather than being immune to her daily work by now, she was freshly horrified by it. Guards yanked her up and dragged her, stomach thumping on the hard ground, to a dingy cell where many had faced final punishment before death.

Alone in the dark cell, Katarina screamed. She felt the ooze between her legs as her water broke. Guards passed back and forth as her labor progressed, ignoring her agony. The labor pains intensified with each abandoned hour, and Katarina's fear for her child heightened. Frau Messer strolled in and laughed wickedly, threatening to sweep the baby off to the lab, where scientists would cut out its heart for experiments.

On September 30, 1944, Alexandra came into the world screaming to survive. Katarina had nothing in which to wrap her new daughter, so she ripped apart her pants from the knees down. She wrapped Alexandra's tiny body in the thin, tattered fabric and held her baby tightly against her heart, praying she would have enough milk to feed her.

Hell came knocking as Frau Messer again entered the tiny cell and ripped the baby from Katarina's arms. Two guards held Katarina down as the demented Messer held a lit cigarette first to one and then the other of Katarina's nipples. Katarina's screams split the air. She looked up to see her baby being held upside down like a rag doll, the child's face red and distorted. Katarina begged for mercy for her child. Help finally came when the prison commander heard her pitiful cries and ordered the torture to cease. Relieved, Katarina slowly slipped into unconsciousness.

When she awoke, the baby was in her arms, and she was back in her dirty bunk. Barren though it was, it was a refuge. She buried her face in her arms, sobs racking her exhausted body till she could not even hold up her head. The baby was soon covered with her mother's tears, her tiny little fingers desperately wrapped around her mother's index finger. Katarina knew she had to try to feed this child; it was the only hope the child would survive. Katarina offered her breast, and despite the burned tissue, the baby latched on well. Katarina shivered in pain with every suck and swallow.

Early the next morning Katarina was ordered back to work, this time in the lab, the baby held against her chest. The sadistic Frau Messer accompanied her, a smug look of satisfaction apparent when Katarina did not work fast enough. Messer struck a blow to Katarina's back, knocking her to the ground.

"Looks like Countess Von Rahmel is no different than the Jews," Messer sneered. "They fall easily, especially when they are ready to die. Do you think Colonel Gold will protect you forever?" She snorted, her fat tongue wagging against jagged yellow teeth.

"When he is gone, I might strangle the little brat myself. It wouldn't be the first baby I've squeezed the life out of."

Katarina pulled Alexandra closer. At least the lab work kept her out of the cold and away from the burning flesh and bones. Colonel Gold allowed the baby to stay with her, but it was of little comfort as she listened to Alexandra's wretched cries and could do little to comfort her.

Katarina had a rabbi say prayers over the baby, and in her own makeshift way baptized the baby with the help of an imprisoned nun. She saw Herr Weissman only once, but for years she remembered their brief exchange.

"Fräulein, it might have been better if I had been

gassed. Here I am helping them hurt my own people. How can I live with myself when this is over?"

She had only that moment to look into his sad eyes. "You must stay alive. You must tell the world what happened here so that it can never happen again."

****

October came. Once a marvelous month of change, it now brought cold and hunger to Katarina and her daughter. Despite her burned nipples, Katarina breastfed as best she could, storing her tears and refusing to give the guards the satisfaction of seeing her cry. The beatings persisted, however. Her back was criss-crossed with slash marks, her legs black and blue from heavy clubs. She grieved that whatever the outcome of the war, her days of professional dancing were over. How could her body possibly recover enough to be what it had been? Once again guards put her in the windowless cell because she was unable to walk fast enough for roll call one morning. They took the baby away as they locked her up. Her screams echoed within the black walls as she begged relentlessly for her child.

Colonel Gold demanded that she be released and reunited with her baby, then ordered her to take a bath and wash her hair. It was payback time. Shuddering with shame and degradation, she presented herself to him in his private quarters. Instinctively, she tried to pull away from him when he approached, but he slapped her hard enough that the room began to spin, and she submitted. The pain of his rape was excruciating. Each time she screamed, though, he struck her again. In between, Gold stroked her cheek and kissed her and told her she was the most beautiful woman he had ever seen and he would enjoy her in his bed often. Finally, an eerie silence overwhelmed her, as she withdrew within herself to a place where no one could touch her.

And so began a routine of repeated rapes and repeated withdrawals to her own world, a world where she could not feel him kiss her, touch her, hurt her, enter her. If this was what it took to keep Alexandra alive, so be it.

In the final week of October, when the night was equal to the day, Katarina knew her baby was ill. Each night she wondered if the baby would be alive when she returned from the colonel's bed. How much longer could Alexandra survive in a concentrate camp, when her mother was barely surviving?

One day as she was scrubbing countertops in the laboratory, a tap on her shoulder startled her. She turned to see the camp commander and held her breath as she waited for his demand.

"Come to my office." With Alexandra strapped to her chest, she followed him reluctantly, thinking he wanted something from her that she did not want to give.

Katarina studied the lamp on his desk while the commander paced in his small office. Feeling suddenly nauseated, Katarina realized the lampshade was made from human skin. She looked away.

"Fräulein," the commander began slowly, "I do not like the Jews. I agree with the Führer that they need to be eradicated from the earth, along with all the undesirables with weak genes. We cannot have a perfect race with their existence. I wanted you to know how I felt before I told you that your brother Anthony is a traitor."

"Anthony?" Katarina's heart pounded. "What does he have to do with anything?"

"Katarina Von Rahmel, your brother is a traitor, a renegade priest." He sighed deeply. "He is right, however, that we must get you out of here. This is a place for Jews and those who do not have good German blood. Despite what you are accused of doing, I am compelled to save you."

"I don't understand! Why would you help me? Or Anthony?"

He actually found a smile for her, then quickly restrained himself. "Two things. Your child is a true-blooded Aryan. I do not want my children and grandchildren to think I killed Germans like you. Your brother has also convinced me by kidnapping my eight-year-old grandson."

Katarina gasped. A child for a child. It was ingenious. She knew Anthony would not hurt the child, but all that mattered was that the camp commander did not want to take that chance.

"I never dreamed a priest could be capable of so much hate. I believe that his little group of criminals would actually kill the child. When you are released, my grandson will also go home."

Katarina let loose a hysterical laugh. Her legs felt as if they were going to buckle as she watched him continue pacing nervously. "You really don't care about these people, do you? You alone have decided they are not worthy to live. How dare you try to take God's place!"

"Fräulein Von Rahmel! You have no right to question me. I care for the German race. You were unfortunate enough to get caught in the middle of all this. There are those who were not faithful to Hitler—nuns, priests, homosexuals, gypsies—and those that would teach against Hitler in the universities. And let's not forget those who want to undermine Hitler, like your brother, who cannot see what good Hitler is doing."

He pounded his fist on the desk, his eyes narrowing in anger. "Katarina, you are different. I would never let them kill you as long as I was here. We need your pure bloodline."

Katarina shook her head. She had hoped there was some humanity left in him. "It's over. Hitler will lose. It's only a matter of time."

"Do you have a secret radio I am not aware of?" He rolled his eyes. "I must concentrate on the release of my grandson. My daughter is already frantic with worry about him."

He indicated that Katarina should sit down and listen to the escape plan. The following night, she would be sent to the infirmary with several other prisoners. The truck would stop, and from there she would flee. If she didn't make it, neither would his grandson. The commander would make sure the searchlights were diverted for a fleeting amount of time, enough for her to escape. After that, it was up to her and those who ran with her.

****

The next night, Katarina pleaded with the guards that she and the baby had both fallen very ill. As she expected, word reached the commander, and he returned an order that she be transported to the infirmary. Leaving her bunk, she forced herself not to look around. Some of these women had become her friends, but only she was being given the chance for freedom.

They bumped along the road in the darkness, ten of them, none knowing what would transpire in the next few moments. A man emerged from the shadows and forced the van to stop. Soon after the first guard got out of the truck's cab to investigate, Katarina heard his body slump to the ground with the gurgling of his last breath. The other two guards jumped from the back of the truck, but before they could raise their weapons, each had his throat cut from one side to the other.

"Come quickly," a hoarse voice said. "The searchlights will go on soon, and more guards will come." The stranger pointed to a hole in the fence, and one by one the ten prisoners squeezed through the hole and began to run.

Katarina scanned the landscape—seven towers. So many eyes watching. Could she really escape? Her shoes fell off as she ran, and frost clung to her roughened feet. Her lungs burned as she kept running toward freedom. Open fields gave way to trees. Katarina heard shouts and, in the distance, gunfire. People around her fell, but she never looked back. She didn't know who else was surviving. She only knew that she herself was alive, and so was her baby. How far would she have to run before someone helped her?

A car pulled up in front of her, its bright lights blinding her. Katarina screamed, thinking she had been caught. Then she saw a glimpse of a face she recognized. Nicholas reached out and pulled her into the car. He loosened his grip only when the baby began to cry. The car sped through the night.

At last the car came to a stop, and Nicholas indicated she should get out.

Trembling, Katarina opened the door and stepped into the darkness. Unable to tame her racing heart, she literally fell into Anthony's arms. She gave little thought to what she left behind—thirty-two barracks, including one for clergy, one for medical experiments, one for camp administration, plus accommodations for the guards and those who manned the main entrance. Most came from Auschwitz. Of the nineteen women guards, there was one Katarina would never ever forget, and her heart filled with dark hate for Frau Messer. She would find her and repay, even if she had to make it her mission for the rest of her life.

****

Katarina sat in the warm bath, hardly able to believe what had happened was real.

Frau Schmidt, the Von Rahmel's housekeeper for more than twenty years, scrubbed Katarina's head. How did she get here? Katarina wondered.

"My baby—" Katarina said. She was startled to realize she had actually dozed off again.

"Father Anthony has the child," Frau Schmidt said.

Katarina smiled. "Anthony doesn't know how to take care of a baby."

"He's managing. The child is asleep in his arms."

"Where am I?" Katarina asked. While she was glad to see Frau Schmidt, the surroundings were not familiar.

"You are safe, that's where you are."

****

Anthony held the baby close in his arms for a long time, gently rocking. Oh, what this little one has endured. He wanted to cry, but he had spent his tears.

For the first time since she was born, in this forested inn Alexandra was warm and had been bathed in clean water. Anthony stroked her soft blonde hair and speculated that the girl would have the same violet eyes as her mother. He kissed each perfect little finger and watched the perfect little round, red mouth yawn. Anthony recalled the joy of baptizing the fat, red-cheeked babies born into his parish, especially before the madness had begun. This little one was pale and thin beyond imagination.

But she was there. She was alive. She was their miracle, the good triumphing over evil.

For Anthony, the first order of business was to get the baby and Katarina to Switzerland where their parents were. Everything had been arranged. It was the first of November, and Anthony and his renegade friends were in full swing helping the Americans and British. The war would soon be over, he was confident, but to be on the safe side it was better to get Katarina out of Germany.

Anthony and Nicholas would soon leave to meet Grigory, who had vital information needed by the Americans and British before they could march on Berlin. He shivered, remembering the rumor that the Russians were also moving toward Berlin.

What was to come? He dreaded the thought, as he looked down on the little face of his niece, now quiet in slumber.

Chapter 12

Outside Munich: November 1944

Every time Anthony delicately encouraged his sister to talk about the months she had been gone, she turned away. She wouldn't answer questions or volunteer information. As a parish priest, Anthony was experienced with situations of loss and grief. However, he was much less experienced in dealing with the kind of trauma Katarina had been through. As desperately as he wanted to do something to help her, he didn't know what that would be. She needed time to heal, and he would have to accept that she would go to Switzerland without his knowing anything more about what had happened to her.

Anthony looked in on the baby frequently while Katarina slept for long stretches at the secluded inn. He loved holding Alexandra and giving her soft kisses. He sat with her for hours as she slept, looking at her little face, her curled-up fingers that moved so slowly as she brought them to her mouth. How could anyone not marvel at the smallness of her fingers and toes, how perfectly her eyebrows were drawn? Anthony remembered that this was how he'd felt the first time he held Katarina, as well.

He hated that he had to tell Katarina that their brother Heinz was dead, but he knew he could put it off no longer. His parents knew, and soon Katarina would be with them. She had to know.

Anthony found his sister sitting alone by the window of the bedroom she occupied, dressed in a warm sweater and slacks. She smiled when he came in and inquired about her well-being. He knew he was probably asking her the same questions too often, but he couldn't seem to help himself. Anthony sat on the bed and sighed.

"Anthony, what is it?" Katarina asked.

"I have news," he said quietly. "I wish I didn't have to tell you, but you need to know."

She turned to face him squarely. "Then you'd better get down to it and tell me."

"Shortly after you were arrested, the French Resistance contacted us."

"This is about Heinz, isn't it?"

Anthony nodded. "The Gestapo took him in for more questioning about my activities. He didn't know anything of substance. I made sure of that years ago. I wasn't going to put Hans or Heinz in danger while they were in the military. After what happened to Edwin…"

"Anthony, just tell me."

"He really knew nothing about any of us, but they didn't believe him. Our sources tell us that Heinz had had enough of the Gestapo when they told him that both you and Edwin had been killed. He thought he had the protection of the general at Templehof, but something went wrong."

"Heinz is dead," Katarina said flatly.

"They shot him in the back of the head. He may have gotten too outspoken with the Gestapo, or maybe they had planned it all along. But he's gone. They left his body on Elvia's doorstep. Of course her neighbors were frightened, thinking they were in danger as well."

"Where is Elvia now?" Katarina asked.

"Still in Cherbourg. But I have a letter that Heinz sent to Mother asking us to take care of his wife if something happened to him." Anthony paused. "The thing is, Katarina, Elvia is pregnant. When the war ends, we need to bring her here to Germany. She has no other family left. I've already told Dietrich he must get Elvia out of France as soon as it is safe for her to join the family."

Katarina nodded. "French women who consorted with Germans will not be treated kindly in France. People won't understand the predicament Heinz was in."

"It's just the three of us now," Anthony said, "you and me and Hans. We won't hear any more poetry out of Edwin, or the songs Heinz loved to sing. But we can't give up now."

Katarina pulled her knees up to her chest and set her chin on them. "Anthony, I can't even cry. I want to. But the tears will not come anymore. I feel like a thousand people are walking on my chest, but still I can't cry. Forgive me."

Anthony fought for words that would make even a little sense. "This madness will be over soon, I'm sure of it, and the family will be together again."

"How soon, Anthony?"

"A matter of months," he answered eagerly. "The Allies have turned the war around in France, after Normandy. Nicholas and I are leaving soon for Munich to wait for more information. But I am convinced we are only talking about months, Katarina. We are almost out of this hell."

"Good."

"Katarina, you must go to Switzerland. It's simply not safe here, even as close to the end as we are. Hitler is making one last gasp and stepping up the killings and violence. Your baby needs to be with the family, and so do you."

Katarina was shaking her head. "No, Anthony, I'm staying."

"But traveling with a baby will be a dead giveaway if they are looking for any of us."

"I won't be traveling with a baby. Send the baby to Switzerland."

"Without you?"

"Yes, without me. Someone else can take the baby to Mother and Father."

"Katarina, be sensible. She's a newborn. She needs to be with her mother. How can you send her away after all you've been through to bring her into this world?"

"This is my decision, Anthony. I want you to send Alexandra to safety, but I am staying."

He couldn't change her mind, though he kept trying until the last moment.

Katarina, on the other hand, never looked back after placing her daughter in the arms of a priest who would take Alexandra to the Von Rahmels in Switzerland.

"Katarina, there is still time," Anthony had said. "Go with them." But Katarina already was walking away.

****

Nicholas, Anthony, and Katarina plotted their journey to Munich carefully. After leaving the inn, they planned to stop at another nearby safe house to retrieve a radio transmitter; then they would continue to Munich.

The minute they entered the safe house, they knew something was wrong. "Let's get out of here," Nicholas urged hoarsely.

Instead, Anthony motioned for the others to follow him further into the house. In the small dining room, they saw the blood on the floor, and behind the table found the bodies. They were backing out of the room when a movement caught Anthony's eye. "Get out now!" he hissed.

Bullets began shattering windows and furniture. Nicholas and Anthony grabbed their weapons and returned fire, but they couldn't see what they were firing at. The trio ran out of the house, with Anthony clutching his chest.

Slowly and painfully they backtracked to the inn. Each step for Anthony was agony; it was painful just to breathe, much less move at a hasty pace. He kept moving only because he heard Katarina's voice behind him urging him on. Later, he had no recollection of how Nicholas had carried him much of the way back to the inn.

When Anthony awoke, he heard a barely audible voice. "Be quiet, Anthony," Katarina said as she gently washed his face. "We removed the bullet that came close to your lung, but you are very sick."

Anthony decided to try out his voice. "How long have we been here?" Finally he recognized the attic room of the inn.

"One week."

"A week! But—"

"You've been in and out of consciousness. You probably won't remember much."

"We can't stay here."

"Shh. When you're better, we'll go on to Munich, just as we planned."

"Where is Nicholas?" Anthony tried to prop himself up on one elbow.

"I'm right here," Nicholas said from the other side of the bed. He gently pushed Anthony's shoulders back down.

Anthony drifted back to sleep and slept soundly until midnight. When he awoke, he heard voices and laughter but couldn't tell where they were coming from. He forced his eyes to stay open long enough to focus on Nicholas standing at the small attic window. Silently, Anthony swung his feet over the side of the bed and took a few painful steps toward Nicholas.

"What's happening?" Anthony asked as he moved closer to Nicholas's side, recognizing the laughter from outside. "My God, Nicholas, what is Katarina doing? That Nazi has his hands all over her. She's leading him inside!"

"Anthony, go back to bed," Nicholas urged, lurching toward Anthony to offer support.

"Nicholas, you tell me right now what's going on."

Nicholas closed his eyes and exhaled. "We didn't have a choice. The soldiers were looking for us. You were in no condition to travel. Katarina knew she could divert the officer's attention by flirting with him. He took the bait and ordered his men to leave. He has no idea you're up here."

"She's sleeping with him, isn't she?" The thought made the bile rise from his stomach.

Nicholas shuddered visibly. "She had no choice. They would have searched every inch of this inn, and we would all be dead, including Frau Schmidt and her husband."

Anthony shuffled back to the bed and lowered himself wearily. "I'm sorry. I put you both in a bad situation. You should just have left me."

Anthony wanted to sleep. Most of all, he wanted to chase away the image in his mind of his sister in the Nazi's bed.

****

Katarina forced her mind to drift back to that place of peace, that place to which she had escaped so many times in the last few months in order to survive. There she could block out the world. There she did not even feel the Nazi's touch on her skin or recognize the sex act that dishonored her body. She reminded herself that Anthony and Nicholas were safe because of her beauty, and that was all that mattered. She told herself it wasn't as bad as it was in the camp. This fool of a man on top of her actually thought she liked him. He was old and clumsy, but he showed no inclination to hurt her. She stayed in the dark so he would not see her scars, and in the morning, she always dressed before he woke. Katarina avoided her brother's eyes when she visited the attic. While she knew that what she was doing was saving all of them—it was her weapon—it still caused her shame.

After nearly another three weeks, the officer explained he had to leave. Katarina laughed inwardly when he promised he would return to her when the war was over.

Silently, she wished for him a long and tortuous

death.

Anthony still had some healing to do, but he was well enough to travel to Munich. After much discussion, Anthony and Nicholas reached the heartbreaking decision that it was too risky to try to help anyone else. The Nazi search for the three of them was not likely to let up. It was time to seek help from the safe houses to get themselves out of Germany.

****

Munich: January 1945

Once they reached Munich in early January of 1945, anxiety struck Anthony when he left Nicholas and Katarina at the Marienplatz, the historic square in Munich. It could be difficult to find anyone to help them, with so many members of the Underground dead, imprisoned, or in hiding, and as much as Anthony hated to leave the others, he thought he could be more fleet of foot and unobtrusive if he were on his own. He wanted nothing more than for Katarina and Nicholas to find a safe hiding place and stay put until he had their papers.

"Meet me at Theaterinstrasse in two days," Anthony told them. "Father Gruen will hide us until time for us to move again. Until then, stay at the Blumenstrasse. I should be able to get papers for us to travel either to Rome or Switzerland. Meet me on the northwest corner at two o'clock, day after tomorrow."

"Be careful, Anthony," Nicholas said. "The Nazis here don't seem to have heard the message that the war is nearly over. They're fighting to the end."

Anthony put a hand on his friend's shoulder. "I'm depending on you to protect my sister."

Their eyes met, and the look spoke volumes.

****

The magical papers were in Anthony's pocket on the second day. So much had transpired in such a short time, Anthony almost felt like whistling, but he was afraid to draw attention to himself. He had papers that included false identification and passports that would enable all three of them to get to the Vatican. They would be on their way in only a few minutes. Anthony turned the corner into the square that had once been so charming and was now mostly a pile of rubble. He waved when he saw Nicholas and Katarina's smiling faces. Then he stopped abruptly as his worst fear came into focus.

They had been found out. A unit of Gestapo was only a few feet behind his sister and friend and obviously headed toward them.

Anthony could only shout, "Run!" as he turned and sprinted in the opposite direction.

Nicholas reacted quickly, pulling Katarina down an alleyway and climbing over debris from fallen buildings. A volley of bullets whistled by them, and others in the street ducked for cover. Katarina screamed as another round erupted and Nicholas was hit.

Finally the pain was too much, and he had to stop.

"Katarina, go! I'll keep them from following you." Nicholas's breath was already coming in large gulps.

"No, please, I can't leave you! Lean on me. We can do this." Determined, she ducked her head under his shoulder and slung one of his arms over her own shoulders.

Nicholas spotted the back door of a bakery. "There!" he shouted, and they lurched together toward the door. The sound of Gestapo boots closed in, but the door would not budge. Nicholas gasped in pain as he cocked his pistol and took aim. One of the pursuing Nazis fell. Then from the corner of his eye, Nicholas saw Katarina slump beside him. Instantly blood began seeping through her dress. Now ignoring his own distress, he braced Katarina to keep her from landing on the pavement. He had no choice but to abandon the shooting and seek another alley. Grunting with every step, he dragged Katarina to safety. The sound of guns dissipated behind them. Nicholas collapsed against the stub of what had once been a brick wall and turned Katarina to face him.

"Katarina!" he whispered urgently.

Her eyes fluttered open. "Nicholas, go. Save yourself. I don't think I can move."

"I promised Anthony."

Before either of them could say another word, tires screeched behind them. Doors slammed, and Gestapo thundered down the alley. Unable to keep her eyes open, Katarina felt the cold iron of the gun at her temple. Blood flowed from both her and Nicholas as Gestapo dragged them through the alley and heaved them into the back of a dark van.

Only a few blocks away, they were pulled from the vehicle and thrown to the ground.

Katarina's eyes blurred as she crawled inch by inch toward Nicholas. Finally she intertwined her fingers with his.

"Princess, tell Anthony I'm sorry. I was supposed to protect you." Nicholas's voice was barely above a whisper as he reached for her face. "Katarina, you must survive."

Before Katarina could respond, the Gestapo fired. Nicholas convulsed and was gone.

"Please, Nicholas," Katarina whispered, "I don't want to be alone." His blood formed an enlarging pool beneath him.

Katarina couldn't lift herself. Her chest burned terribly, and she longed for this moment to be over. She heard the click of the gun once again at her temple.

****

Anthony kept running, his lungs burning as sweat poured from every pore in his body. He wasn't sure when his wound reopened. He pressed his hand inside his jacket to try to stem the bleeding.

"Halt!" The shout came from behind him. "Stay where you are."

Anthony pressed his body up against a tree, nauseated at the thought of what was coming next. He hadn't come this far to fail. He had to stay alive. Against the security of the tree, he silently fingered his weapon. The young soldier never knew what happened. Anthony took him down with one shot, and the young man lay motionless in the dirt. The priest didn't look back. There had been a time when he would have paused to give last rites, even to a Nazi soldier, but no more.

He barely made it back to Theaterinstrasse, staggering and falling between the pews of the seventeenth-century church there. He had looked everywhere and found no sign of Katarina and Nicholas. Looking up at the surprisingly intact ceiling, Anthony saw the angels and saints looking at him from all sides.

Father Gruen found him there and carried him to a bed.

When Anthony awoke later, Father Gruen was

sitting next to him saying prayers. "Am I dying?" Anthony asked.

Father Gruen smiled and shook his head. "No, you're much too hardheaded. Your lungs filled with fluid, but a doctor has been here."

"How long—?"

"Three days," Father Gruen said. "You've had a hard time with pneumonia, but the good doctor believes you will be fine in time."

"My sister?"

Father Gruen shook his head. "I'm sorry. It seems she and Nicholas have disappeared off the face of the earth."

"It's my fault. I led them right into a trap."

"You were trying to save them, Anthony. Maybe they survived. We honestly don't know where they are. They could have gotten away."

Anthony shook his head. "Father, I have a terrible feeling."

"Anthony, you must get well so we can get you to Rome. The Americans are there, and you will be safe. If you stay here, the Nazis are sure to find you, even though most of the military has left, cowards that they are. They still have those in places of authority who will make life hell. I don't know how much longer we can hide you. Fortunately, you had only a minor flesh wound; it looked and bled worse than it was."

"But how can I leave without Nicholas and Katarina?" Anthony asked.

"You have no choice," was Father Gruen's response. "Go to Rome."

Turning his face away, Anthony longed for Rome, the beloved city that gave him peace. He would stretch his arms wide in the great church that housed the bones of St. Peter and cry out, "God, save me! Forgive me for what I have done."

Chapter 13

Munich: January 1945

"What are you doing?" Katarina flinched. Her eyes darted around the strange room where she had come to consciousness. A man she didn't know was changing the dressing over her right breast. Slowly his features came into focus, and she remembered her last sight of him. He had shouted, "Stop!" to the Gestapo, then reached down to feel her unsteady pulse. She remembered his worried look as he picked her up and carried her to his car, then ordered his driver to go quickly. "She is more valuable alive than dead," the voice had said.

Katarina's relief at being alive dissolved as she recalled pressing her ear to Nicholas's lifeless chest. She had desperately wanted to hear a heartbeat, or see the breath rise from him, but there was no sign of life.

As Katarina retreated into unconsciousness, the stranger barked, "Fräulein Von Rahmel! I'm General Von Dimitri Schwartz."

Her eyes remained closed.

"Fräulein, you must wake up and listen," the general persisted. "You cannot stay here much longer. If I don't deliver you to the Gestapo, I will end up in prison right next to you."

What is he talking about? Katarina wondered. Why

didn't he just let them shoot me?

The general was undeterred. "I took you into my home and got help for your wounds to keep you alive. I refuse to let you put me in danger by dying now."

"Why do you care?" Katarina asked.

"The Gestapo still has questions for you. Those ignorant soldiers didn't realize your value."

Katarina turned her head away, unimpressed.

"Fräulein, this is not the war most of us wanted," the general said softly. "We have known honor as military men, but now we will be known only as murderers." He smoothed the edge of the bandage over her wound, now freshly wrapped. "I'm sorry I was too late to stop them from killing your friend."

"So you know who I am," Katarina said flatly.

"I have seen you dance," he answered. "I know what your family has done for Germany for generations." He turned away slightly. "And I know what they have been doing the last few years."

"Then why—"

He waved off her question. "You are in my home, but I cannot protect you much longer. You will have to face the questioning; I simply want you to be strong when it comes."

"The war will be over soon," Katarina insisted.

"Yes, but perhaps not soon enough."

As it turned out, he was not home when the Gestapo came. His housekeeper's face blanched as soldiers took Katarina away, showing none of the kindness of General Schwartz.

****

Unknown prison: January 1945

Katarina saw a faint glimpse of light in the hallway

of the prison where they took her. Her legs were shackled to the bed unnaturally far apart, causing excruciating pain even for a well-toned dancer. But Katarina had no time for self-pity as she heard anguished cries arising from other cells. What would they want with her now?

When the interrogation squad finally arrived, Katarina steadfastly refused to say anything. Ironically, she discovered she was still being charged with stealing mail of military importance from her husband. The Gestapo hammered her with questions about people she had worked with, where she had been, what role she had played. Wishing only for her life to end, she said nothing.

Over the next few days, she realized she was incarcerated along with resistance fighters from France, Holland, and Norway. She had no idea where she was. The cold and dampness, and the gunshots at all hours, provoked nightmares about her imprisonment in Dachau. She shuddered as she relived the repeated beatings, the regularly scheduled rapes, the inhuman work she had been forced to perform. The shackles never came off her feet, and they left her to lie in the indignity of bodily functions.

Sometimes Katarina would curse God for standing idly by while all this happened. At other times she decided he simply did not exist. She could not believe in Anthony's God any longer.

Anthony. Where was he? He had managed to get her out of Dachau. Had they finally taken her beyond his reach?

The days began to merge together as Katarina retreated to the recesses of her own mind to shut out the horror that entombed her in darkness. Numbness of body and mind crept through her, like a glacier moving almost imperceptibly, until she nearly convinced herself she was not in this place and this was not happening to her. Not again.

****

In the spring of 1945, the war finally ended. The Soviets reached Berlin in April, with the Americans and British on their heels, cutting the heart out of Hitler's reign of terror. Camps and prisons emptied rapidly and mercifully. The world saw firsthand the atrocities that had happened behind fences and guard towers. Liberated cities sprang to life once again, and people all over Europe breathed the air of freedom. Over the months that followed, Europeans began to believe that some sense of normalcy would return as they rebuilt their nations.

****

Paris: September 1945

Grigory stood outside a hotel in Paris, pulling the late summer scent of the city into his lungs.

"Peter," he said, "this is a day of celebration! We are walking down the street talking to one another, no secret meetings, no need to whisper."

Dietrich and Peter had joined Grigory in Paris, and they were on their way to a local café. The pall of Nazi uniforms had disappeared almost overnight when the city was freed in August 1944. Now, a year later, the faces around Grigory and his friends were at once drawn with grief and the unimaginable loss the French nation had been through and with joy and relief that they had emerged from hell alive. The generals of the German army stationed in Paris had loved the city.

When Hitler ordered the destruction of Paris, they defied his orders. The city had sustained minimal damage, especially in comparison to other cities around the continent.

The three men found a table at the small café.

"Peter," Grigory said, "I have done exactly as you asked me to. I sent out a message to all the hospitals for someone to notify us if they see anyone who fits Katarina's description."

"That was months ago," Peter said. "Anthony has asked every Red Cross agency he can find."

"I know. But I think I finally have something." Peter and Dietrich's faces lit up.

Grigory extracted from his pocket a letter from a British military officer and handed it to Peter. Peter read aloud.

"We have found a woman meeting your general description. She has not spoken since she was found four months ago and is obviously still in deep shock. She was discovered in a prison under the bodies of people who were shot during the last hours of the war, just before the British reached the prison. No one realized she was alive. Bodies of the dead had been piled on top of her. It would seem she was there for several days before being found alive.

"The woman is in our local hospital being well cared for. However, the doctors have not been able to identify her or get her to speak a single word. I would advise a family member to come quickly. If she is the one you seek, her family may be the only hope she has of reviving."

"Grigory!" Dietrich exclaimed. "Good work!"

Peter sighed heavily. "I truly did not expect her to

be found alive. Now I wonder if she is alive only in body—if it's even Katarina."

Dietrich brushed away the concern. "It's her, all right. I'll tell Anthony. He's still in Rome but plans to go back to Berlin to try to rebuild his church. His parents are already there."

"And Heinz's wife?" Peter asked.

"Yes, she's there, with her baby girl."

Peter shifted in his chair. "I'd like to go to Rome and tell Anthony myself, but I can't go to Berlin or to the hospital with him. I'm not sure I can stand to ever step foot in Germany again. Every time I think about what the Germans did, the bile burns in my throat!"

Dietrich's face fell.

"I'm sorry, Dietrich," Peter said quickly. "That was thoughtless of me to say. I am half German myself, after all."

Dietrich spoke softly. "But you have the privilege of returning to another country, one the world does not blame for causing hell on earth."

The waitress brought three large glasses of wine and three plates of cheese and ham on rolls.

"Peter," Grigory said, "I know what's on Anthony's mind. When I saw him a month ago, he said he would not tolerate the divided Berlin the Allies are suggesting. He wants a democratic government. He wants the family factories to start up again, but some of them are in the Russian sector."

Peter stared at Grigory. "What were you doing in Rome? And why are you and Anthony even considering becoming involved in the politics of Germany? Let it go, man. You have done more than your share these past years."

Grigory glided his finger across the top of his glasses and avoided looking directly at either Peter or Dietrich. "Whatever I do in the next few months, just don't ask questions."

"Oh, Christ, someone has recruited you!" Dietrich looked at Grigory as the truth sank in.

Grigory gave a slow smile. "Remember me? I'm one of the good guys."

Peter ordered more wine. They ate without speaking until the next bottle arrived. Peter narrowed his eyes and stared at Grigory. "You're not going to involve Anthony, are you?"

Grigory did not speak.

"For God's sake, Grigory, leave him alone. Hasn't his family been through enough?"

"Anthony speaks for himself," Grigory said firmly. "You can't expect him to suddenly become a docile priest who minds his own business. He has paid too high a price to have Berlin fall to the Russians."

Dietrich groaned. "What was it all for, if the Russians take control? We will have traded one hell for another."

Peter rolled his eyes and blew out his breath. "I'm going to tell Anthony to just stay in Rome—although, if he keeps this up, they'll excommunicate him!"

They all laughed. More relaxed now, they drank their wine and listened to the sounds of the city around them. Peter insisted once again that he would be the one to go to Rome and find Anthony, and even promised to accompany his cousin to the British hospital where an unidentified young woman might be Katarina Von Rahmel.

****

They found her in Holland, not Germany. A doctor filled them in on what was known about this young woman. Found in a prison near the border, she had been admitted to a hospital in Amsterdam as a displaced person. Her condition was severe, and the doctors had not been sure at all that she would survive. But she had—at least physically. They had tried to reach her mind, knowing by the scars on her body—fresh wounds overlapping old ones—that she had been tortured extensively. But the doctors had been unsuccessful at getting her to say anything about what she had been through or to confirm her identity. Most likely, she had selective amnesia. It was a defense mechanism, one that had kept her alive through more horrors than any of them could fathom.

"Will she ever remember?" Anthony asked.

No one could answer his question, and Anthony wondered if it might be best if she didn't ever regain full memory.

Anthony and Peter took a deep breath as they entered the room where a young woman sat in a rocker, staring vacantly out the window.

It was Katarina.

Choking on his tears, Anthony pulled a chair in front of her and took her hands in his. Peter stood behind him, wondering what magic words his cousin might say to revive his lost sister.

"Katarina, it's Anthony," the priest began slowly. "I've come to take you home." Katarina turned her head about an eighth of an inch, her eyes not meeting Anthony's.

"She doesn't know who I am," Anthony murmured. "How am I going to reach my sister if she doesn't even know who I am?"

Peter knelt next to Anthony and took one of Katarina's hands. Touching her chin gently, he turned her head toward his face. "Katarina?"

No response.

Peter stood up. "Anthony, I'll let the doctors know you will stay as long as you can. When it's safe, they'll let you take her home."

"But when will that be?"

Peter shook his head. "I don't know, Anthony. I don't know. I'm sure they'll let you be with her as much as you want. However, I've got to get back to England."

They went into the hall to say goodbye. Anthony embraced Peter tightly. "Thank you so much, Peter."

Peter thumped his cousin's back. "Stay out of trouble in Berlin. Just rebuild your parish church and lie low."

One corner of Anthony's mouth turned up. "Lie low? Peter, after all these years I thought you knew me!"

"Then at least promise me you'll stay safe, Anthony."

"I'll do my best to try. I always have."

"And look where that has landed you!"

They laughed together. Peter threw his hands up in the air, rolled his eyes, and left.

****

Anthony stayed a week, hardly leaving Katarina's side. He talked to her and showed her pictures of Alexandra that his mother had sent to him in Rome. He brushed her hair while he spoke of happier times. Still, there was no life in her eyes.

"Why can't she recognize me?" he demanded of the doctors in frustration. Their silence only reminded him that Katarina might never come back to him.

Another four days passed. She was staring out the window while he brushed her hair, longing for its silky texture to return. He almost didn't notice when she raised her hand and pointed out the window.

"Father's horse."

The horse did indeed look like one Jona Von Rahmel had once owned. Anthony spun her around to look him in the eye. "Katarina, do you know who I am?"

"You're Anthony. What a silly question." A weak smile passed her lips as she looked directly at Anthony for the first time.

"Katarina, do you remember how you got here?"

She looked around, bewildered. "I…I…I don't know." She scanned the room further. "I only remember Munich. I feel ridiculous for not remembering, but I don't."

She stared at her forearm, with its distinct remains of a deep wound, then raised her questioning eyes to Anthony.

"How…?"

"I don't know, Katarina. They say it happened in the prison, after you were captured in Munich."

"What prison? I was never in a prison!"

Anthony breathed slowly and evenly.

"Nicholas!" she cried out. "What happened to Nicholas?"

Anthony swallowed hard, not knowing what to say.

"Nicholas died." Katarina answered her own question. "I was there."

Katarina snatched a sweater off the bed and slung it over the wound on her arm.

"The past is the past," Anthony said softly. "The war is over. We can go on to the future now." He pulled out a photo of Alexandra. "Here is your future, and she's waiting for you."

Katarina barely glanced at the photo.

Chapter 14

Holland: October 1945

It took powerful convincing to get the doctors to release Katarina to Anthony's care. He agreed with the doctors that his sister still had a long way to go in healing, but he firmly believed she would make faster progress in the care of her own family. Surely the warmth of her family environment would stimulate her to health better than the sterile hospital setting. Would she ever remember what she had gone through? Perhaps not; but Anthony was intractable in his belief that Katarina would be better off with her family, and in the end the doctors reluctantly agreed to release her.

Katarina barely said a word during the trip. The train rumbled through the countryside and past endless checkpoints. Thanks to Peter and the right papers from the Vatican, special arrangements eased their travel through occupied regions. Anthony frequently caught Katarina wiping away tears and wondered what memories the sights might be stirring. Still, though, she offered no information.

Berlin, of course, was even further destroyed than the last time they'd seen the city. Nearly every city in Germany had taken the same beating; still, when they got off the train and looked around, Katarina stared at Anthony in disbelief, as if she could not understand what had happened.

Has she forgotten the entire war? he wondered.

"We can't stay here, Anthony," she said. "The whole city looks like a skeleton. The people, the buildings, the animals, the trees, everything is gone!"

"The city has been through a lot," Anthony said cautiously, not knowing how much Katarina understood about what had happened.

"Look at the people! Everyone looks so old! God, Anthony, it's as if we've entered hell all over again."

So she does remember she has been in hell.

"We have to go to Munich," Katarina insisted, "where the mountains are, where we can breathe, where we can see the winter snow on the Alps."

Anthony held Katarina's hand tightly. "Katarina, the Alps will always be there, but we can't go to Munich right now. The house there is not livable. The Nazis burned much of it as their last act. The horses are gone, the library destroyed, the vineyards trampled. There's nothing to go back to right now."

"But I'm already suffocating here," Katarina protested.

"Let's go see Mother and Father." He steered her toward the street, and they began walking toward the Von Rahmel home, which miraculously had survived reasonably intact. Of the four apartments they owned, only one had remained livable, in Kreuzberg near Templehof. And they had the estate house in Grunewald, in one piece because the generals had used it during the war. "Thank goodness both our apartment and Grunewald are in the American Sector. Fate could have been worse." Determined to sound upbeat, Anthony continued talking. "Hans and Father are starting up some of the factories again. The apartment building is gone, but we still have our wonderful garden home here, and soon we can go to Grunewald, where we can have boat rides and plant summer vegetables. The food Mother and Helena canned and buried under the house is still there. We've managed better with rations than most."

"I suppose…" Katarina's voice drifted off, and Anthony could only guess what she might be thinking.

Anthony persisted in making conversation. "My church is coming along nicely. Most of our valuable artifacts came through without a scratch. Have faith, Katarina; we'll be fine."

Katarina looked at her brother and started to laugh. "You're asking me to have faith? I had faith. I believed. And what did it get me? Your God abandoned me."

She remembers something, Anthony thought, but what? How much?

A military jeep stopped them just then, and once again they presented their papers. Anthony was becoming impatient. There had been too many stops, and Katarina was not faring well. In the past, he could simply have said who he was, and he would be recognized and acknowledged. Now no one cared. He was a German. The Americans at the checkpoints and patrolling the streets saw only a German.

"Father, your paperwork is in order," a young American officer said. "You are entering the American sector. Welcome home."

Before Anthony could respond, Katarina brushed aside the wispy hair from her face and interrupted. "Gentlemen, could you possibly drive us? We have come a long way. My brother has brought me from a hospital where I had to heal from wounds the Gestapo inflicted. The long walk is tiring me."

Anthony was startled by her frankness. He had not expected Katarina's first words about her wounds to be to a stranger from another continent. He gazed at his sister, as her violet eyes remained fixed on the American soldier.

"I'm afraid that's against our policy, ma'am," came the reply.

But five minutes later, Anthony and Katarina were riding comfortably in a jeep toward home. Anthony let an amused smile cross his lips. How quickly she had charmed them. Just as quickly, though, she became withdrawn once again.

The soldiers left them at the end of their street, and Anthony watched his sister take in the sight. Surrounded by rows of debris, the family home stood, almost completely unscathed. They climbed the steps slowly and stood outside the front door.

"Anthony, I'm not sure I can enter. What do I tell Mother and Father?"

"You don't have to say anything until you're ready. They've been waiting so long for you to come home. That's all that matters."

Katarina involuntarily stepped back when she heard the sound of a child laughing inside the house. However, Anthony pushed the door open and took her hand to lead her across the threshold.

The hallway seemed dark and damp compared to the last time Katarina had stood there, when lights glowed and paintings of lovely scenes in colorful detail hung on the walls. Now the walls were bare and the lights were gone. But Jona Von Rahmel stood in the hallway, waiting for his daughter. Katarina stared at the lively toddler in her father's arms. The girl's eyes were the same color as her own; golden hair curled around her angelic face as she laughed and grabbed Jona's mustache.

"Lisa, come quick!" Jona called out. "Our Katarina is home."

In a moment, Katarina was surrounded by family hugging and kissing her. In a tangled herd of arms and legs, they moved Katarina to the living room and insisted she sit in her old favorite chair. Can't they give me room to breathe? she wondered.

Anthony took Alexandra from Jona's arms and started to hand her to Katarina. It was as if someone had struck her, and she motioned him away. "No. Not now."

****

How lovely she is, Katarina thought. But still she could not hold her. Mesmerized by the child's enchanting beauty, she nevertheless saw some resemblance to Frederick Spitz and could not lift her arms to hold the girl.

"I just want to sleep," Katarina said. "I'll get to know her later. Not right now."

Anthony helped Katarina to her room. Her bed was still in the same spot, as were the rugs. Instead of her beautiful chintz curtains, however, were boards covering the windows. Anthony helped Katarina lie down on the bed and spread a light blanket over her.

"Katarina, it will take time, but soon you will be in the rhythm of life again. You have a beautiful little girl."

"I hardly recognized her."

"She was only a few weeks old the last time you saw her. Now she is over a year old. I'm sure she will soon bring you as much joy as she does the rest of us. She seems to heal all the splintered hearts she meets with her smile and laughter. Father has been spoiling her, and Aunt Helena manages to spend a whole day with her every week. No one can resist her."

"I will see her tomorrow. I am so tired, Anthony."

"Of course you are. There's time to meet everyone tomorrow. Heinz's Elvia is here too, with their little girl. Hans married Gertrude, and they have a little boy."

Katarina sat up in the bed sharply. "Who is Gertrude? I knew nothing of Hans marrying. Has he forgotten about Anna?"

Anthony panicked. Had Katarina forgotten that Anna was killed in a bombing?

"What am I saying?" Katarina said, lying back down. "Anna is gone, killed with the rest of them."

Anthony's heart slowed to a more normal beat. "Yes, Hans loved Anna, but she is gone. Gertrude is very nice. She's a nurse. Hans met her when he was wounded."

"When did they marry?"

"A year and a half ago. We had no idea, though, until he brought her home, along with Ernst."

"Ernst?"

"Their little boy. The house is bursting with children these days!"

Katarina stared at him blankly, and once again, Anthony wished he had some glimpse of what she was thinking, what she was remembering. He kissed her on the forehead and left her to rest.

****

Katarina got out of the bed and locked the door behind her brother. Even though she was exhausted, she did not actually want to sleep. In sleep, the nightmares returned, like a black death enveloping her. In sleep, she smelled the burning bodies. In sleep, skeletons reached out from the grave, begging for her help, latching onto her legs as she tried to run to save herself. In sleep, stinking guards forced themselves inside her. Inevitably, she woke terrified. No, she did not want to sleep.

Katarina moved to a window and pried off the board. Only fragments of glass remained in the frame, but she was desperate for clear air. The late afternoon sun filled the room, and she let the cold breeze dry her perspiring face. As she peered down the street, a sudden chill ran down her back. Someone was watching her; she could feel it.

But she saw no one. She forced herself to take a deep breath and calm down. Katarina knew she had been in the hospital a long time when Anthony found her, but she did not remember the end of the war. She only remembered waking up on clean sheets, with nurses bathing her frail, beaten body. The nightmares had plagued her through the months in the hospital. Her body had healed physically, and she had put on lost weight, but even Katarina knew that her mind was far from healed.

Here in her family's home, she hoped the nightmares would be banished. She moved to the full-length mirror in which she had admired herself in dancing costumes for many years. This time, instead of a performer's trained and toned body, she saw a gaunt, sickly sight. Slowly she let her thin wool dress fall from her shoulders. The scars on her breasts were fading, but the long ones on her arms were fresh enough that it frustrated her not to know how she had come to have them. It must have hurt, she thought. Why wouldn't I remember something that created this?

Turning slowly around, she looked at the reflection of her back and saw the long white scars. Instinctively she snatched up the dress and covered her body. She tied her long hair back in a simple fashion with a rubber band, making her face appear even thinner. How will anyone ever find me attractive again? But the real question was whether she wanted anyone to find her attractive again.

****

Katarina warmed to Elvia and her daughter almost immediately, but she could not make herself like Gertrude or Ernst. Gertrude's presence was a walking reminder of Anna's absence. Gertrude was not even attractive; how could Hans have fallen for her after having been in love with Anna? In contrast, Elvia was a startlingly tall and slender woman with coal black hair and clear blue eyes. With Elvia, Katarina spoke mostly French, which automatically excluded Gertrude from conversation. Elvia was still learning German, and it was just easier to use French as their friendship developed. The fact that Gertrude spoke almost no French was an added bonus.

While she befriended Elvia's daughter, Katarina virtually ignored her own. She knew Anthony was encouraging everyone to just be patient with her, but she also knew patience was wearing thin. Katarina had been home for two weeks and had not spent a moment engaged with her own child. One day Aunt Helena showed up for her usual visit with Alexandra, and this time she decided to take the child home with her. Katarina stood quietly at the kitchen door listening to her aunt speaking to her mother.

"Lisa, how can you accept Katarina's coldness toward this child? She cannot blame Alexandra for the circumstances of her birth. Why are you all tiptoeing around her?"

"She's been through so much," Lisa said. "We're not sure what to do."

"She's a lot stronger than you think," Helena retorted. "A lesser person would not have survived what she went through. Stop coddling her."

Katarina stormed into the kitchen at that moment, taking both her mother and her aunt by surprise.

"How dare you question me, after what you did to me? You stand here acting as if you have not committed any sins. You with your self-righteousness! You had no trouble walking away from me as soon as I was born, yet you're judging me for how I treat my daughter. If you want to love a baby, you can have her. Take her!"

Lisa gasped. "Katarina, stop this moment! How dare you speak of your child this way? You don't just give a child away."

Katarina pointed her finger at Helena. "She did!"

Helena closed her eyes and took a deep breath. "Katarina, you're right. What I did was wrong. There is one difference. I love you. I always loved you. I've always been part of your life, watching you grow up. So many times I wished I could undo what I had done, but it was too late." Helena rubbed her temples in frustration. "Look, I didn't come here to argue with you, Katarina. But I will not stand here like the rest of the family and pretend that what you are doing is right. This is your baby. You fought to make sure she was born alive, and to keep her alive. You fought to keep yourself alive. Why are you giving up now?"

Katarina dug her nails into her hands, barely keeping herself from stepping into full-blown rage. "I do not want her," she seethed. "You take her. I was thinking of giving her to the orphanage anyway."

Lisa pressed her hand over her mouth. "Mother of God, child. What has become of your heart? She is your baby!"

"She is Frederick's baby! Her own father didn't want her, so why should I? I couldn't get down the steps because of her. I couldn't run because of her, and look what happened."

Katarina slid down the wall as a cry surged up from deep within. Lisa reached out for her, but Katarina pushed her mother away.

Helena stepped into the other room, scooped up Alexandra, and left.

****

Berlin: March 1946

During the seasons after the end of the war, Berliners faced hard times in their divided city. The harsh winter of 1945-46 left them hungry and without heat. Anthony compared it to the rape of a woman, what the Russians were inflicting upon his city. The family mostly kept to the American sector, especially Katarina. It took only one look and people were drawn to her, even now with her body so thin and her eyes without the spark they used to have.

Convinced they were doing the best thing for

Katarina, the Von Rahmels never discussed Katarina's rejection of her daughter, instead being silently grateful for any morsel of attention Katarina threw in the direction of Alexandra. She held her occasionally, and as the weather warmed took her for walks on sunny days. More and more, though, Helena took the child to her own home for protracted lengths of time, and each time Katarina was more relieved to be left on her own without the pressure to tend to her daughter.

The family began to restore their summerhouse in Grunewald, five miles outside Berlin. They began with tilling the small plot of land they used for a vegetable garden. They didn't have much in the way of seeds, but they planted what they scrounged up: cabbage, cucumbers, beans, and potatoes. The house itself needed extensive repairs.

Everyone took turns working on it as much as possible, when they weren't busy trying to hold life together in the city.

Katarina talked almost non-stop about getting out of Berlin. Her sleep had not improved, and many nights she did not even want to try. She convinced herself that if she could just get out of Berlin, she would feel normal again. Anthony was virtually the only person she could bear to have around her, but he was busy rebuilding his church, and Katarina did not see him as often as she wished.

Once again the Von Rahmels were involved in political activities not entirely welcomed by the Russians, while the Americans watched closely, as did the British. Hans and Anthony organized small meetings at the family factories to stir up movement toward a truly democratic government. A friend with a printing press provided the leaflets the brothers handed out throughout the city, both East and West. Some of the family's business interests were in East Berlin, giving Hans and Anthony reason to cross sectors frequently. Anthony also used his priestly identity to cross the various sectors of the city.

Once a week, Anthony said Mass at a church in East Berlin that had no priest. The Soviets had thought the Von Rahmels were just a bug on the wall to be swatted; instead they were turning out to be troublesome.

One day, as Anthony worked on restoring the well-worn altar in his church, he was startled to see a shadow behind a pew. Then a smile lit his face.

"Grigory!"

The two men greeted each other with broad grins.

Anthony gestured. "Come, my study is surprisingly habitable. My good furniture became kindling long ago, but I still have a couple of chairs." His eyes twinkled. "And some good brandy under a floor board. I believe you know the way."

The warm drink oozed down their throats a few minutes later. "So, Grigory, what really brings you to Berlin?" Anthony asked.

"Anthony, we know what you're up to. You're holding meetings and working toward elections for a democratic government."

Anthony raised an eyebrow. "And?"

"And it's clear we have the same agenda. We cannot let the Soviets take over Berlin."

"If they get Berlin, they get all of Germany."

"Exactly. I have two missions. There are ex-Nazis working for the Soviets that need to be brought to justice, and at the same time, we need to know what the Soviets are doing so we can divert them. In other words, we want to confuse them as much as possible."

Anthony calmly sipped his brandy. "Grigory, I will do whatever it takes to keep Berlin free. My family paid too high a price to have it occupied by immoral leaders again." He paused. "You're doing more than looking for information, aren't you?"

Grigory smiled. "You know I can't talk about that. I can only ask if you are willing to help in a bigger capacity."

Anthony ran his finger around the lip of his glass. "You know the Americans watch every move I make. I must admit, though, it's quite different from having the Gestapo on our backs. These people actually seem to care."

"Tell me about your meetings."

"We hold them at the factories, especially in the West. Sometimes some men come from the East and stand at the back and call us traitors. They sing the praises of the Nazis or Communism, trying to provoke a fight, because if a fight breaks out, the Americans will stop our meetings."

"And are they successful?"

Anthony shook his head. "We just ignore them. Perhaps if they listen long enough they will see the light." He leaned forward to refill their glasses. "I'm sure you know that a lot of Nazis escaped to East Berlin and found protection under the secret police there."

"Anthony, what will the Vatican say about your activities?"

"Well, it's a fact I will never make bishop, much less cardinal, but they haven't excommunicated me yet.

They were silent all through the war; why should they say anything now?"

"I believe Peter might still come to Berlin."

Anthony's eyes widened in hope. His cousin had met him in Rome but had steadfastly refused to return to Germany after the war.

"The British want him here," Grigory explained. "He's objecting, but he can't hold out forever." He paused. "How is Katarina?"

Anthony's eyes darkened. "Sometimes I don't think I know her anymore, she's changed so much. Not physically, you understand. She's recovered from her wounds. The doctors say the scars will fade a great deal over the years, and she has gained weight and looks healthy. Her charisma is overwhelming when she wants her way and smiles at you. But there's a hardness to her now. At times she laughs as if nothing ever happened and other times I can't get through to her."

"I'm so sorry, Anthony. We put her in a terrible position when we asked her to help. In hindsight, I wish we hadn't."

Anthony shook his head. "It wouldn't have mattered. Frederick would still have been there. He would still have done what he did because of the rest of us, no matter what Katarina did or didn't do."

"Be careful, Anthony. There are still people out there who could be dangerous for you."

"I'm always careful, Grigory."

"I'm serious. The Russians are as dangerous as the Gestapo was. Your name is on a list, and they wish you would disappear. They don't like all your talk about democracy."

Anthony leaned his head back on his chair and

thought, Here we go again. But this time Katarina will have nothing to do with it.

Chapter 15

Berlin: August 1946

On the small broken-down stage, Katarina felt free again.

It wasn't the opera house in Munich or a prestigious venue in Berlin. She wasn't a prima ballerina and didn't expect to be ever again. But it was a stage, and she was free to move and dance as much as her tortured muscles would allow. And she could teach. Even thoughts of leaving Berlin faded when she glided across the stage absorbed in the music. A local group was behind the effort to revive the arts in Berlin along with the physical infrastructure. Frau Simmons, who had competed against the Meister for the best dancers in all of Germany, was heading up the project. Katarina was only too happy to participate.

Even a year and a half after the end of the war, food was scarce in Europe. A nation that historically depended on importing much of its food had few friends and the thinnest of economic networks. Food rations dropped to even lower levels than during the Hitler years. The threat of mass starvation was far from over. The Allies strategically had divided up Berlin and Germany, but the Soviets were determined to have the whole pie.

In their quest to rout the British and Americans

from Berlin, they managed to control all electricity and railways flowing into and out of the city. The Russians changed border regulations seemingly at whim, making it almost impossible to rebuild a system of free trade that would feed the nation. Without a reliable supply of electricity, factories—including the Von Rahmel enterprises—could not operate at capacity.

Katarina watched helplessly as her father and Hans tried to keep their factories open and productive. It was the hunger and cold of winter that Katarina desperately wanted to escape. Not a day went by that she did not formulate a plan to leave Berlin. She wanted food. She wanted warmth. She wanted to have enough—of anything, of everything. She wanted to forget. Convinced that life in Berlin would take far too long to return to pre-war qualities, she just wanted out of the struggle. Other than when she danced, escaping the impoverished city was on her mind every waking moment.

Through her dancing, Katarina was slowly learning to put reason before temper. She lived on the edge of her roiling emotions, so this didn't always come easy. Often she experienced such melancholy that her whole body ached, and this presented itself in chronic ill temper. Her family's pity only made things worse. No one could begin to grasp what she had been through in the last months of the war—she didn't even remember herself—so how could they pretend to understand? The evenings haunted her. Darkness was the enemy, the habitat of nightmares poised to lunge at her the moment her guard was down. She constantly believed someone was watching her; occasionally she even asked her mother to look out the window to see the person who must be there—but wasn't. Anthony stuck to his position that it was just her frayed nerves, and she merely needed more time to heal. Numbing her senses with quantities of wine or brandy soon became a nightly routine for Katarina, and the family complied by somehow managing to keep enough on hand to satiate her. When Katarina fleetingly wondered what sacrifices they were making to do so, she dismissed the thought even before it could take full form.

She had promised Anthony she would make an effort with Alexandra, but when the child came near, her skin crawled. She swallowed the bile and tried to smile. At night, when she herself could not sleep, she often watched Alexandra sleep. Her heart would even skip a beat as she looked down at the perfect face of her daughter. But in the daylight, when the child might return her forced smile with her own dancing violet eyes, Katarina cringed inwardly and could not bring herself to hold Alexandra.

Katarina knew this was wrong. This was her child, and she had sacrificed greatly to bring her into the world alive. Alexandra was not responsible for who her father was; that had been Katarina's free choice. Alexandra was innocent. She was a child learning to walk and talk, not someone who had willingly harmed Katarina. But Katarina could not love her. Try as she might to be a normal mother, her rage erupted at the most unpredictable moments, leaving her family flabbergasted and their patience waning.

One night, in the deep hours, Katarina heard Alexandra crying. She made no move to comfort the child. When the crying changed to laughter and singing, though, she flew down the hall. Opening the door, she saw Gertrude with the child in her arms, swaying back and forth as she sang. She even heard her brother's wife promise to love the baby even if her own mother did not.

Katarina was furious. Gertrude, this ugly woman who had taken the place of beautiful Anna in her brother's heart, would not have her child, as well.

At dawn she gathered the necessary papers to cross through the sectors of Berlin. She bundled up Alexandra and left the house before anyone would know what she was up to, hoping all the while the trains would be running. She only needed to go to Weimar, scarcely two hours to the east.

Her family was panic-stricken when Katarina returned in the afternoon and did not have Alexandra with her. She wouldn't say a word about where she had been or what she had done.

Two days later, Jona Von Rahmel could wait no longer. He barged into her bedroom.

"Katarina, I have loved you more than you can imagine. We have all tried to understand what you have gone through. But I promise I will banish you from this family if you do not tell me what you have done with my granddaughter."

The fury in her father's eyes stunned her, and she knew he meant what he said. Never before had he challenged her in such a way.

"Katarina," he continued, "you can walk the streets with the rest of the refugees if you do not tell me where the child is."

Katarina stared into her father's eyes. "I couldn't look at her any longer," she said softly. "She wanted kisses. She wanted to hug me. I couldn't stand it. Every time I looked at her, I saw Frederick. I bore the devil's child, and I cannot love her."

"Just tell me what you have done."

She turned her head and stared out the window, but she told him.

Anthony stepped into the room just in time to hear Katarina's answer. This was his fault, he was sure of it. He should never have involved Katarina in the resistance activities. He should have insisted that she stick to dancing and mind her own business. After all, she was barely twenty years old when she began helping him. He couldn't undo all of that, but he could have listened to the doctors who did not feel she was ready to go home. He could have insisted she be under the care of a psychiatrist when she got home, instead of giving in to her insistence that she didn't need help and everyone should stop hovering over her.

"Father," Anthony said firmly, "go get Helena. Give me a few minutes with Katarina, and then Helena and I will go and find Alexandra."

As his father, shocked at what he'd heard, left the room, Anthony moved closer to his sister. Many times since the war began Anthony had clung to the words of Psalm 18: "The Lord is my rock, and my fortress, and my deliverer, my God, my rock in whom I take refuge." Sometimes it felt as if his prayers fell on deaf ears, yet every morning Anthony lifted his arms and cried for help.

Anthony went to where Katarina sat leaning against the wall, her arms wrapped around her knees, staring blankly. He sat on the floor next to her and stroked her long hair, gently moving it away from her face.

"Katarina, why the little one? Why take it out on her?"

Katarina stared straight ahead. "I just wanted her to go away. Everyone kept pushing her on me. Sometimes I look at her and my heart swells. I think of kissing those chubby little hands. Then I remember, or think I'm going to remember. And it makes me sick. I just wanted her to go away."

Anthony gathered his sister into his arms, feeling her heart pounding against his chest.

"Promise me you won't stop loving me, Anthony," she pleaded, her nails digging into his arms. "I don't know why I behave in these horrid ways. I am dead inside. They should have left me to die."

"Shhh," Anthony murmured, at a loss for any meaningful words.

"God, Anthony, half of my life is branded into my memory, while the other half is somewhere I can't find. I catch only glimpses, faces I don't quite recognize, feelings that are ugly. I can't sleep, I can't remember, and I'm not sure I want to remember. But don't give up on me, Anthony. Please don't leave me!"

Anthony raised her chin and gazed into her violet, teary eyes. "Katarina, I will always be with you. I will always love you, always forgive you. But you must learn that forgiveness sets us free. It heals. You must accept it so you can be free of the pain. Don't you see that you can never heal the past memories if you don't start living for your future? Alexandra is your future."

"I'm sorry, Anthony." Katarina sobbed openly now. "I hope it's not too late for Alexandra."

****

Anthony and Helena sought help from friends for a

ride. The trains would take too long. Grigory was the one who came through. Anthony called him at the hotel he frequented, and surprisingly, the phone in the lobby was working. Grigory made a few calls, and soon a British soldier appeared with a vehicle at the Von Rahmel home.

Anthony and Helena got in it.

"Don't feel sorry for your sister," Helena said as they rumbled along. "What do you think that little girl is going through right now? She has been ripped apart from the only family she has known. Two days is an eternity to a toddler."

"We'll find her, Helena," Anthony answered.

"She might already be adopted," Helena said.

"We'll find her."

"And then what? Take her back to a mother who gave her away?"

"None of us can imagine what is going on in Katarina's head," Anthony said.

"Don't try to justify her actions!" Helena was clearly incensed. "Katarina isn't the only one who suffered in this war. Alexandra was born in a concentration camp, for God's sake. You aren't helping your sister by coddling her."

"Helena, I have to try to help her. It's my fault all this happened in the first place."

"This is not about you," Helena said coldly. "This is about a little girl who doesn't deserve what happened to her. I don't claim to have made perfect choices, Anthony. I should never have given Katarina to my sister. But that does not make me responsible for what she has chosen now. You choose your own path when you think it's right."

When they arrived at the orphanage, Anthony was thankful to see it was a Catholic institution. He was wearing his priest's collar and could prove who he was. Anthony found the mother superior and quickly explained a mistake had been made. They were there to pick up a child who never should have been brought to them. The nun led them to a large room filled wall to wall with cribs, with narrow aisles between the rows. Anthony quickly scooped up Alexandra—who was clearly glad to see him—and after pressing her close to his cheek, put her in Helena's arms.

Alexandra coughed, and Helena put her hand against the child's forehead. "She's sick, Anthony. That sounds like croup."

"We'll be back in Berlin in a couple of hours. I'll call the doctor as soon as we get there."

They signed the papers the nun placed in front of them and within minutes were back in the British vehicle.

"Anthony," Helena said determinedly, "I'm taking Alexandra home with me. There's a doctor in my building who buys penicillin on the black market."

"We don't know that she needs penicillin."

"I'm not taking any chances. How could Katarina do this? I will never forgive her!"

Anthony was determined not to go around that loop again. "Helena, take Alexandra home with you. I agree that's a good idea. Keep her for a while, even after she's well. Give Katarina some time to come to love Alexandra."

Helena glared at Anthony as she swayed with the baby, trying to soothe the crying. "When are you going to stop making excuses for her, Anthony? Have you considered she might never find this peace that you think is just around the corner? She needs help. Your whole family is so guilt-ridden about things that aren't your fault that you'll never be able to help her. Lord knows we can't change the past."

"Helena, you're not being fair."

"Don't throw that in my face," Helena seethed. "Yes, I gave away my daughter. But I gave her to my sister, to a family who would love her, and never was I cruel to her. Never did I hate her."

The child began to scream and pulled on her left ear.

"I think she has an ear infection," Helena said. "She caught it in that place."

"Helena, if you had only seen what I saw. I can't forget Katarina running for her life across a field outside a concentration camp with a baby in her arms. I can't forget what she looked like when I found her in that hospital. I just want to make her life easier."

"Then find her some help," Helena insisted. "You can't just say Mass and fix this."

"Katarina protected this child and kept her alive in the camp. Deep down, she loves her, I'm sure of it."

Helena sighed deeply. "There is no reasoning with you when it comes to Katarina. Let's just drop it. But I am keeping Alexandra indefinitely."

Chapter 16

Berlin: October 1946

The weeks went by. Residents of Berlin scrabbled to find enough food to keep alive. They cut trees to burn for warmth and cooking. The Von Rahmel family was fortunate to have an auxiliary food supply from the canned reserves they had buried behind the summerhouse. Jona Von Rahmel had rescued a female goat from the desecrated Berlin zoo, and the family now kept it hidden in the back of the kitchen, searching daily for food to feed it and in return being rewarded with desperately needed milk for the children in the household. They could also make cheese, which they shared with their neighbors. Because of the valuable milk, everyone tolerated the smell of the creature and took turns cleaning the mess in the kitchen.

Anthony continued organizing meetings with German workers, the everyday citizens who bore the brunt of the political jockeying. He warned them that before Germany could become healthy again, they must have free trade unions and a solid democratic government. As the Christian Democratic Union rose from the ashes of Berlin and united Catholics and Protestants, politicians and laborers, Father Anthony Von Rahmel was not afraid to press for his convictions and what he believed in his heart was essential for the future of his country. The church had already given him warnings to simply concentrate on his church, but he would not listen. After all he and others had endured, he couldn't allow Berlin to fall to the Soviets, for the Russians to replace the Nazis with the same kind of bullying regime.

Anthony didn't reveal to his sister the secret activities that took him in and out of East Berlin. When she questioned him about the oddities of his comings and going, he managed to change the subject, determined not to suck her into his renegade activities again. He knew it was only a matter of time before she found out what he was up to—the rest of the family knew—but he persevered in protecting her for as long as possible.

It seemed to the whole family that Katarina was improving. With each day her mood swings moderated, and the angry outbursts came at less frequent intervals. Her old self was beginning to surface as her friendship with Elvia deepened, and she even managed cordiality with Gertrude. Most important, she began to visit Alexandra several times a week at Helena's home. Although she still hesitated to hold her daughter for any length of time, even Helena agreed Katarina was making progress.

Katarina's involvement with the small dance studio and work on the summerhouse kept her occupied, though she faced limitations on both counts. She loved dancing, but her muscles were not the same after the beatings she had endured during the last months of the war. When pain shot through her legs, she sometimes saw the steel rod coming down on her again, but just as quickly, the memory fled—or was pushed out by

Katarina's refusal to remember. She enjoyed working in the garden at the summerhouse, but it soon became evident it was useless to plant until the family could live in the house again. The crops disappeared to foraging animals and neighbors as soon as they became edible. Seeds were too scarce to keep trying to replace them.

One day as she walked slowly in the cold, the wind blowing through her thin coat and the stockings that had been mended so many times, Katarina decided to stop and see Hans and her father at the one factory they managed to operate continuously because it was in the American sector. She saw little of them. They left at dawn every day, and came home late in the evening.

Near the factory, Katarina paused to watch the traffic on the street corner. Many of the German women made themselves readily available to the American soldiers in that sector. The soldiers invited them into a local bar, hoping for a night of dancing and with a little luck some physical pleasure. Often the women went into the bars because they knew they might get a badly needed meal out of the arrangement. Katarina was not tempted in the least to join them. Watching the pairings on the street, Katarina realized how much she had seen Elvia and Dietrich together lately. They would also go for a walk in the evening, after Elvia's daughter was asleep, and remain gone for hours.

So engrossed in the scene in front of her, Katarina did not hear anyone approach her. A sultry voice startled her.

"Are you interested, Fräulein? I promise you a good time, and maybe you could show me something in return."

Fury welled up as she turned on the American soldier. "How dare you! Perhaps you thought I didn't speak English, but I do. The girls who go in there with you soldiers are just hungry and want to get out of the cold. If you want a prostitute, go find one in Potsdam."

"I'm sorry, truly sorry," the soldier stammered and turned away.

Incensed, Katarina turned and walked as quickly as she could toward the factory. She didn't know if the tears running down her cheeks were from the cold or from sadness and anger. How she hated Berlin! Would she ever stop being cold and hungry? Would she ever get out of this desolate city? Her parents were barely getting by. How long could they keep a goat in the kitchen? How long could they keep feeding it enough that it would continue producing milk? How long before a neighbor was hungry enough to eat the goat instead of depending on its milk?

Soon Katarina was standing in front of the factory. It was sadly in need of repair, but of course there were no supplies. The building had been patched together enough to be functional, but not much more. Limited by short spurts of electricity that lasted only a few hours a day, only one machine was operating much of the time. Katarina chuckled to herself. Did Anthony really think no one would wonder what all those people were doing inside a factory that clearly did not employ them all?

Katarina eased herself inside and heard loud voices, with cheering and clapping. It was not the first time. She had attended several meetings, taking care to stay hidden in the shadows. She smiled as she heard Anthony's voice swell in oratory.

"And we cannot allow a German unification under

Soviet terms. The Soviets' long fingers will stretch into Eastern and Central Europe. They will try to force Moscow's policies on us. We must not believe the rumors they have broadcast that the Americans are leaving. The Americans are not here to bleed us or find revenge. They have come to help us rebuild, re-educate, cleanse."

The crowd was listening intently. Anthony inhaled deeply and continued. "We must not allow the Soviets to sow seeds of another war by separating Germany into sections. The Soviets know we long for reunification. We might look like a ragged humanity to the outside world, but we must show the world that we want to go to the polls. We want elections for a democratic government. We must not let the lack of water and the epidemic of pneumonia and TB sweep us into a panic. We cannot let these living conditions cause us to side with the Russians and their propaganda. We will not be defeated!"

Anthony paused to look at the faces nodding in agreement. He also noted the Russian henchmen standing defiantly at the back of the room.

"We must let the British and Americans realize we want democracy, not Russian dictatorship. We must prove we support their efforts. We must pull the conservatives and Christians to the democratic side. No one will hand us freedom; we must fight for it!"

This is better than a homily at Mass, Katarina thought, though she had not been to church in years. Anthony has found his calling.

Katarina eyed two men just slipping into the crowd. Why did they look so familiar? Almost certainly they were with the new Gestapo of the East, the

Communist action squads who rampaged through Berlin, kidnapping, beating, and killing those who resisted Russian rule. They preached peace with the Russian brothers and tried to engineer election campaigns by giving out free cigarettes and food. Keeping an eye on the Communists, Katarina wasn't paying enough attention to where she was going. Her scarf fell from her head as she bumped into an American army officer.

"I'm so sorry. I wasn't watching where I was going," Katarina apologized. She took in his features. How tall he was, with light brown skin, high cheekbones, and eyes slightly slanted. His hair was black as night, gently graying at the temples. On his captain's uniform, she read the name Lee.

"No, it was my fault," he said. He seemed at a loss for words, staggered by her beauty. Finally he murmured, "My apologies."

They both turned as a roar went up from the crowd and everyone began to pound their feet on the floor and yell, "Freedom! Freedom!" Like everyone else in the room, they became once again entranced as Anthony continued speaking.

****

Captain Francis Lee's orders were to attend these meetings and report what he observed. The brass wanted to know just what support these new leaders were gathering and how hard they were willing to fight for democracy in Germany. Of all the meetings he had been to, Captain Lee preferred listening to the Von Rahmel brothers, though he thought they were putting themselves in far more danger than they realized. Because of his research on the family, it did not take him long to realize that this stunning young woman was their sister, Katarina Von Rahmel.

The speeches over, the room was beginning to empty. Fräulein Von Rahmel negotiated her way through the crowd to her brothers as Captain Lee watched. He expected Anthony Von Rahmel to welcome his sister. Instead, he seemed distressed and pointed at the back of the room. Von Rahmel was turning red, clearly having trouble breathing. Lee followed Anthony's gaze, easily spotting a known Gestapo agent still enjoying his freedom. When the agent exited the building, another man swiftly ducked out after him. Lee casually moved toward the Von Rahmels.

"Don't worry, Anthony," he heard Hans Von Rahmel say. "Grigory will take care of him. He won't make it back to the East."

Katarina opened her brother's shirt and urged him to take deep breaths, her own breath falling shallow. "He was there," she said, barely audible. "The day Frederick arrested me. I saw that man."

"That was not the only time he tried to hurt our family."

Captain Lee stepped forward. "Hello. I'm Captain Francis Lee. I hope you are not seriously ill."

Anthony breathed deeply and raised his hand to stop the captain's stumbling German. "We speak English," he gasped. "There's no need for you to struggle with German."

"My brother is fine," Katarina was quick to say. "He is simply exhausted from speaking."

"Father, I would like a word with you," Lee said. "I've been following your meetings."

Anthony raised an eyebrow.

"Would you come to my office in Templehof tomorrow?" Lee asked. "I would like to discuss some of the issues you are promoting. We may be able to help you."

Lee wrote down an address, then bid a polite goodbye to the Von Rahmel cluster. He paused at the back of the room and turned to watch the young woman once again. Lee no longer could hear their words, but she seemed to be admonishing Anthony. She was simply the most ravishing woman Francis Lee had ever seen. He had read briefly about a sister in the Von Rahmel file, but he hadn't paid much attention. He resolved to go look at the file again.

Katarina refused to be left behind. She stood at the church door after early Mass, waiting for her brother. She didn't attend Mass anymore. Her mother and Aunt Helen went nearly every morning. Katarina had not been a single time since returning to Berlin, since she did not believe God existed. The only pull to the church was to see Anthony.

She was here this morning because she was determined to accompany Anthony, Hans, and Dietrich when they met with Captain Lee in the Templehof borough where the Americans had set up their headquarters. She didn't intend to take "no" for an answer. Her brothers had protected her long enough. Even Grigory reluctantly agreed it was time to include her once again—not because he thought it was wise, but because she would nag them to death if they excluded her any longer. Somewhere behind his agreement he realized how much he had missed her. Every time he went back to Israel, he was drawn back to Berlin, just to see her.

When they arrived at Templehof, every head turned to look at Anthony, so impressive was he in his clean, white collar. Like many citizens of Berlin, he was thinner now than in the years before rationing, but he was still strikingly handsome, and Katarina knew it. She teased him incessantly about it. On this day, Katarina had deliberately chosen to dress more femininely than she had in the last few months. She wore a simple dark silk dress, the tight belt around her tiny waist accentuating her curved hips. Her long blonde ponytail hung to her waist, tied in a bow of white lace, and wisps of bangs fell over her forehead enchantingly. She had found some very old lipstick, and with her finger had managed to dig out the last bit and smear it on her full lips. With her flawless complexion and big round violet eyes, she was still a classic beauty. The heels she wore belonged to Elvia. They were two sizes too big, but they went well with the dress.

****

As the Von Rahmels entered his office, Captain Lee once again felt something catch in his throat, just as he had the moment he'd bumped into Katarina at the rally. He cleared the lump with a slight cough and invited the entourage to sit down. Knowing they most likely had not enjoyed sweets for a very long time, he asked his secretary to bring a plate of cakes.

This family intrigued him. He had stayed awake most of the night rereading their history. He knew everything they had been through—he was stunned Katarina's ordeals had not caught his attention earlier—and knew everything there was to know about their co-conspirators, Peter and Grigory.

Grigory, he had decided, was not someone you wanted to cross. He had every reason to believe Grigory worked for the British intelligence office in the most confidential matters, and he seriously suspected that Grigory was connected with the body that had turned up in the river last night with a clean shot to the head and no other wound. Captain Lee had taken one look at the photo and known that this was the man who had made Anthony Von Rahmel's pulse race the previous day.

Lee looked at the Von Rahmels and their friend Dietrich closely as they sipped their coffee. He was transfixed by Katarina, and he forced himself to stand up and walk to the window to break the spell.

"Father, you are aware of the great strides General Clay is making with the Truman Administration to have Berlin become its own seat of government, with occupied forces staying in place for a time. We have to listen to Churchill's Iron Curtain speech. No longer can anyone claim reactionary pessimism, but prophetic realism. The man we must watch, the one who would like to undermine everything, is Sokolovsky in Moscow. If he continues to convince those who are in most need, those who are starving and without fuel, that the Western powers have evil motives, we will run into the same problems we have in the past."

Seeing that he had their attention, the captain continued. "We, in the United States, have limited resources. Everyone in the world seems to need our economic and military assistance. We promise not to let anyone communize Eastern and Western Germany, but 1947 and 1948 will be difficult years."

"What exactly are you trying to tell us, Captain?"

Anthony asked. So far the captain had not said anything the Von Rahmels did not know.

"We believe you should continue your meetings," Lee said, "but you must realize that the East considers you the enemy. You and your family might be in danger. We ask you to limit your activity. Cut back, and let the professionals who know how to handle the Russians do their job."

Anthony smiled blandly as he set down his coffee cup. "Captain, the world has not seen the demons we fought. This is only a small problem. With the help of the Allies, we can make this go away. Let's face it. How many of those soldiers we saw as we walked down the hallway believe there are any good Germans?"

"You have proven yourself quite persuasive, Father Von Rahmel," Captain Lee responded.

Anthony leaned forward in his chair. "Between 1934 and 1937, Germany had over six thousand political prisoners in concentration camps. Some of them were there just for being educated, not because they'd ever said a word against Hitler. Then all hell broke loose in 1939. I was a priest. I could not stand by and watch this injustice, so I joined the resistance. If you think I am going to step back now, after all I have risked to this point, you are sadly mistaken."

"Please don't misunderstand," Captain Lee said quickly and smoothly. "We simply want you to be cautious. There is no need to put your family in danger when others are standing by to help. Change will not come overnight, but I assure you the United States is no more interested in the Russians ruling Germany than you are."

Hans spoke up. "Captain Lee, I'm sure you have read everything about us and realize our family took the ultimate gamble with the Nazis. In the process we lost our home in Munich, two of our brothers, family heirlooms, my father's irreplaceable library. We are an old country, and I grant you that we are not very experienced with democracy. The Weimar Republic after World War I was a disaster. But we will not stand by and let the German people become passive about their own future."

Katarina listened to her brothers' passionate speeches, and at the same time tried to gauge the response of the handsome American officer.

"No one is asking you to give up your convictions, Mr. Von Rahmel," said Captain Lee. He looked at the four seated before him. "I can see your determination is unswerving. We are only concerned for your safety."

"The Russians are blockading and trying to starve us to death," Anthony said. "They can shut off the electricity entirely, but we will continue to fight. We will not live under the likes of someone like Stalin."

Captain Lee smiled graciously. "Perhaps this is the first of many conversations we will share as we come to understand each other better."

****

The American officer stood at the window for a long time watching the Von Rahmels walk down the street. Katarina had hooked her arm through the priest's and reached up to kiss his cheek.

No, not a German girl! he could hear his father say. His own mother was French and had arrived in Hawaii as a two-year-old, when her family established a plantation there. When she married his Hawaiian father, she had brought all her grace and style to his home, until her death three years ago. His family owned a large part of the island of Kauai, complete with sugar and pineapple plantations. Francis Lee had two younger sisters. He was also engaged to a lovely Hawaiian woman named Maria. Their families were longtime friends.

After he'd seen Katarina Von Rahmel, however, he thought only of her.

****

Katarina had found her ticket to freedom, and his name was Captain Francis Lee. She began to plan.

Chapter 17

Berlin: November 1946

Katarina busied herself making flyers for Anthony and the freedom movement.

They could give out the flyers openly in West Berlin and had been successfully smuggling them into East Berlin for secret distribution. Only yesterday she had stood on Unter Den Linden under the awning of trees that lined the historic street in the center of Berlin.

Today she walked slowly to the Brandenburg Gate, remembering the grandeur when she had danced at the opera house and the cabaret had been full. The beautiful domed cathedral was now gutted and looted. Her beautiful flowered Tiergarten was no longer. Most of the trees were gone, and only random stubborn flowers managed to bloom. She stood and looked at the Reichstag with tears in her eyes. It would be better if the whole building had been destroyed; so much evil had come from it.

A hunched-over old man shuffled toward her. Katarina averted her eyes. The last thing she wanted to see was another beaten old man.

"There is no reason for you to cry, Katarina," a voice said. "You did the best you could."

Katarina's head snapped up, and she met the man's eyes. "Grigory! Oh, my God! What are you doing here?" If the disguise hadn't been so brilliant, she would have burst out laughing.

"Don't look directly at me, Katarina," Grigory said, shuffling slightly to one side. "I knew you were handing out leaflets here. I just happened to have crossed through that magnificent structure to pass on information."

"Grigory, please stay and talk to me. Maybe we can find a little bench. It's been so long since we talked."

He chuckled. "No, my dear. That would be a most unlikely sight. Someone is always watching you, you know. I came here to tell you to go home and tell Anthony the Soviets plan to use American engravings and plates they have stolen to print occupation currency. They want to flood our zones to cause inflation, just like we had after World War I. Anthony needs to get this information to Captain Lee."

"Captain Lee?"

"He is a lawyer. Let him strut his stuff. Now go. The goon squads will beat a woman as quickly as they will a man."

Reluctantly, Katarina turned away and casually continued walking away.

Desperately, she wanted to turn around and watch her friend shuffle down the sidewalk, but she didn't dare. American MPs passed her, as they had several times that day. Young GIs smiled at her, and Katarina giggled in return and kept on walking.

Katarina had begged Anthony to let her help. Twice she had secretly crossed to the East and personally passed on information packets. Each time, her blood raced, but she felt as if she were really doing something other than surviving the cold and hunger. As Katarina made her way to Anthony, her mind wandered to the black market and how it was now in full swing. The Tiergarten appeared less ravaged when it buzzed with people working their deals, however illegal. Everything began to look hazy as she stared at these strangers who were her countrymen, searching the faces for those who had tortured her. Katarina told no one about these moments of paralysis, when she could not make her feet move and felt herself being drawn into a pit of blackness.

Standing outside the Tiergarten, she pressed her fingers to her temples, determined she would not go to that place. Instead, she began to walk faster, knowing she must get to Anthony immediately. Perhaps she could convince him to let her take the news to Captain Lee. It would fit well into her plan.

Anthony was not at the church. No one knew where he was or when he would be back. Katarina smiled to herself. Her pace picked up as she walked toward the Templehof.

****

She had been up and down the block four times before she heard her name. When she turned toward the voice, there he was, behind the wheel of his jeep, one arm stretched over the brown back of the front seat.

"Captain Lee! How delightful to see you."

"I am delighted to see you, as well," he said.

Katarina approached the car. "Captain Lee, I have some information for you." With a smile on her face for the sake of any onlookers, Katarina relayed the information she had received from Grigory.

Captain Lee picked up on her tone flawlessly,

smiling back flirtatiously. His cheeks were red with cold; his dark brown eyes narrowly focused on her.

"Fräulein Von Rahmel, I would like to invite you to a small bistro. It's in the English sector. They have a limited menu, but delicious." It was against the rules, but he seemed eager to be with her. It was forbidden for soldiers of any rank to fraternize with German girls.

She didn't want to appear too eager by answering immediately, though she had to bite her lip to keep from doing so. Finally she said, "Captain Lee, I would love to go with you. I'm not exactly dressed for a place that might call for a good dress." She laughed suddenly. "I wonder if any Germans dress up any more."

"I can't imagine you could ever look anything less than beautiful, Fräulein."

With a sense of satisfaction, Katarina climbed into the jeep. She had passed on the information, and she had furthered her plan, in one fell swoop. They made nervous small talk until they arrived at the small eatery full of British and American soldiers. Many of them seemed to have German women on their arms. Katarina stopped short before entering the bistro. For her plan to work, she had to do this right.

"Captain, may I speak frankly?" she asked timidly.

"If you're uncomfortable, I know of another place."

"This looks like a lovely place," she said. "It's just that many of my people are selling themselves for a meal or a pair of stockings. What will you think of me if I go in there with you?" She met his gaze levelly.

"Fräulein, you are nothing but a lady. Anyone can see that. I asked a lady to have dinner with me. That is all I'm asking."

As they entered the bistro, every head turned. She was dressed in a dark pair of slacks and a long, black cotton sweater and wore no makeup. Her hair was pulled back in a long braid. Katarina deliberately held her head high and her shoulders straight.

The owner knew the captain and led them to a corner table and quickly produced a bottle of wine. Katarina wondered just how many other women had been lucky enough to share a table with this man and in the next moment resolved that he would never bring another woman here again. Francis ordered a cheese-and-sausage platter for both of them.

"I hope you don't mind my ordering," he said. "I have found this is the best item on the menu."

"Captain, I would betray my country for a good piece of cheese."

He laughed. "I can hardly take that seriously, given your background."

"Captain, tell me where you are from. You know so much about my family. What can you tell me about yours?"

He smiled, responding to the warmth in her eyes and the dimness of the bistro. "I come from halfway around the world, Hawaii. My mother is French, my father Hawaiian. Before the war, I had only left Hawaii long enough to study law in California. Now I am here as a legal advisor."

She laughed lightly. "How lucky you must feel to have ended up in Berlin when you could have been in Paris!"

"Actually I could be home, but I decided to stay on a bit longer. My father hates the paperwork on our plantation and would much rather have me doing it, but

188

I'm afraid I don't much care for it either." He paused. "Am I boring you already?"

"Not at all. Tell me about Hawaii."

Francis sipped his wine. "I can look out the back window of my office and see the clouds covering the top of the mountains. Our house sits at the entrance of a valley, with the mountains on one side and the ocean on the other. We see whales and dolphins from the bedroom windows, and we look down on the beautiful garden my mother built over many years. It's full of pathways and flowers, with small lily ponds, and benches."

"Sounds like you love it there," Katarina said. Hawaii did not sound cold or hungry. She decided at that moment she could easily live in Hawaii. She added, "Except for the paperwork."

He chuckled. "Hawaii is the most beautiful place in the world. Soft breezes kiss your cheek like a lover. The mountains, flowers, water—it all gives your soul new life every time you take a deep breath."

Katarina didn't take her eyes off him, knowing he was captivated by her own violet eyes. She let out a sigh as she cupped her chin in her hand. "I've read about Hawaii. It sounds as beautiful as the pictures I've seen. I wish I could go to your paradise. Look around you. This isn't exactly what a girl wants to wake up to every morning."

"Germany will be beautiful again someday," Francis said softly.

She sighed again. "I used to ride through beautiful forests as a girl, and breathe fresh air and look at the trees towering over me. Even here in Berlin our summerhouse sits on the edge of a forest. But of course most of the trees are gone now."

"Who knows what your future holds, Katarina? You may see my paradise someday."

When they left the restaurant, Katarina shivered in the night air. Francis gently laid his coat around her thin frame. She smiled her gratitude and sat as close to him as the seats in the jeep would allow.

They drove past the Brandenburg Gate, stopping to let a man with a horse and carriage pass. The city was dark and dreary, windows lit mostly with candles.

"It's such a dark world, isn't it, Captain?" Katarina said slowly.

"And you have seen more than your share of the darkness," he replied.

"My husband was the worst of them all," she said, her voice barely audible now. "He was Gestapo, with unlimited powers to arrest and torture. Now the Gestapo works with the Russians and can walk freely among us. I ask myself every day, since we know who they are why do the Americans and English not arrest them?"

Francis put one arm around her shoulders and pulled her closer to him. When they reached the front of her home, she genuinely wished the evening was not ending. It was so nice to have a night out. Even so, when he pulled her toward him and it seemed he might kiss her, her arms instinctively folded across her chest protectively.

She hadn't meant to become defensive. "I'm so sorry," she said. "It's just that the old wounds still haunt me. I have nightmares... But you know all this from our files." She closed her eyes, expecting him to be irritated.

Instead he kissed her on the tip of her nose. "There will be another day," he said softly.

She pressed one finger lightly into his chest. "Is that a promise?"

"That is a promise, Fräulein Von Rahmel."

Katarina stepped out of the jeep and gave him a smile that would have melted any heart. "Thank you for a lovely evening," she said. She watched him drive away, both of them smiling, then scampered up the front steps of the house. Once inside, she heard voices coming from the living room and realized both Anthony and Dietrich were there, along with Hans. But as she slipped into the living room, she saw several strangers seated in the far corner.

"I can't believe anyone is going to allow this from the Soviets," Anthony said.

One of the strangers, who appeared to be in his eighties, answered. "Anthony, my dear boy, you must understand that if the Soviets can ration food and give favor to those who convert, anything can happen. Isn't that how dictatorships are born? Food is the one thing people will always follow."

Anthony bowed his head. He respected Herr Bowman's opinion. Bowman had been a university professor before the war but was taken as a political prisoner because he spoke out against Hitler early on. Many had thought he was dead—how could an old man survive the camps?—but he had surfaced after the war and stepped back into university life.

"Herr Bowman," Anthony said, "even more than food rationing, we must be concerned that the Russians are able to infiltrate our government and education systems with communists. Their action squads are scaring so many of our people, I sometimes wonder myself if we can win. The Americans and the British just don't seem to know how to handle the Russians. It's a different war than the world has ever known."

"Yes, I know," Bowman responded. "They call it the 'cold war.' "

Just listening to that snippet of the conversation had made Katarina weary. She slipped out of the room, without anyone ever acknowledging she had entered, and went upstairs to her bedroom. She was tired of the fighting and the political discussions and the strategizing. She was willing to do what she could to help Anthony while she was in Berlin, but she was determined to get out of Berlin before the insanity of it all killed her.

A very pleasant evening with Captain Francis Lee had been the first step of her plan.

****

Anthony looked in on Katarina before he left for the rectory. She was sitting at her vanity brushing her hair.

"Katarina, Mother says you were out late."

She raised an eyebrow in the mirror and continued brushing. "I'm a grown woman, Anthony. I can stay out late if I want to."

"Of course."

"I saw the way you looked at Captain Lee the other day. Were you out with him?"

"What if I was?"

"Katarina, it's not wise to go out with an American. Besides, you are not ready to be seeing anyone. It's too soon."

She slammed her hairbrush down and turned to

flash her eyes at her brother. "Anthony, I think you'd better mind your own business. What I do or don't do with Captain Lee has nothing to do with you."

"You hardly know him, Katarina, yet somehow I sense there is more to this than you are telling me."

"I had a pleasant evening out with a man—and a good meal, with no strings attached. If it should lead to something in the future, would that be so terrible?"

"That depends what it leads to."

"What if it were to lead to my getting out of Berlin?" She never could keep a secret from Anthony.

Anthony sighed. "You can't possibly be thinking of using this man just to get out of Berlin. What if he comes to care for you?"

"Yes, what if he does? So much the better."

"If you don't care for him, is that fair?"

"Maybe I will care for him," Katarina countered.

"Somehow I don't think that will matter to you."

"Actually I like him a lot. He's very good-looking."

"And?"

"And nothing. He lives on a beautiful plantation in Hawaii, where there is plenty to eat and all the buildings are standing."

"So for this you would give yourself away like a whore? That is not how we raised you!"

Katarina stormed to her feet and glared at him. "You didn't raise me to give my body over to filthy guards so I could stay alive, but I did that. I kept you alive that way, too. I guess you think that was all in a day's work."

Before either of them realized what was happening, Anthony slapped Katarina across the face.

She looked at him aghast, her chest heaving for breath.

In the next instant, Anthony gathered her in his arms. "Katarina, forgive me. I'm so sorry. I can't believe I did that. I know what you've been through, and I understand why you feel you need to get out of Berlin."

"I think you should go, Anthony. Let's forget this conversation ever happened." After Anthony left the room, Katarina lay on her bed, making plans in the darkness, touching her cheek. He had never been angry with her. Tears fell till early morning, and she smothered her cries in the pillow.

Chapter 18

Berlin: January 1947

As the weeks flowed, Katarina saw Francis Lee nearly every day. Her family benefited from the courtship because Francis managed to provide generous portions of food for the household, including special treats for the three children. Even when he could not come personally, baskets appeared on the front porch. On some days, Katarina was not hungry at all, and she was glad to see her mother smiling more.

Katarina continued helping at the dance studio and running errands—or even short missions—for Anthony. She popped in on meetings at the factory and visited Alexandra. On the surface, her life was coming together. Underneath, she still wanted nothing more than to get out of Berlin. She would gladly exchange secret trips into East Berlin for the security of a lush Hawaiian plantation. Russians robbed Germans at gunpoint in the street and continued their intimidation strategies, and the Allies didn't seem to be able to manage the Russians. Ordinary German citizens didn't know whom to trust. Attendance at Anthony's meetings waned in a cloudy fear of recriminations.

Francis did not like Katarina attending Anthony's meetings. Whenever he protested that she was putting herself at risk for no good reason, she gazed at him with her wide violet eyes, and he softened. He asked her to please consider his feelings—he would be devastated if something happened to her—and she would kiss him without making any sort of promise at all. When his hands began to roam over her body, she didn't resist. It wasn't love on Katarina's end; she knew that. But she was becoming increasingly fond of him, so it was easy enough to lead him to the ultimate moment when he agreed to visit the summerhouse in Grunewald with her at the end of his duty shift.

Even in its state of disrepair, Katarina enjoyed showing off the summerhouse, with its large entryway and winding steps leading to the second floor. She moved through the house lighting candles and chatting enthusiastically. The family had managed to move most of the rubble out of the ground floor, though they had been able to replace very little of the furnishings. French doors opened from the foyer to a grand living room, with heavy drapes framing large bay windows looking out over a lovely courtyard of rose bushes and now inoperable fountains. Hans had recently painted the walls a light shade of butternut, which provided a hint of the former glory to which the family hoped to restore the home. With a glint in her eye, Katarina described the grand piano that used to stand in the middle of the room and the Queen Anne chairs in which friends and family would gather for impromptu concerts.

Most of the family's remodeling efforts so far had gone into the kitchen. A large butcher-block table stood in the middle, and freshly shined copper pots hung above it. Handmade cabinets had been painted a soft ivory and held the few surviving pieces of good china.

Old paint cans and mismatched remnants of furniture filled most of the other rooms—except one bedroom. Katarina had made this room her special project starting the day after her first dinner with Francis. Kerosene lamps sat on the fireplace mantel, and she had dragged in a worn but soft Oriental rug and arranged it in front of the stone hearth. She had found a set of lace curtains in the attic—probably they had belonged to her grandmother—and had washed them and hung them on the window. In another time, the window had overlooked a beautiful garden and drawn one's gaze to the riding stables in the distance. Though cracked, the walls were still a beautiful rose color.

Francis was impressed. With a smile on his face, he lit the fire that Katarina had laid ahead of time. They both knew what they were there for.

Katarina had not expected her body to come alive under his touch. No man had ever touched her in a way that showed any concern for what she was feeling. When he carried her to the bed and methodically undressed her, she was grateful for the darkness. She was not ready for him to see her scars, though she felt his fingers lightly tracing them down her back. Her eyes fluttered closed as he entered her, and his lips enveloped her full mouth, while his hands gripped her buttocks. In only a few minutes she shuddered in orgasm—something she had never felt before and never expected to feel. But behind her closed eyes rose the smell of the camp to replace the sweet scent of her lover's skin. She saw not his face, but the others, the demons of her nightmares. With a gasp, he came as well; then they lay still, listening to the pounding of each other's hearts.

He kissed her throat, his lips then wandering down to her breast. "I have wanted you since the first day I saw you," he whispered.

She let out a long sigh and pushed his damp hair out of his eyes. "I have no regrets, Francis. This is something we both wanted."

"Let's stay all night." His mouth sought hers again, and she responded. "My parents will worry," she said, "and my brothers will come looking."

Francis leaned on one elbow and sighed. "Why do your brothers have such control over you?"

She shrugged. "It's been that way since I was born. You take me, you take my family, especially Anthony." With one finger she traced the line down the center of his chest.

"Then I guess I take your brothers," he said, leaning in to kiss her deeply again. Pulling back again, he sighed in contentment. "And what about your little girl? She's the most delightful part of the package."

Katarina held her tongue. She had made up her mind long ago that Alexandra would have no part of her life with Francis. But this was not the time to speak that thought aloud.

They made love again. It was late into the night when she dressed for him to take her home and blew out the last candle. Instinctively she knew she had accomplished what she had really come there to do.

Within a few weeks, Katarina recognized the familiar nausea when she awoke each morning. She kept her secret for a few more weeks, as the nausea became more pervasive and lasted all day long. She was having dinner with Francis one evening when her hands shook and her face blanched against the black sweater she wore.

"Katarina, what in God's name is wrong?" Francis asked. "Let's get you outside for some air."

She willingly went with him outside and leaned against the restaurant's cool brick wall. A chill ran up her spine—that feeling that someone was watching her. She peered into the shadows across the street and was about to say something to Francis when another wave heaved through her system. She turned away from Francis to vomit.

"Katarina! I'd better take you home."

Francis helped her back to the jeep, then returned to the restaurant to settle the bill.

When he came back to the jeep, she knew the moment had come.

"Francis, I know this is not ideal, but I am pregnant. A doctor has confirmed it."

He looked at her perplexed. "But how?" he asked as he pulled away from the curb.

She laughed. "I think we both know how."

"That's not what I meant. We've only had that one night. When we talked about it, you said it wasn't the time of the month for you to conceive."

"Apparently I miscalculated," she said. "Look, I'll take care of the baby. I just thought you should know. Just drop me off at Anthony's. He'll know what to do."

Francis stopped the jeep abruptly and turned sharply to face her. "Jesus, what can I say? You'll have to tell your parents there will be a wedding."

"A wedding?" Of course she had known all along he would do the right thing.

"Yes, a wedding. I love our child already, and my father will be overjoyed to have an heir." He pulled her into his arms and kissed her. They would marry in the church, but they would have to travel to Frankfurt for the Army to give permission.

"An heir?" she asked when he released her.

"My father has been trying to marry me off to the daughter of a family friend for years. Maria. He wants grandchildren. But she is nothing like you. He will love you the minute he sees you, just as I did."

So he did love her. He had never actually said so before.

"Katarina, it will take some doing to get the paperwork through, and you will be questioned by the American military, but I promise I will push this forward as quickly as I can so we can be married." He grinned. "And I'll come with you to tell your parents."

She stopped him cold. "No, I have to tell Anthony first. He has to be the one to break it to my parents. They'll listen to him."

"If that's what you want. I'll take you to Anthony's now, if you feel well enough. But tomorrow I will be at your parents'."

****

Katarina climbed the steps slowly, dreading the moments ahead as she entered Anthony's office. He was bent over an open Bible, reading by candlelight. Looking up, he removed his glasses and motioned that she should sit down.

She sat across from him, her head lowered and her legs not completely steady. "I might as well just come out with it," she said. "I'm pregnant, and I'm going to marry Francis."

Anthony's eyes blazed. "Katarina, how could you do this? You don't love Francis Lee."

"How do you know what I feel?" she responded defiantly.

"If you loved this man, I would see it in your eyes."

"I'm quite fond of him," she said.

"That's not the same."

"It's enough. Anthony, I do believe I love him. It's different from when I was eighteen years old. He is good to me, and his tender love doesn't hurt my heart. When he holds me, he makes me believe there is hope."

Anthony sighed and leaned back in his chair. "You wanted out, and you got what you wanted."

Katarina was having trouble controlling her exasperation. "Anthony, look at Germany. Hundreds of thousands of refugees are still coming in from the East. Times will be hard here for a long time. It's not as if I were being promiscuous with occupation soldiers. I developed a relationship with one man, a very good man."

"Someday this nightmare will end," he said.

She shook her head. "I can't wait that long. I can't miss this chance to have a tomorrow of my own."

"You are going into a marriage without love. May God help you."

"Stop, Anthony! There are far worse things than this. Look at you. You love someone you cannot even see. You depend on God, and what has he done for you? For our family? If that is love, I would rather live without it."

"You can't make God responsible for Hitler!"

"Can't I? Francis will take care of me. I'll have a good life. In the meantime, you just keep on loving your God."

"How can you talk like that?" Anthony was on his feet now, furious.

"Because I've called on your God, and he did not answer. What love did he give me? Not once has he helped to ease my pain. I will take a full stomach over your God's love, thank you very much." Katarina stood up to leave.

"Katarina, you're not really disturbed that I love God. You're disturbed because you don't know how to love anyone. Turn back to God, and he'll show you the light in your darkness."

"Stop trying to be my priest, Anthony. I need you to be my brother. Come with me to tell Mother and Father."

He moved out from behind his desk to embrace her. "Does Francis Lee want this child?"

"He says he loves it already."

"And he loves you?"

She nodded. "I believe he does."

He blew out his breath forcefully in surrender. "I guess we should be glad that a good man like Francis Lee can offer you a small piece of happiness."

Chapter 19

Berlin: March 1947

On March 15, 1947, Katarina Von Rahmel arrived at the church early, hoping to see Anthony before the ceremony. She found him, as usual, in his office behind his desk. Katarina rolled her eyes in amusement as she leaned across the desk. She thought perhaps he was working on a homily for her wedding, but instead he was rehearsing a speech for an upcoming rally.

She cocked her head to one side and waited for his attention. He looked tired, the lines in his face deeper than a few weeks ago. Katarina wondered when the last time was that he'd had a good night of sleep. He was a priest, after all. Between rallies and writing speeches, he had been rebuilding his church, saying regular Masses, and working with the nuns at a nearby orphanage. He never gave up hope that Germany would rise to greatness once again, and her people would enjoy prosperity.

Katarina was getting married in a few hours. Why was the officiating priest paying no attention to her?

"Anthony, my dear brother, you look much too occupied for this lovely day. Stand up and give me a hug."

Anthony looked up at last. "You look happy today." He complied with her request for an embrace.

"Why shouldn't I be happy?"

"Shouldn't you be getting gussied up for your big day? I heard you have a lovely dress."

She laughed. "It's a good thing I'm getting married today, because the gown is getting a little tight."

"I'm sure you'll be beautiful. You always are."

"Are you aware we have real butter and cheese today? Not that stuff we get from that silly goat. And real coffee! Francis has worked miracles in procuring food for the reception." She reached across the desk to grasp his hand. "I just wanted you to wish me well before the ceremony. It means a lot to me."

"I give you my blessing, little sister," he said. "I have seen for myself how Francis cares for you and how much he wants this child."

Katarina leaned back in her chair again. "The other reason I came here today is to thank you for making Frederick disappear from all of my paperwork. I know what you've done for me, and I'm sure if your bishop knew he would not be happy. Francis wants to be married in the church, so getting my first marriage annulled is a great gift to us. And I'm relieved Alexandra need never know who her father was. She only needs to know that her father died before she was born."

"There's no connection between Frederick and Alexandra. And when we looked for proof of her birth, we found she had been registered at the prison outside Dachau, not the camp. Most of the children born in the camp were never registered."

"Because no one expected them to survive," Katarina said.

Anthony nodded. "But we found a record of

Alexandra's birth in the prison, and there is no longer any mention of her father in the official paperwork."

"Thank you. It will be better for Alexandra that way. Someday Helena can explain everything."

"Helena?" Anthony's eyes blazed into Katarina's. "Why would Alexandra's mother not explain this to her?"

"Don't start that today," Katarina pleaded. "It's my wedding day. Just be happy for me."

Anthony blew out his breath and relaxed. "Of course. Today is a day of celebration."

Katarina nodded. "I'd better go. Mother has great plans for my hair today."

A few hours later, Captain Francis Philip Lee married Katarina Von Rahmel, making her happier than she had been in a very long time. She could almost smell the Hawaiian breeze.

****

The perfect place for Katarina and Francis to live was the summerhouse. In the weeks before the wedding, the family had intensified their fix-up efforts so that the living room and formal dining room downstairs were inhabitable, along with the kitchen.

Upstairs, Katarina and Francis would occupy the room where they had conceived their child, and Katarina was already hard at work preparing a nursery next door.

Francis let Katarina sleep late the first morning he had to return to duty. He had only managed a weekend leave, and they had hardly left the bedroom in thirty-six hours. On Monday, he had a long day ahead of him. The Russians were causing more concern every day. Noticing the house seemed cold as he dressed, Francis spread an extra wool blanket over Katarina. She woke with a jolt.

"I'm sorry, darling," he said, "I didn't mean to wake you. Go back to sleep. It's only six in the morning."

She cleared the sleep from her eyes and said, "No, I'll get up and make you something to eat. Let me see what's in the kitchen."

"Don't bother. I'll get something later. Just stay home and relax and take care of our baby. I'm sure you can find something to do around the house that is not too taxing."

Katarina sat up and put out her hand. "How do you do, Mr. Lee? My name is Katarina Lee."

He shook her hand, baffled. She sat up so abruptly that the bedding slipped away and exposed her naked white skin. Francis's eyes went straight to her breasts.

"Let's start this marriage out right, Francis. Please don't tell me what to do."

Francis pulled his eyes away from her beauty. "I should have chosen my words more carefully."

She got out of the bed, leaving the sheets behind, and opened her arms to him. He held her closely. Katarina felt his arousal as she pressed her breasts against his chest and held his head in her hands, kissing him deeply.

"Enjoy your day," she said, breaking the kiss. "I'll see you tonight."

After Francis left, Katarina slowly gathered her thoughts while she dressed. In the kitchen she enjoyed hot tea, bread and jam, luscious leftovers from the wedding reception. As she carried her dishes to the sink, she spotted a piece of paper on the floor. Francis must have dropped it, and she bent to pick it up. It didn't say much, nor did she understand it. There was something about stacking and holding patterns for a theoretical airlift. The goal was 45,000 tons of food and essential items.

Katarina quickly put the pieces together. Everyone knew the Soviets were lobbying for control of Berlin by rationing electricity and threatening blockades of major transit routes in and out of the city. It looked like the Americans were finally preparing a response.

Anthony Von Rahmel was doing his part to oppose the Soviets. Katarina knew he was helping to organize an enormous march on the Brandenburg Gate. He'd been rallying people all over town for weeks. His purpose was to show the people's desire for democratic elections and for the Russians to leave Berlin. Francis knew about the rally and discouraged it. It would only stir up trouble, he said. Anthony needed to be patient; he wasn't realistic about how long things would take.

Katarina rationalized that the information might be of interest to Anthony and made it her excuse to leave the house. She packed the rest of the bread for Anthony, who looked too thin, in her opinion. Her brother gave anything but minimal rations to the nuns for the orphanage, and what little bit of food he retained he shared with a stray collie he had adopted for companionship. She and Francis had no personal vehicle, but her father had repaired a bicycle for her to use to cover the distance between the summerhouse and town.

When she arrived at the church, Katarina carried her bicycle inside with her. She took no chance that someone would steal her only mode of transportation.

Anthony's head was on his desk, buried in his arms. He looked up when Katarina called his name.

"Oh, my God, Anthony! Oh, sweet mother of God!" Katarina ran to her brother. "What happened to you?" His lower lip was badly swollen, and his left eye bruised shut. A noise across the room made Katarina jump. She gasped at the sight of Grigory and Dietrich slumped against a wall, also beaten.

"Katarina, what are you doing here?" Anthony asked, his speech thick. "Aren't you still on your honeymoon?"

Curiosity overwhelmed Katarina along with the fear that gripped her as she looked at the severely beaten men. "My husband had to return to duty today. Just what did the three of you do after the wedding?"

Dietrich dragged himself to his feet but deferred to Anthony for an explanation.

"We went to the East for information we were told was waiting for us. The Russians are promising every Berliner free food and milk for their babies. Our people are confused. We wanted to pick up a package that would prove it's all lies."

"So what happened?"

"The good news is we did get the paperwork. The bad news is we got caught leaving the building."

Grigory opened his one good eye. "Your brother actually tried to reason with these goons. It would have been easier just to stab them, or shoot them, but oh, no, Anthony wanted to avoid violence. Only after they went for their guns did Anthony decide it was okay to fight back against these ex-Nazis. There'll be hell to pay when their bodies are found."

Anthony groaned. "Grigory, do you have to use

that tone? The killing days have to stop."

"It's easy to kill when you know these are the people who killed my brother, and two of yours, and tortured your sister, as well."

Katarina didn't know who to help first. Finally she moved behind the desk to get a look at Anthony's cut. "Anthony, stop worrying about heaven and hell and what punishment will be inflicted on us. Learn to survive against the Nazis and the Communist demons in the East."

"Listen to your sister," Grigory said. "They want revenge. They must die or they will never give us peace."

Katarina picked up a cloth from the desk and pressed it against Anthony's head, where blood still seeped. "I would suggest that you begin thinking about where and how you got these bruises," she said. "You will not be able to avoid Mother and Father long enough for them to heal."

Grigory stood, still leaning against the wall. "Don't worry, Katarina. Dietrich and Anthony had a beam fall on them while they were working in the church hall. Who would doubt it? I'm leaving for a few days; no one will see my injuries." He looked at all his co-conspirators. "I expect all of you to stay out of trouble while I'm gone. Whatever you do, stay out of East Berlin."

A wave of dizziness reminded Katarina that it was time to eat again. The baby must be hungry.

The baby.

As soon as she had announced her intention to marry Francis, Helena had been after her about taking Alexandra to live at the summerhouse and eventually to travel to Hawaii. She insisted the toddler needed her mother. Now that Katarina was married, Alexandra could have a real family. That was the true motivation for Anthony to do what he had for Alexandra's birth certificate. So far, Katarina had not said a word to anyone about her intention to leave Alexandra behind when she left for Hawaii. But the point was not negotiable.

Katarina scrounged in Anthony's kitchen for food for all of them. The choices were limited, as always. After feeding the men and tending their wounds as much as she could, she rode back out to the summerhouse late in the afternoon and saw that Francis still was not home. Realizing that she had forgotten all about the paper with the airlift information, she slapped the side of her head for not telling Anthony what it said.

Inside, she lit the kerosene lamp and laid kindling for a fire in the bedroom fireplace. Joseph, the sometimes groundskeeper, had found wood, she saw gratefully. As she gathered an armload outside the back door, she saw Joseph at the stables with the stray dogs that had started to call the summerhouse home. Through squinted eyes, she saw someone with Joseph, and the sight made her drop her wood and bound over to the stables.

"Father! I'm glad you came!" She kissed her father's cheek.

"I was not going to intrude on your third day of marriage."

She slung her arm through his. "Come inside and keep me company. I was just about to start a fire and warm the place up."

Jona shook his head. "I must leave before it gets

too dark. I just wanted to bring some food for Joseph and the animals."

A pang of guilt stabbed Katarina. "I'm sorry. I should have thought of that this morning. I could have asked Francis to bring something back." Katarina smiled brightly at her father. "You are as bad as Anthony. He shares his last morsels with that dog. How many animals are you feeding these days? And that goat! You must get it out of your kitchen."

Now Jona shook his head. "Not as long as she keeps giving us milk. Besides, with all the cracks in the walls, the breeze blows the smell right out."

Katarina raised her arms in mock exasperation. "What am I going to do about you?"

"There's nothing to do. Go inside and take care of that little one you're carrying." With a last smile, he turned and began his trek back to town.

Francis was pacing the kitchen when she entered the house.

"Francis, what's wrong?"

He stopped and approached her, framing her face in his hands. "I just missed you. I wanted you to be here the minute I got home."

"I was just outside. I'm here now."

He took her hand and led her into the formal dining room. On the small table—all they could scrounge up for the room—were several lit candles, with a roasted chicken and dumplings and a bottle of white wine.

"Francis!" she gasped. "Where in the world did you get this?"

"It was meant for the general," he said, smiling, "but he was called to Frankfurt unexpectedly, so I brought it home. But I felt guilty when I saw your father and Joseph. I'll take them some extra bread tomorrow. And I'll find bones for the dogs."

"Let's light a fire in here," Katarina suggested. "I'll get wood."

"Let me do that," Francis said.

"Don't be silly. I can still carry a couple of logs."

She stepped outside the back door once again and picked up the wood she had dropped earlier at the sight of her father. A chill ran down her back, and she glanced around, convinced someone was watching from the edge of the forest.

Katarina screamed.

Francis was there in an instant. "What is it? Is it the baby?"

She shook her head. "No, the baby is fine. I saw someone."

"What do you mean?"

"Someone was watching me, I'm sure of it. There, at the edge of the forest."

"I don't see anyone."

"He's gone now."

Francis stood behind her and massaged her shoulders. "It's shadows, Katarina. No one is following you."

****

Katarina was glad when spring gave way to summer and the icy winter seemed to be behind them at last. Not much was left of the forest on their land. Wood had been free for the taking to anyone with an axe during one of the coldest winters in German history. Where would the warmth come from the next winter, Katarina wondered. Of course, she hoped by then she would be basking in the year-round warmth of

Hawaii. Francis anticipated leaving Berlin soon, hopefully before fall and the advent of cooler weather once again. Katarina was as eager to go as Francis was. She yearned to live in a place where things were in order and people weren't hungry. She would miss her family, of course, but she was sure Francis would agree to send money and care packages to make their life easier. The time would come when travel between the two countries would be easier.

Then, to the surprise of both of them, Francis was promoted to colonel, which meant the army wanted him to remain in Berlin longer. A few American wives had arrived to join their husbands, bringing their children with them. The U.S. seemed committed to stopping Communism and showed no sign of vacating Berlin.

Though the division of Germany into East and West and the presence of military forces from four different countries was difficult, the Von Rahmels were grateful Germany had not ended up like Czechoslovakia—twice victims of takeovers, first the Germans, then the Russians. Even France and Italy showed Communist leanings.

She knew the American presence was good for her country, but still, Katarina wanted to leave. With Francis's promotion, however, their departure looked indefinitely postponed. To Katarina's dismay, their baby was sure to be born on German soil.

Katarina sat in the garden one day, admiring the blooms that had fought their way through winter and spring to burst forth in summer colors. The dogs startled her when they began to bark. She looked up and spied Elvia approaching the house. Katarina rose to meet her.

"What brings you here?" she asked. "Francis brought home some wonderful lemons. Even with this horrible water they taste quite good."

They sat in rocking chairs on the patio, sipping their drinks.

"I just came from Anthony's," Elvia said. "He thought it would be nice if I told you myself."

"Told me what?"

"Dietrich and I are going to be married."

Tears sprang to Katarina's eyes as she took Elvia's hand. "I'm so happy for you."

"Katarina, I loved your brother dearly," Elvia said. "When he came to pick me up for our first date, he saw a German patrol driving through the streets. Heinz could hear the tapping in my father's bedroom, and he warned my father to stop the radio signals and hide. The German patrol was looking for the hand-operated radio my father used. Heinz saved my father's life that day. But two days later, my father was shot in an alley when he was caught sending another message.

"Heinz did everything he could to help our village, even if it brought danger to himself. Eventually they came for him. I loved him more than my own life, and I would gladly have taken his place. There will never be another Heinz. But now I love Dietrich and he loves me. He knows I want my daughter to know her own culture. When the time comes, we'll go back to France together."

Katarina's throat knotted up at the memories of Heinz. "Elvia, Dietrich is a good man. He deserves happiness, and I know you make him happy. Marry him, and be happy!"

She would miss Dietrich and Elvia. But she was

leaving Germany as soon as the Americans would let her husband go home.

Chapter 20

Berlin: August 1947

Apprehension mounted as summer yielded to the fall of 1947 and winter loomed.

The previous winter had taxed the German land and people heavily; how would they survive yet another harsh season when general circumstances in the country had not improved significantly for many people? Paired with the threat of winter was the threat of a full-fledged Soviet invasion. The division of Berlin, and the country, was not sitting well with the Soviets. Clearly they felt they had earned the right to govern Germany by their military victory from the East, without which Berlin would not have fallen. Soviet muscle tactics came more to the forefront all the time. The German people were weary of coping. They just wanted to be fed and warm, to be able to provide for their families once again.

Anthony was weary as well. He sat at his desk and poured himself another brandy. Darkness was descending, and in a few hours he and Grigory would make their way to East Berlin once again, seeking information about the Soviet plans to invade the West despite the presence of the Allies. If the Soviets launched a war, would Allied forces just hand Germany over to them in order to be rid of the whole mess?

It was becoming more difficult to cross to the East. Document requirements changed frequently, and action squads acted belligerently and randomly. Anthony had so hoped he would never see this type of violence again in his country after Hitler was routed out, but violence was alive and deadly in Berlin. The difference was that this time the people were not being led like sheep to their deaths. The majority were fighting back.

Anthony chided himself for telling Grigory he would go on this expedition. Wasn't it enough that he held meetings and passed out materials? He even dared to speak his mind from his pulpit. And despite his own instincts, his sister was deeply involved once again. Her pregnancy had provided interesting cover more than once.

Francis's attempts to keep Katarina safe at home awaiting the baby had failed miserably. On the one hand, Anthony valued what Katarina did. She intended to leave Germany, but as long as she was here, she wanted to help.

At the same time, he understood Francis's perspective. Katarina was expecting a child—why put herself in danger? She was married to an American officer—why not enjoy the protection that afforded and let the Americans do their job?

But in the end it mattered little what Anthony thought. Katarina did what she wanted to do, just as she always had. She made sure she was home every evening before Francis came home from work, but what she did with her daytime hours or when Francis was working nights was her own business.

On the night of this mission into East Berlin, Katarina lied to Francis. Knowing that he had duty that evening, she said she planned to spend the evening with Helena and Alexandra, and Anthony would bring her home the next day. She knew Francis would not object to her spending time with her own daughter.

In truth, Dietrich was waiting outside the café when Katarina arrived with Grigory. Dietrich pulled Grigory aside. "Grigory, this is a hell of a position you're putting Katarina in. Is this really necessary? Can't we just tell the Americans and the British what we've learned about the Soviets?"

Katarina saw Grigory raise his eyes to her. He made no effort to keep his words from reaching her ears. "Not this time. We have to prove they are planning to invade Berlin and willing to kill Americans, English, and French to get what they want. The Allies are being naïve in thinking that their negotiations are working."

"The Americans and British are organizing an airlift," Dietrich countered. "Relief is coming."

"It could be too late," Grigory responded. "You know the action squads are getting out of hand. We have to come up with irrefutable facts. This is our best shot at getting them."

"I'm not afraid, Dietrich," Katarina said, stepping forward.

"I don't like the way we're using you," he said.

"You're not using me," Katarina retorted. "I'm choosing this. Believe me, I know the difference."

"If we find what we need tonight," Grigory said, "we can distribute the information all over Berlin. We'll get the support we need for the September 9th rally."

Hans and Anthony came around the corner.

Katarina giggled. "You look ridiculous all dressed in black. Why not dress like ordinary people? It would attract less attention."

The brothers looked at each other and shrugged. It was too late now. They all climbed into the waiting jeep and quickly reviewed the plans for a mission that could put all their lives at risk.

****

When they arrived at the Brandenburg Gate, Grigory kept the car out of sight. Katarina got out and walked toward the gate, her hands wrapped around her swollen belly. She reached the young guards and widened her eyes.

"I know it's late," she said, "but I've been trying for a month to reach Colonel Poltive. You see, he promised to marry me. Look at my condition. He thinks because he is an officer he has the right to ignore his responsibility."

Katarina's bottom lip quivered as she pretended to wipe tears from her eyes. Clearly the guards had recognized the name of the hated officer, and even with their limited German they understood her predicament. They hardly looked at her paperwork and quickly waved her through. She gave each guard a slobbery kiss on the cheek, as she pointed to her belly saying, "Half Russian baby."

As the guards were distracted by this woman in distress, four Germans silently pushed a jeep through the checkpoint behind them. Once on the other side, they hung a Russian banner on the vehicle. Never looking at the men, Katarina walked slowly through the gate and continued on the road until she spotted the jeep in a side alley, exactly where they had told her it would be.

"Quick, get in the jeep." The urgent whisper was Hans. "We're going to the building right next to the opera house. We'll show you where to stand so you can let us know if anyone is coming."

Katarina knew what to do. If anyone came near, she would fake labor pains and scream the name of the Russian officer.

Moments later, Katarina stood alone outside the building.

Anthony and Grigory crept up the back stairs ahead of Hans and Dietrich to the third floor and headed down a dark, empty corridor. Everyone but Anthony carried a grenade, knives, and a gun. When they heard footsteps, they slipped through an unlocked door and waited breathlessly for a soldier to pass.

Suddenly a side door opened and rays of light spilled across the floor. In an instant, Grigory crossed the room and was ready. The Soviet soldier never knew what happened. After one well-aimed stab to the neck, Grigory eased the man's lifeless body to the floor.

Seeing what Grigory was capable of with such ease reminded Anthony that this man had no remorse when he snapped a soldier's neck or their enemies were found in the Spree River; he said so himself. What was he doing on those trips he was always taking to Israel and to England?

Instinctively Anthony crossed himself as he moved to give the blessing for the dead. Grigory stepped in his path. "Leave him," he whispered. "He is not worthy of prayers. He would have killed you just as easily without a care." Anthony looked from the dead soldier to his friend, then stepped past the soldier toward a filing cabinet. Hans and Dietrich split off to rummage through another room.

Only moments later, Anthony grinned and held up a file. He had found what they were looking for. Hovering by the window, he and Grigory used the moonlight to scan the papers. It had all gone so smoothly.

Just then their heads snapped up. Katarina was wailing. They looked down at the street and saw her pointing to her stomach in serious discussion with two Soviet officers. She grabbed a soldier's sleeve and begged for help in finding the elusive Colonel Poltive. The Soviets looked uncomfortable, and she hung on their arms and clutched her abdomen.

"Find the others," Grigory ordered, stuffing the file under his jacket.

A bang told them where Hans and Dietrich were. Anthony slithered across the hall and warily opened a door, with Grigory right behind him. Looking in, they saw two dead Soviet officers, with Dietrich standing over them, knife in hand. Hans was slumped in a chair pressing his hand to his side. Blood stubbornly seeped between his fingers.

With no time to lose, Grigory pulled Anthony and Dietrich close. "We have to go out on that ledge, into that tree, and down to the ground below."

Anthony was flabbergasted. "That's a long drop, Grigory. Hans is wounded. How will he manage to climb down a tree?"

"I can make it, Anthony," Hans interrupted. "It looks worse than it is."

"The building was supposed to be empty," Anthony said, "and now we have killed three men."

"We'll have to have this ethics debate later," Grigory said. "This tree has survived being cut for firewood for a reason. We have to move now!"

One by one they climbed out on the ledge, then into the oak tree that virtually leaned into the building. They took turns helping Hans get a foothold.

In her peripheral vision, Katarina saw the movement from the ledge to the tree. Her eyes never left those of the officer she had attached herself to.

"Walk with me, please," she pleaded. "I am supposed to meet him at the entrance to the building. But the pains have started. I don't want to be alone." She gripped one arm of each officer.

She gave them no choice but to move with her.

Grigory landed on the ground with a thud and reached up to help Hans. Dietrich and Anthony quickly followed. By now Hans was bleeding profusely. They still had to find Katarina and get back to the jeep. Anthony looked at Grigory, who gestured they should move toward the alley.

A jeep roared toward them. A voice ordered, "Get in. Now!"

Anthony caught the eye of the man who wore a Russian uniform and gave the smallest of laughs.

"Get in, you bloody fools," his cousin Peter demanded.

Seconds later, Peter screeched to a halt in front of Katarina and pulled her into the jeep while the soldiers attending her looked on in shock. One of them recovered enough to reach for his side weapon, but he wasn't fast enough. Grigory threw a knife, hitting his target perfectly in the heart. The jeep lurched forward.

Once they cleared the area safely, Anthony spoke.

"Peter, where the hell did you come from?"

Peter smiled. "You ask too many questions, Father Anthony." He turned and glared at Grigory. "This was dangerous. Grigory was not supposed to involve any of you."

"This is not the time, Peter," Grigory said simply as he applied pressure to Hans's wound.

They sped down Unter Den Linden toward the guardhouse at the Brandenburg Gate. The guards were temporarily confused by the banner flapping from the car, and before they could recover, Peter rammed the barrier. Shots rang out from behind them, and they ducked low in the seats.

They were safely in West Berlin.

Peter parked the jeep in a dark alley.

"What happened back there?" quizzed Anthony. "The building was supposed to be empty. The Soviets were all supposed to be at a rally of their own. And where did you come from, Peter?"

Grigory and Peter looked at each other. Anthony knew then. "You two were in this together from the start, and you didn't tell the rest of us."

"I've been assigned to work under cover for a while," Peter explained. "I speak fluent Russian and German, so it was easy. We have tunnels all over the city. We listen in on the Russian squads, and we have heard the Von Rahmel name come up often. It's clear they want all of you dead. Congratulations—you are no longer just a bug on the wall, but a problem they are serious about removing."

"But what does that have to do with tonight?" Anthony demanded.

"An informer gave you up to save his own hide. He

gave you the right building and the right information, but the plan was for you to get caught. If it had worked, the informer would have ingratiated himself with the Russians." Peter was shedding his Russian uniform as the spoke.

"And you were willing to break cover for us?" Anthony asked.

"I guess we won't use him as an informer again, will we?" Grigory said.

Everyone laughed, including Hans in his pain.

Grigory looked at Katarina, who was hushed and pale. "Katarina, are you okay?" She nodded, but could not speak.

Peter revved the motor again and drove as fast as he dared to the Von Rahmel home. Peter and Anthony carried Hans inside, while Dietrich and Grigory helped Katarina out of the cramped vehicle. Inside, Lisa and Gertrude were already crying and wringing their hands in anguish. She pushed past them, wondering why they were not responding to Anthony's demands for someone to bring water and get the doctor.

"Gertrude," Katarina said sharply. "Do something for your husband!"

Katarina sank to the floor beside Hans as Gertrude finally got enough of a grip on herself to bring a pan of water and some clean rags. Katarina took the water and didn't move. She was not about to yield her brother's care to his frozen wife. She began sopping up blood and trying to uncover the wound to clean it.

"Don't do this to me, Hans," Katarina whispered into her brother's ear. "Don't you dare leave me."

Hans smiled weakly. "Not to worry, Princess. I'm not going anywhere."

The doctor arrived a few minutes later. He asked no questions, for he had worked with the Von Rahmel family for years. Anthony helped Katarina get up from the floor and move out of the way. Gertrude stood in the doorway, her face contorted and glaring at Katarina.

"Stay away from my husband, Katarina," Gertrude growled as she clenched Katarina's arm. "You have a husband and a daughter of your own. Go take care of them."

Katarina pushed Gertrude's hand away. "Don't touch me! And don't ever try to bully me. You have no right."

"And neither do you," Gertrude hissed. "These are your cousins, not your brothers. Everybody knows the truth. Why don't you face up to it? They didn't even change your name on the birth certificate, because they didn't want you."

"Gertrude!" Anthony said sharply. Gripping her elbow, he steered her out of the room, out of earshot to Hans.

Katarina wobbled out of sight, but she heard the exchange that followed.

"Gertrude, get control of yourself," Anthony said. "You're being cruel."

"And Katarina is not?" Gertrude challenged. "You're all so pathetic when it comes to Katarina. You're so convinced she can do no wrong that you're blind to the things she does."

Anthony pivoted on one foot and walked away. He found Katarina standing in the kitchen, shivering in anger.

"Ignore her," Anthony said.

"Why is she talking about my birth certificate?"

Katarina asked, not moving her eyes off the floor.

Anthony sighed. "Please, Katarina, ignore her."

"No, Anthony." Her head snapped up to face him. "Why is she talking about my birth certificate? Why is that any of her business?"

"I suppose Hans told her at some point," Anthony muttered.

"Hans told her something even I don't know?" Rage welled up in Katarina, even against this brother she loved best of all.

"We were all furious when we found out Helena had told Uncle Richard you died at birth. We wanted to believe she would tell him the truth some day, and he would want you to bear his name."

"So my birth certificate?"

"You have two. It's as simple as that. It's not so unusual with adopted children."

Katarina sighed. "Some days I don't know who the hell I am."

Anthony moved close to her and took her cold hands in his. "You are Katarina Von Rahmel. You are my sister."

"Anthony, I had planned to stay the night, but I think I want to sleep in my own bed. Please take me home."

****

They drove in silence. Grigory was behind the wheel, and Anthony sat with Katarina in the back seat of the jeep. After seeing his sister into the house, he reluctantly left. She had made it clear she didn't want him to stay.

As they drove away from the summerhouse, Grigory said, "Well, priest, I guess you need to pray for all of us tonight."

"This is no time to mock me," Anthony replied as he adjusted his clerical collar against his sore neck.

"I'm amazed you still try to say prayers over the enemy."

"Grigory, we don't really know who the enemy are. We might face them in heaven some day."

"I rather expect hell has a special spot reserved for me," Grigory said. "Or maybe this earth is hell, or maybe there is no life after death. Then what will you do?"

"I know my God," Anthony answered. "He is always there. He hears my prayers even for you."

Grigory stopped the jeep abruptly. "We have to go back. I have this terrible feeling; the hair just stood up on the back of my neck." He turned the jeep around and sped back to the summerhouse.

They found Katarina on the floor, doubled over in pain.

"My water broke," she gasped, "and I'm bleeding. Get me to the American hospital."

Francis was turning into the driveway just as they turned out. Anthony gestured wildly that he should follow them. They reached the hospital in record time, with Francis right behind them.

Katarina was more pale than anyone had ever seen her, even in the days of recovering from her camp injuries. The hours crawled by. Anthony never stopped praying with his rosary. Francis glared at Grigory and Anthony, clearly suspicious that they had something to do with his wife's current crisis.

Dawn was approaching when finally the doctor entered the waiting room. "Well, gentlemen, someone's prayers worked a miracle. She lost a lot of blood, but she is stable now, and the baby is healthy in spite of the early delivery." He looked at the faces of the three men. "Where did she get such scars?"

"She was beaten by the Nazis," Anthony answered simply.

"In what country, Father?"

"She's German, Doctor," Anthony said. "She just didn't believe the way Hitler believed."

Francis stood up abruptly. "Doctor, I'm her husband. If you need to know anything, you may direct your questions to me."

"Yes, Colonel. I'm sorry, sir."

"I believe Father Anthony needs to go say the morning Mass." Francis looked at Anthony. "Does it not start at six?" Lee was leaning against the wall, looking smug, and from the glances he gave Grigory, Anthony knew their presence was causing an issue.

****

Francis walked softly into Katarina's room and sat next to her. He took her hand in his and held it to his cheek. "I looked in on the baby," he murmured. "He is a strong little fellow. I've decided to call him Douglas."

Her eyes fluttered open briefly. "Anthony! Where is my baby?" She fell immediately back to sleep.

Francis dropped his wife's hand. This was exactly why he needed to take her away from here. *You wake and who do you think of first? Your brother, then the baby. You don't even see me.*

Disgusted, Francis stepped out into the hall. Perhaps he would go see the baby again. Then he heard the blood-curdling scream come from Katarina's room. Her doctor was nearby and dropped his clipboard and rushed into the room. Francis was on his heels.

The doctor could find nothing wrong.

"Colonel Lee, she was most likely dreaming," the young doctor explained. "During delivery she told some horrific tales. We were not sure if she was having delusions or dreams or what. She kept begging us not to hurt the baby, not to burn her breasts, not to let the SS have the baby."

Francis sighed.

"Colonel, I have to ask. Did any of these things really happen?"

"Doctor, just tell me when I can take her home. It's no concern of yours what her life was like before."

"Of course, sir. She'll need to stay a few days. She seems particularly exhausted."

"Will she be able to have more children?"

"I believe so. She lost a great deal of blood, but time will take care of that."

"Then if you will excuse me, I'd like to go see my son."

"Yes, sir."

Francis returned the doctor's salute and strode down the hall toward the nursery.

Chapter 21

Grunewald: August 1947

Katarina didn't leave the hospital for almost two weeks. The dream came nearly every night she was there. She was always running with a baby. Anthony was always at the end of the forest waiting for her. She cried for Anthony to take the baby. Then came the rain, and it was Frederick's hands, not Anthony's, that reached out and took the baby from her.

Convinced Francis would never understand, Katarina never told him about the dream.

On the day Katarina returned to her summerhouse, Anthony visited to play with the new baby. He was pleased to see that she seemed to have genuine affection for little Douglas. It was so different from the way she still treated Alexandra, and to Anthony it seemed like a good sign. Perhaps there was still hope that her feelings about her daughter would soften.

The next morning, Francis opened the bedroom door after preparing breakfast and saw that Katarina was still sleeping soundly. He stood close, studying her face. He wanted to let her sleep, because she had nearly waked the dead a few hours ago with her screams. She had gone to the nursery to feed the baby, but suddenly she came tearing down the hall to wake him, demanding he look out the window to see who was standing there watching her. She swore, as she had for the past year, that someone was out there. So he wished he could let her sleep, but they already had visitors.

"Katarina," he said gently as he shook her. "Your mother is downstairs with Aunt Helena and Alexandra."

"Mmm." She acknowledged his presence without opening her eyes.

"They said to tell you to take your time coming downstairs. They're looking after the baby, and breakfast is waiting for you when you're ready."

Francis left without kissing her goodbye, and Katarina mused on this point behind her closed eyelids. In fact, he had barely touched her since Douglas was born. He said it was too soon after the baby. *Too soon for a kiss? For a hug?*

Her husband had not asked her any questions about the night she went into labor. But that night seemed to have changed things between them. He didn't want to know what she'd done, but he made it clear he knew she'd done something and was emphatic that now the baby was here she was not to participate in anything her brother and Grigory were doing.

Katarina had made no promises.

A few minutes after Francis's departure, Lisa and Alexandra entered the room.

Lisa cradled the new baby in her arms. "Katarina, he is mighty hungry again. I'm sorry to wake you."

Katarina propped herself up in the bed, and her mother settled the baby in her arms. Alexandra climbed up on the bed as well and watched in fascination as the baby suckled.

"Your father is down at the stable," Lisa said. "He's trying to repair a stall so we can bring that goat out here. Phew! I do believe I'm beginning to smell like her." She laughed. "The neighbors call us 'the goat people,' but that doesn't stop them from lining up for the cheese."

"Mother, it's time you depended on us for a little help," Katarina said. "You know as long as I am here Francis can provide you with extra food. Almost every day he manages to bring something home."

Helena cleared her throat as she entered with a tray of hot tea and bread with jam and fresh butter.

Alexandra's little hand reached out. "I have some too." Her little nose crinkled as she leaned over the baby. "I love the baby."

Lisa reached over and lifted Alexandra off the bed. "Let your mama eat her breakfast."

"Go and find Mama's brush," Katarina said. The child scampered down the hall to the bathroom.

"The baby seems to be finished eating," Katarina said. "Why don't you take him to the nursery and change him while I get dressed."

Lisa took the baby and left the room with Helena.

Katarina had just removed her nightgown when Alexandra ran back into the room with the brush. The child stopped, clutching the brush.

"Mama, you have a big boo-boo," Alexandra said, pointing to the scars on Katarina's back.

Katarina grabbed a robe and quickly put it on.

Alexandra pointed to her knee. "I had a boo-boo on my knee. Grandmother kissed it and made it better. I can kiss your boo-boo."

Katarina turned on her daughter, who was not quite three. "I have these boo-boos because of you. I couldn't run down the steps because of you."

A shadow filled the doorframe once again. Katarina looked up to see Helena standing there. Alexandra began to cry and ran to Helena.

Helena gathered the child in her arms and turned the girl's face away from her mother. "You will never be alone with her again. I will not let you blame an innocent child for the decisions you made. We warned you about Frederick Spitz, but you wanted him in your bed anyway. Don't you ever blame this child again."

Katarina returned Helena's icy stare. "Why don't you adopt her, if you feel so strongly about her?"

Helena held the child closer. "We'll talk about this later. Right now I'm going to tend to this precious child. I hope you can find it in yourself to be a mother to that baby down the hall."

Katarina couldn't wait for Helena and Alexandra to leave her house.

****

A few days later, Katarina arranged for her mother to stay with the baby so she could take some extra food to Anthony at the rectory. She was grateful that Peter could come for her in his jeep; she was in no shape to get back on a bicycle, her only independent method of transportation. Besides, it was such a treat to spend time with Peter. He had stayed out of Germany for so long. On the way to the rectory, Peter let it slip that Anthony had received a visit from a bishop from Rome, who had suggested that Anthony curtail his activities, particularly his plans for the September 9th rally. The bishop had politely warned the priest that if he did not cut back his extracurricular activities and focus on his parish, they would move him out of Germany and assign him duties elsewhere.

As they pulled up in front of the church with expectations of unloading a basket of food, they saw Anthony carrying one of his altar boys to an American jeep where MPs were waiting. Anthony had already run back inside the church by the time Katarina and Peter got out of their jeep.

"My God, what happened?" Katarina asked the MPs. The boy was barely breathing, his face beaten to a pulp.

"We're not sure," the MP replied. "We think an action squad from the East was here. The priest waved us down and asked for help. We have to get him to a hospital."

"Of course." Katarina stepped out of the way, and the jeep carrying the boy drove off.

Peter and Katarina ran up the church steps. Inside, many pews were smashed, and the walls Anthony had spent so much time restoring with his parishioners were once again cracked and blood-smeared. The communion host was strewn around the sanctuary.

Then they saw where the blood had come from. Katarina's fist flew to her mouth to stifle her sobs.

Anthony knelt in front of the altar in the jumbled hues created by sunlight streaming through a stained-glass window. The collie's head rested in his lap, the lifeless bodies of her six puppies tossed ruthlessly around them. The collie whimpered weakly against her own wounds.

Anthony's chest heaved convulsively as he cried out, "My God, why this? Why have you let them do this in your holy house? They brutally beat a child and took the lives of innocent creatures. Why, God, do you not believe my love for you?"

Peter quietly began moving the puppies out of Anthony's sight. Peter and Katarina helped Anthony out of the sanctuary and to his living quarters in the rectory before Peter went back for the collie. The unspoken understanding was that she would have to be put down.

Anthony sprawled on the couch. "Do you think the Lord despises me?" He lifted his gaze to Katarina, who could think of nothing to say. She had never seen Anthony break down before. To avoid looking at him, she went into the kitchen to brew tea.

Peter finally returned. Anthony didn't ask any questions about what he had done with the dog. Peter moved his chair close to Anthony. "Listen, Anthony, you told me a long time ago that God is all-loving and does not hold grudges for anyone who is sincere in asking for forgiveness. Do you recall that conversation in Rome? You can't take back those words now. You're like the custodian of all our integrity."

A feeble smile crossed Anthony's face. "I remember, Peter. I never knew you actually listened to me."

"I always listen to you. Don't you know that by now?"

Katarina poured tea for all of them and handed Anthony a cup.

Anthony sat up and directed his attention to Peter. "They will pay for what they did to my altar boy, my church, my animals. Grigory was right. They are evil, and I have been too naïve for too long. How stupid I've been to think that Satan is no longer walking around. Let him return to hell without me!"

After tea and something to eat, Peter drove

Katarina home. Anthony went to the hospital to check on the altar boy.

"I want Anthony's faith, Peter, but it just isn't in me. After what he went through today, his faith is even stronger. Everything he goes through does that for him. But everything I go through makes me believe less and less."

Peter drove on, silent, unsure what to say.

"I saw children shot and pushed into a pit. I saw children buried alive, burned alive. I saw my baby held upside down by a guard who is probably living the good life now. There is no room in my heart for faith."

"I have faith," Peter said, "but not like Anthony."

"He shouldn't be alone tonight," Katarina said.

Peter nodded. "I'll go back and spend the night with him."

Katarina kissed Peter farewell. Before she went into the house, for the first time in a long time she said a silent prayer for Anthony.

Chapter 22

Berlin: September 1947

On the morning of September 9, 1947, Colonel Francis Lee gave his wife explicit instructions to stay away from the rally for which she had been distributing pamphlets for months. The Allied Forces were not enthused about this demonstration, and he didn't need his own wife to make his job more difficult. She was not to even think about going into town.

Katarina, of course, made no promises. She had already arranged to take Douglas to her mother's. In contrast to her first baby, Katarina was thoroughly enjoying this one. She never tired of watching Douglas, marveling for hours at the wonder of his perfection. He had his mother's blonde hair and his father's olive skin. Anyone could see he would grow up handsome. And he didn't cry nearly as much as Alexandra had. Of course, he was warm and well fed, not cold and hungry like his sister. With Alexandra there had been no hugs and tickles, no baths or belly kisses. It had been all about survival.

To Katarina's annoyance, Francis continued to bring Alexandra to the summerhouse for overnight visits. Clearly he was preparing to take the girl with them when they left Berlin, but Katarina had been inwardly determined from the beginning that Alexandra would have no part of her life in Hawaii. The time would soon come to speak those words aloud to Francis.

None of that mattered at the moment. Katarina had to get Douglas to her mother's so she could meet Anthony at the church, and they would go together from there. Peter had lingered in Berlin after the attack on the altar boy and the killing of the dogs in the church. Katarina was glad, because Peter was always good for Anthony. The spark was starting to come back to her brother's eyes.

Katarina pushed open the door to Anthony's office. "Sorry I'm late," she said. "I thought Francis was never going to leave the house this morning. Of all mornings, he picked today to give Douglas a bath. Then the baby started fussing when I left him at Mother's, and I had to stop and feed him."

Anthony was busy arranging books on shelves that he and Peter had built recently. "I'll be finished in a moment, Katarina." He cocked his head. "I sure hope I won't have to use these shelves for firewood this winter."

She crossed the room and kissed his cheek.

"Well, my dear sister, today is the day we show everyone how we feel about Berlin. Just think, we'll end up in the history books!"

"Do you really think the demonstration will be successful?" Katarina asked. They'd been planning for so long; she hadn't stopped to imagine what the day itself would be like.

"It's been hard to persuade our people not to follow Stalin blindly, the way they did Hitler. They have to see that the Soviets are trying to turn Germans against

Germans, but if they're successful, only the Soviets win."

"Let's get it done!" Katarina said enthusiastically.

****

The size of the crowd at the Tiergarten was more than encouraging. Weeks of canvassing and distributing literature and holding meetings had yielded the desired result. Mayor Ernst Reuter spoke, promising the people of his city that the rugged existence of 1946 and 1947 was not the end of Berlin, not a permanent condition. The city would rise again to rebuild its industry and agriculture and the character of its people.

And then it was time to march. Anthony stood squarely with Hans. Right behind them, Katarina stood shoulder to shoulder with Dietrich. Peter was somewhere off to the side, prevented from marching because he was a British military officer. The crowd stretched through the historic Tiergarten and along the Charlottenburger Chausee and on to the Victory Column, which was in the British sector. Anthony estimated easily a half million Berliners had come out to stand up for their city and for their nation.

This mass of patriotism began walking to the Allied Control Council, where they presented documentation from East Germans proving Soviet terror and kidnapping of influential people out of the West. Soviet soldiers had strict instruction not to let anyone near their zone, but a half million people gave no heed to the raised rifles as they approached the Brandenburg Gate.

"For freedom we will fight!" rose the cheer of the throng.

Then the firing began.

Utter chaos ensued as the Soviets and People's Police fired directly into the crowd. A tangle of bodies fell to the pavement, some wounded, some seeking safety.

Katarina had her hands over her head, paralyzed with fear. As soon as the firing began, her whole being was transported back to 1944. Chills ran up and down her spine, and she could not move, could not speak, could not think. The pressure of the crowd had ripped her apart from Dietrich and her brothers. Suddenly she was amazed to see Grigory and found her voice.

"How did you find me?" she asked, tears springing to her eyes.

He wrapped an arm around her shoulder and began directing her toward a vehicle. "Katarina, you are never out of my sight for very long."

Before them, a student was tearing down the hammer and sickle from the Brandenburg Gate. They safely reached the edge of the crowd and Grigory's vehicle. Somehow Katarina was not surprised to see Peter there as well, with Dietrich and Hans and Anthony. Peter was shouting orders at soldiers; the British were determined to take control and disperse the German people for their own safety.

Katarina's stomach lurched at the sight of the blood in the street. A drizzle came from the sky, but it would take far more than that to wash away the evidence of what had happened on this day. Her eyes were drawn to someone standing behind a car, and just a glimpse gave her assurance this was the person who had been her shadow for more than a year. She turned to speak to her brothers.

Gunfire rang out from the stranger's direction.

Peter yelled for everyone to get down just before an explosion shattered the sidewalk. Someone was throwing grenades. A second explosion came much closer. A strong arm pulled Katarina behind Grigory's vehicle. Dietrich covered her body with his as Grigory and Peter pulled their weapons and began firing. She flinched as bullets dug up the dirt next to her face. Fear shot through Katarina's flattened body; her mind raced through all the moments she had thought she was going to die and had not. Would this be another one of those, or was this the end?

Darkness squeezed through her as she felt herself descending to that old familiar place of silence and escape, the place where the beatings meant nothing, where the men using her were nothing. In a few seconds she would be there once again.

At last the sirens of the British MPs blared and the gunfire ceased. The group slowly unpiled and stood once again to survey the scene.

"Who in the world is trying to kill us in particular?" Anthony asked. "Peter, you must know something!"

Peter shook his head. "Let's just get out of here."

"Wait," Katarina protested. "Listen to me. I saw him. I saw the man who has been following me all these months."

Peter and Anthony glanced at each other. "Are you sure?" Anthony asked.

"Yes! You must believe me. I saw his eyes. They seemed familiar, somehow, but I couldn't quite see his face. Anthony, I swear to God, he aimed his gun right at me when this all started."

****

Katarina didn't want to take the chance that Francis would see her with this group of men he disapproved of, so after they picked up Douglas, she asked to be dropped off a few blocks from the summerhouse. She would walk the rest of the way. She picked up her pace as the rain turned from drizzle into a full-fledged shower, hoping to beat Francis home. As she reached for a lantern, a match was struck. In its small light, she could see her husband in the rocking chair. He lit the lantern and blew out the match without saying a word.

Her teeth started to chatter, both from the cold and from fear.

"Francis, you scared me half to death." She forced herself to breathe slowly in defiance of the fury on his face.

"You walked in the rain with the baby? How could you?" He rose from the chair and took the baby from her. "I'm going to give him a warm bath. You do what you want with yourself, but don't you ever put my son in danger again. We'll talk later about your little adventure today."

****

Katarina knew she couldn't lie as she stepped out of her own warm bath. Angry as he was, Francis had still heated enough water for her to have the luxury of a bath as well. Bundled in a robe, she was drying her hair with a towel and trying to come up with an explanation when he came into the bedroom. Wordlessly, he walked over to the small table where he kept his whisky and poured himself a drink. Katarina hated that smell, and Francis knew it. It reminded her too much of the guards in the camp. After throwing back the drink, he came close enough to her that she felt his breath on her cheek.

She tried to stand up, but he pushed her back into the chair.

"You sit, and you listen!" he demanded.

Pushing her still-wet hair from her face, she glared at him in defiance. How dare he push her! She began twisting the long ends of her robe's belt into knots, her anger growing with each one she tied.

"Katarina, from this moment on you will no longer have anything to do with tacking up pamphlets or going to meetings. You will see your brothers and parents when I am with you, and you will let me know when your parents plan to come and visit here."

She let out a hysterical laugh and pushed past him, successfully this time. "Don't you ever try to tell me what to do! I swore when I came out of the camp that no man would ever again push me around or tell me what to do. That includes you!"

Against her will, Katarina began to tremble. She and Francis had argued occasionally, but never like this.

"Look, Francis, you knew when you married me that I was involved with my family in political activities. It was all there in the file. Did you expect that just because I married you that part of me would go away? Don't blame my family for your black moods."

Francis huffed in disgust. "Don't try to put this on me. You have issues you have never resolved, and you don't want to resolve them. I will not have you dragging my son into them."

"I don't know what you're talking about. I did nothing to put Douglas in danger."

"You ignore anything I say, Katarina. I asked you to stay home today, and not only did you go out, but you dragged Douglas out in this rain. He's a newborn!

He could catch pneumonia. I've asked you repeatedly to invite some of the other officers' wives over so you can start being part of my world. They would love to see the baby. But you want to stay in your own world. You are my wife. Some things ought to change now."

"I'm not a perfect wife, Francis. I know that."

"I'm only asking you to try a little harder," he said. For the first time that night, his tone was softening.

"I will," Katarina said, "I promise." She widened her eyes and looked at him expectantly. In a few seconds, she knew she had him where she wanted him. He took her hand, and she touched his face, letting her finger trace his cheekbones, his mouth. They had grown closer, she knew, and she enjoyed his tenderness. She told him she loved him, and he gathered her thick, long strands of hair in his hands and murmured how he could not think of life without her. As she stood to leave the room, he pulled her into his arms.

"Katarina," he murmured into her ear, "come downstairs. Douglas is tucked in, and I have a treat for you."

"A treat?"

"I brought hamburger meat home. I think it's time I show you how to make a good old American hamburger."

****

She ate every bite of the meat on her plate. It was so filling, and she didn't often get to fill up on meat. Picking up her wine glass and sipping it slowly, she watched as Francis tilted back in his chair with his eyes closed. He was such a good-looking man.

Why couldn't she muster the enthusiasm for him that he had for her? She didn't have long to ponder the question, because Francis leaned over and kissed her fervently, and a moment later lifted her in his arms and carried her upstairs to the bedroom.

Her robe dropped to the floor when he untied it, and the moonlight fell softly across her white shoulders. Francis undressed quickly while gazing at her nakedness. He moved to kiss her full breasts, and worked his mouth from there to her neck, to her waiting lips. Pressing his naked body against hers, he walked her backward to the edge of the bed and nudged her to lie down and spread her legs. He soon entered her, and she wrapped her legs high around his back, her nails digging into his thighs as he thrust himself deeper and deeper into her. All the while, he repeated her name over and over, saying he loved her, until he released his passion inside her.

It was always easy for Francis to fall asleep after lovemaking. Katarina, however, lay sleepless throughout the night, wrestling with guilt for not feeling warm and loving toward Francis, especially after such a passionate night. But no matter how hard she tried, turmoiled shadows from the past haunted her.

Finally the morning light brought release. Douglas stirred, and she went to feed him. Satisfied, he returned to slumber. Katarina looked out the window toward the stables. When her father brought three horses that he and Joseph had managed to keep hidden throughout the entire war, she couldn't contain her happiness. She had run to Sasha and laid her head on the horse's neck, while the horse gave a slight neigh and scratched her hoop on the ground. Almost as good as dancing, riding was Katarina's second love. She hadn't wanted to ride in a long time, but suddenly she had an irresistible urge.

Back in her own bedroom, she dressed quickly, left Francis a note, and slipped out.

Down at the stables, Joseph had just finished cleaning the stalls, and the smell of the hay, though not fresh, lifted her spirits.

"Joseph, I feel like a ride this morning," she said brightly.

He simply nodded and helped her saddle the horse. She started out slowly, then increased her speed. The wind stung her face and brought tears to her eyes. As she urged the horse to a full gallop, the tears fell freely, and she howled into the wind.

This was freedom! How she loved this feeling. Katarina slowed to a leisurely trot back to the stables, while the rising sun flashed shadows around her. The instant the stables came into sight, a chill ran down her neck, and she peered into the gray spaces for whoever was there. But she saw no one. Still, she quickened her pace, and at the stables handed the horse's reins back to Joseph without so much as a glance.

Francis was dressed and ready to leave when she arrived back at the house.

"I watched you ride," he said. "You were magnificent. I've always thought there was no one who could dance the way you do, and now I see that you ride as well as you dance. I can hardly wait to show you the hills and beaches of my home. You will have an entire stable full of horses we can ride."

He kissed her passionately, then left, without seeing her silently wipe the kiss on her sleeve.

Chapter 23

Berlin: January 1948

Another desolate winter set in. By January 1948, the German people once again were braced to wrap themselves in layers against the cold and pretend that hot tea was filling. Action squads from the East still roamed Berlin, provoking outbursts even from reasonable citizens.

Peter and Grigory would disappear for days, appearing unexpectedly at Anthony's door to recruit him on short notice for one of their many well-planned missions. Dietrich and Hans' activities were in full swing, as well.

Francis's consternation about Katarina's activities persisted to the point that he decided to drop in on Anthony. He found him in the sanctuary of his church, replacing hymnals and prayer books in the pew racks.

"What can I do for you, Francis?" Anthony asked. "Is Katarina okay?"

Francis gave a slow smile. "You would be the first to know if something is wrong. Nothing my wife does is not reported to you, after all."

Anthony turned his head to meet Francis's gaze over the three pews that separated them. "Do you want something, Francis?"

"Anthony, it's simple. I want you to stop involving

my wife in your activities. She's done enough for your cause."

Anthony picked up a prayer book from the pew and placed it carefully in the rack. "I would have thought you would have learned a long time ago that Katarina does what Katarina wants to do."

Francis nodded. "True enough. But surely you recognize the influence you have on her. She worships you."

"We are siblings, of course," came Anthony's even reply.

"You know as well as I do that Katarina wants to leave Germany," Francis said. "She does whatever you ask her to do because she wants to please you."

"No one tells Katarina what to do."

"How can you be so blind, Anthony? You're contributing to your sister's problems. All this cloak-and-dagger business has her convinced someone is following her wherever she goes. You just feed her insecurities."

Anthony stopped arranging hymnals and looked at Francis squarely. "I think you should believe her when she says that," he said simply.

"We all saw what the Nazis did in the camps," Francis said. "I want to help her heal, but that's not possible as long as you insist on interfering in her life. You're doing her more harm than good. Let go of her, Anthony."

A voice boomed from the back of the sanctuary. "What makes you think you're the one to help Katarina?" Grigory demanded. "You have no idea what went on in those camps. So what if you've seen a few photographs? Katarina lived through it! She went to hell and back, and you have the nerve to stand there and try to tell us what she needs."

Francis thrust his finger through the air at the man who always seemed to appear from nowhere. "You will stay away from my wife!"

Grigory thundered down the center aisle toward Francis. "Don't ever point anything at me! I could twist your finger off right now, or kill you with my bare hands. Out of respect for Katarina, I won't."

"Back off, Grigory!"

"You will never be the man Katarina needs because you will never understand her. She is a Von Rahmel. You are merely a means for her to get out of Berlin."

Francis's arm drew back, ready to strike. Anthony stepped between the other two men. "Stop it, both of you!"

Madder than hell, Francis shoved Anthony aside. "Grigory, I could have you put in jail just for threatening an American officer. We could arrest you at any time for your clandestine activities in the East. For all we know, you could be training an action squad. You certainly have the qualifications."

"Francis, stop that!" repeated Anthony. "Grigory is an agent for the British. He's an ally to you. How could you accuse him, when he has devoted his life to the betterment of all?"

"If I were not standing in a church, I would spit in your face!" Grigory seethed. "If you have a problem with your marriage, work it out with your wife. Keep your threats to yourself." Grigory turned on his heel and stomped out of the church.

Anthony sighed. "Now I'll never know why he

really came here today."

"Why does it matter?" Francis retorted. "Do you think so little of your sister?"

"Listen, Francis, I'll talk to Katarina."

"No, you will not. I'm capable of talking to my own wife. I simply want you to leave her out of your business from now on. Have you got that?"

Anthony nodded. What was the point in arguing further? Clearly Francis did not know the woman he married.

****

Francis never knew whether Anthony had spoken to Katarina or not, but she did seem to make an effort to reform. He arrived home one day to find a group of officers' wives sipping tea in the living room. His own wife was playing the perfect hostess. After the women left a few minutes later, Katarina moved to the floor to blow bubbles in Douglas's face. Alexandra and Helena were visiting for the afternoon, and the little girl giggled and swatted the bubbles, and in between slobbered her little brother with kisses.

Alexandra reached with open arms toward her mother. "I love you, Mama, and I love little Douglas."

Rather than hugging her daughter, Katarina pushed the child's arms down. "Don't hug me, Alexandra. I don't want to hold you."

Behind her, Helena gasped, and even Francis caught his breath. Helena darted across the room and swooped up Alexandra, who had begun to whimper.

"Katarina?" Francis questioned.

She didn't respond, instead blowing another round of bubbles for Douglas.

Helena stopped at the door and whispered above

Alexandra's head. "Don't even think of including Alexandra when you leave. I will never let her raise this precious child in her sickness."

Francis sat on the floor with his wife and son. "Katarina, why?"

"You don't understand," Katarina said, rubbing Douglas's tummy. "Don't involve yourself in this."

"I have to concern myself, Katarina," Francis said. "I have my orders to go home. I was processing papers for Alexandra. My God, Katarina. After what she went through as a baby, she doesn't deserve this. Nothing that happened was her fault, and she can't help the fact that she resembles her father."

Katarina had no response.

"Look, Katarina, Alexandra's papers say she was born in a prison, and the Army wants you to fill out forms to explain why."

"I don't think I can do that," Katarina said softly.

"I know she was actually born in the camp. There will be many questions to answer when she is older. The one good thing that could come from all this is knowing that her mother loves her, but she doesn't have even that. How can you harden your heart to your own child?"

"Francis, what can I say? It's the way it is. You don't ever have to doubt my love for Douglas. That's completely different, and that's all that should matter to you. Don't worry about the paperwork. I don't intend to take Alexandra with us." She brightened briefly. "When do we leave?"

"I'm afraid I have to go ahead, fairly soon, and you will follow in a few months with Douglas when your paperwork clears. We can always bring Alexandra later."

She spoke sharply. "I told you not to concern yourself with that."

"Okay." He let it go. "For now, we just need to focus on your paperwork. I'm afraid there will be some questions about your first husband."

"Don't ever call him my husband." Katarina shuddered at the mere thought of Frederick. "Besides, Anthony had that marriage legally annulled. That means it never happened. Why is it the business of the American government?"

"They're just being cautious. Some of our officials still have a hard time trusting Germans. But we don't have to be afraid of telling the truth."

"It's cruel to make me talk about it. If Frederick had stayed with me that night instead of having his henchmen take me to prison, there is no question I would have been shot. I'm lucky he was more interested in getting laid than in what happened to me. He didn't care what happened to his own child. I can't look at Alexandra without wondering how I will tell her that her father wanted us both dead! Anthony made him disappear from our records for Alexandra's sake as well as mine. I won't spend a lifetime repeating this story to people when it's none of their business."

Francis knew not to press further. Katarina was turning white, and her chest heaved. Most likely she was already doomed to wake up tonight with nightmares and pace the room until she exhausted herself enough to sleep a few short hours.

"Darling," he said, "I'll go ahead of you to Hawaii and make all the arrangements. I should be discharged soon after I get home, and we'll go back to an ordinary life."

Suddenly Katarina started shaking uncontrollably.

Francis grabbed her hand. "What's wrong? You look like you've seen a ghost."

"You're not going to have me come. You'll go home and forget all about me. You'll leave me here!"

He pulled her to him and held her tight. "Don't be ridiculous. You are the mother of my son. I would never leave him."

****

A few days later, with heartache and tears, Katarina watched Francis load his duffel in the back of a jeep. His first stop was Wiesbaden; then he would spend a month in Frankfurt, and then he would be off to Hawaii. She pleaded with him to stay with her until they could travel together, and he explained over and over that he had his orders, and her arrangements could not be made so quickly. He promised it would be only a few weeks.

Finally, Francis was gone, and she was left standing alone with Douglas in her arms. She didn't relish staying in the summerhouse alone with the baby, but neither did she want to go home to live with her parents. Katarina wanted out of Berlin, pure and simple; nothing else would do. However, even though Katarina stayed in the summerhouse, Lisa and Jona insisted that Douglas have an overnight stay with his cousins and sister, and Katarina had yielded. She would spend the evening with Anthony, she decided. Perhaps she could convince him to stay a few nights at the summerhouse, since her time was short.

Outside the rectory, Katarina had the familiar sense that someone was watching. The shadows were not right. Francis never believed her, but Anthony seemed to, at least some of the time. Desperately hoping Anthony was home, Katarina forced a cry through her throat.

The cry was quickly muffled by a hand over her mouth. His face was now inches from hers, and their eyes met.

It couldn't be. It was impossible. It couldn't be him.

He dragged her down the street, the barrel of a gun against her temple.

"It would be my pleasure to shoot you on the spot, Katarina," the voice said. "But I will enjoy it far more seeing you rot in a Soviet cell. It's waiting for you right now." He looked at her with a sneer. "But first we have some unfinished business."

How could this be happening? Frederick!

Katarina was afraid she was going to throw up as he pushed her against a wall to let people pass. He pressed himself up against her and acted like he was going to kiss her. With one hand he shoved the gun into her abdomen, and with the other he groped her groin.

"Please stop! What do you want? You're supposed to be dead."

With the spectators gone, he hit her on the side of the head with the gun.

Everything blurred, but as he put his mouth close to hers, she bit his lip. He hit her again, then dragged her further from the rectory.

"Please let me go," she pleaded. "I swear I won't tell anyone you are alive."

He let out an evil laugh. To her horror, her assailant shot an old man just because he couldn't walk past them fast enough. Katarina screamed as the blood spattered from the old man's head. He kicked the body aside and jerked her violently toward him again.

****

Anthony was the first to reach the window when he heard Katarina's scream.

Peter and Grigory were on his heels as he scrambled outside and down the rectory steps. When they heard the gunshot, they froze momentarily. Did the sound tell them where Katarina was? Anthony thought he had caught a glimpse of his sister's blonde hair disappearing into a building. He knew the building opened to another street on the other side. A simple gesture sent Grigory around to the other door. Peter appeared next to him just in time to hear another scream and a second shot.

****

Katarina knew it was just a matter of time before Frederick shot her. He had just killed an innocent woman who happened to be going down the steps in front of them. It was obvious, though, he wanted her to suffer first. He would have his way with her and then send her back to prison before taking his final retribution.

****

Anthony caught up with Peter and Grigory. "Anthony, it's Frederick," Peter said.

"That's not possible," Anthony responded. "I saw him go up in flames."

Peter shrugged. "I can't explain it either. But the glimpse I caught of him is undeniable."

The trio heard distressed movement inside the building and uniformly slammed into the door to force it open. Rapid gunfire splintered the floorboards as they hugged the wall for protection. A side door opened and closed. They knew it led to a street blocked by large mounds of rubble.

****

Katarina's legs were rubber beneath her, and blood still flowed from her head. At least she did not have Douglas with her at this moment.

"Just shoot me now, Frederick," she said. The man laughed hysterically.

"Oh, no. I'm not Frederick. You will pay for killing my twin brother, though. I have followed you for months and watched your every movement."

Katarina stared at the wild-eyed man standing before her brandishing a gun. The difference was clear now. This man had a narrow scar above his left eye, and a pale birthmark at the side of his neck. This was not Frederick, though beyond those differences the resemblance was startling. He kept on dragging her over the rubble, faster than she could keep up. Over and over she stumbled and scraped up her hands and knees. On the downside of the mound of rubble, she saw a car and knew he was taking her there.

The first bullet hit the car door. Katarina screamed.

Grigory lunged from the darkness and tumbled into Katarina, breaking the hold her assailant had on her. Peter took solid aim and shot the man in the leg. He howled and cocked his gun again, but Grigory expertly shot the weapon out of his hand. The man lurched into the waiting car.

"Look over your shoulder the rest of your life, Fräulein," he said, "because you will never know when I will come for you or your children." He signaled the driver, and the car screeched away.

Katarina sobbed against Grigory's chest. "Please, no cell. They kept me with a dead body for weeks." She stopped abruptly and realized, clear as day, a memory stifled for years. A dead body, but where was it? Slowly Grigory's face came into focus, and she could feel his caring hand wiping the blood from her face, then his lips on her forehead.

Then Anthony was there, and she ran to his arms.

****

Anthony put her to bed at the rectory. As he looked at her, he silently whispered to himself, "Now she's walking in Helena's shoes. History repeats itself."

Katarina was afraid to sleep, and when she did, she woke up in a drenching sweat, screaming. She was moving dead people off of her, and she kept saying the skeletons were trying to pull her back down into the grave. Anthony, Peter, and Grigory sat with her all night.

"Did any of you know about this man who was following her?" Anthony asked. "I didn't doubt someone was watching her, but I assumed it was the same people who follow all of us."

Peter lowered his head. "We'd heard Frederick had a brother. But we didn't know he was an identical twin."

"Why would he turn up here now?" Anthony wanted to know. "What have you not been telling me?"

"We learned a few months ago he was one of the leading secret police commanders in the East. He's probably responsible for some of the goon squads that have swept through Berlin. It's been hard to keep track of him, but we never thought he would come here."

"I can't believe you didn't think I needed to know this information." Anthony was angry. "It was probably his sick mind that ordered the attack on my innocent altar boy—and those harmless puppies."

Peter sighed. "Quite possibly, yes, he ordered the attack on your church."

"If I had known, I would have done something to protect Katarina," Anthony said. "You should have told me what you knew."

"Honestly, I never thought it would come to this."

During the next few weeks, Katarina was never left alone. She still refused to move in with her parents, but Anthony, Peter, Hans, Grigory, and Dietrich set up a rotation so that someone was always watching her and staying the night in the summerhouse with Katarina and Douglas. The countdown for her departure to Hawaii was down to only three days.

Chapter 24

Grunewald: April 1948

Anthony stood in the warm sun outside the stable and watched Katarina dismount after a robust ride, grateful to see the bright flush in her cheeks. She smiled when she saw him, her violet eyes gleaming with pleasure. Katarina handed the reins to Joseph and embraced her brother. Then she picked up Douglas from the blanket where she had left him in Joseph's care.

"One more day," Anthony said, "and you'll be gone from us."

Katarina pushed back the damp strands of hair from her face as they began walking toward the house.

"I'm not dying, Anthony. I'm moving to Hawaii with my husband and baby." She kissed the top of Douglas's head.

"Will you see Alexandra tonight?"

She shook her head. "We said goodbye yesterday."

"Are you sure that's best?"

Katarina extracted her arm. "Of course. There's no point in confusing her further."

"But... How... What did you say? Does she really understand you're moving halfway around the world without her?"

"She's four, Anthony. How do I know what she

259

understands? Helena will look after her, and the rest of you will dote on her incessantly as you always do. Alexandra will be fine."

"Forgive me for saying this, but you seem unnaturally detached."

"Anthony, stop it! You've known for a long time that I intended to leave Berlin. I'll be back some day, or you'll visit me. Perhaps you'll bring Alexandra with you for a visit."

"But Katarina—"

She waved him off. "I'm so tired of trying to sort through everything that happened in the last few years. I don't remember a lot of it, and frankly, I don't want to. What I do remember is horrifying enough; why would I want to know more? It turned out I was right. Someone really was watching me, and he's still out there. I have to leave."

"But just walking away without truly understanding? Is that really what you want?"

Katarina sighed. They had reached the house, so she pushed open the back door to the kitchen and they went through. "What I'm doing is right, Anthony. Please believe that."

"But you've admitted you don't love Francis."

"He seems to love me, and we have a child. It's enough." Katarina handed Douglas to his uncle and filled a kettle with water to make tea on the small stove. "I have to leave here and start fresh, Anthony. I can't stay here with all the ghosts, and I can't take Alexandra with me, or the ghosts will come, too."

Anthony sat at the kitchen table bouncing Douglas slightly. "Katarina, the actions of Germany killed ten million people. The whole world hates us. I'm so sorry for what happened to you, for the experiences that created your ghosts. But if you and I hadn't tried to save as many people as we could, we would be living with a different set of ghosts."

Katarina slid a mug across the table to Anthony. "Yes. We made a difference. We're making a difference now. Maybe we'll avoid Soviet rule, maybe we won't. Either way, how long will it be before another Hitler comes along?"

"Don't say that!"

"Anthony, just the other day, when the officers' wives were here, I gave a cup of water to one of the drivers. You would have thought I'd committed a cardinal sin. The man was a Negro, and I got a fast lesson on the Negro's place in America—separate bathrooms, separate drinking fountains, separate sides of town. I told the general's wife they might as well put a star on them, the way Hitler did with the Jews."

"What did they say?"

"Not much, only that it's not the same, because they haven't killed ten million people."

"Well, that's true."

"But it could happen!" Katarina turned to the whistling kettle. "We thought we were a civilized nation, and look what we allowed to happen. And now we face the prospect of getting in bed with the Russians, and we beg the Americans to save us. Well, I can't save the whole country, but I can save myself. I am married to an American, and I am going to live on American soil."

Anthony rose, walked around the table, and put his arms around his sister, cuddling her baby between them. "Perhaps you are right. Perhaps this truly is the best thing for you. Maybe you'll see life differently when you are away from here."

Katarina kissed his cheek and stroked her baby's head. "And what you are not saying is that you believe I'll see Alexandra differently if I am away from here."

Anthony only shrugged. Katarina knew him too well.

"I have no intention of taking custody of her," Katarina said flatly. "She belongs to Helena now. I will sign anything Helena wants me to sign."

Anthony sat down and sipped his tea. The baby began to fuss, and Anthony resumed jiggling him.

****

On her last night in Berlin, it was Grigory who was scheduled to keep watch over Katarina. They sat and talked nearly all night before falling asleep in front of the fire for a few hours. They knew then they would love each other forever, that nothing would break their bond. He was the only one who loved her with all her sins, all her moods; he knew her as no other, even better than her own brother.

Anthony didn't want to see her other side, the woman who had learned to survive with whatever it took. He still had the image of a little girl in his mind when he thought of her, the little girl and the quilt on his shoulders.

Grigory loved her and would always love her, but she would soon be gone. So before she awoke he was ready to slip silently out of the house. He didn't want to look at her as he kissed her on the forehead, but the softness of her skin would stay in his memory, and the fresh smell of lavender from her clean, washed hair. He took it all in, and then he left without a goodbye.

He needed to find those who had murdered his people, and he would make those pay who had guarded the camps. He would hunt them down and protect Israel with all of his being. He would never let another Jew become a victim again. He was now part of a great organization in the Holy Land that would go after anyone who dared to attach Israel, but he also knew he would always look out for the Von Rahmel family; he would never let anything ever hurt Katarina again.

****

The day Katarina had longed for finally came. Her family stood with her at Templehof airfield with tears in their eyes. Gertrude had stayed home with the grandchildren, and no one mentioned Alexandra's name as they hugged Katarina one at a time.

She boarded the plane and settled Douglas in her lap. A lump rose in her throat as the aircraft's engines roared and it began its trek down the runway. The take-off was smooth. A long sigh came from inside her as she looked at the lakes and canals. Then she saw the rubble of buildings scattered over the land. As they flew higher and the scene grew smaller, she did not regret leaving it all behind.

From the time she left Germany, Katarina spoke only flawless English. She was traveling with American papers, so why make things difficult by provoking any hostility toward all things German? She flew to Frankfurt, to London, to New York, and finally to San Francisco. There she boarded the ship that would take her to Hawaii.

Katarina had packed lightly. Francis had assured her that she didn't need to bring most of her drab clothing or even Douglas's tattered blankets. In Hawaii he would be able to dress his family the way they deserved, rather than by struggling Berlin's standards.

She took him at his word, but even so was surprised to see the clothing of the people moving through the airport in New York. At last Katarina allowed herself to begin dreaming of a new wardrobe.

On the ship, her stateroom was one of the best, and to her delight, when she opened the door she saw packages everywhere. Just as Francis had promised, he had made all the arrangements for new clothing for both her and Douglas. Katarina hadn't expected this until reaching Hawaii, but it was a delightful treat for the voyage. The colors of her new clothing were bright and fresh. The sleek skirts and shoes fit perfectly. It had been a long time since she had felt nylons against her skin and cotton dresses swirling around her legs. Katarina spent hours trying on all the ensembles and dressing Douglas in one outfit after another. She felt beautiful again, as if the last few years faded from reality.

For the most part, Katarina kept to herself during the ocean crossing. People cooed and fussed over Douglas, as they had in the air all the way across the Atlantic. Katarina remained anxious to conceal her German roots. She listened intently to conversations in the elegant dining room, studying gestures and inflections of the Americans.

Finally the ship wound its way into the harbor at Honolulu. Katarina chose one of the new outfits—a sleeveless green shift she suspected Francis would particularly like because it hugged her form—and gathered Douglas in her arms to go on deck and watch the docking. The dress exposed more of her arms than she was comfortable with, and the neckline plunged lower than she was used to, but this must be the style, she reasoned. She reminded herself that her husband had chosen this dress for her. Her hair flowed freely behind her, gleaming in the sunlight She soon spied Francis in the crowd, wandering as far out on the wharf as he could. Traditional Hawaiian music drifted through the air, and the smell of flowers wafted from every direction.

Though in reality it was only minutes, it felt to Katarina as if it took an inordinate amount of time to actually exit the ship. By then Francis was practically running toward her and Douglas. He snatched Douglas from her arms, kissed her heavily, and spun them both around in a full circle. Breathless, Katarina was overcome with the colors and fragrances of the island. Her head was in constant motion, turning from side to side to take it all in. She didn't hear half of what Francis was saying as he steered her toward the waiting limousine.

In Berlin, even at home Francis had worn a uniform of some sort. Here, he was in a colorful flowered shirt and tan pants with leis around his neck. He was at complete ease behind the dark tinted sunglasses in his beautiful island world.

"My father is waiting with the limousine," Francis said. "Don't worry about your bags. They'll be brought to the hotel."

Gordon Lee, Francis's father, was indeed anxious to greet them. He was as tall as Francis, but more classically Hawaiian in appearance. His striking silver hair accented a face highlighted by angular cheekbones, and he emanated an air of casual confidence, a byproduct of a lifetime of power and wealth.

Gordon placed his own lei around Katarina's neck and kissed her on the cheek. "My son has not done you justice, my dear Katarina," he said. "You are truly stunning."

As they settled into the limousine, Gordon reached to take Douglas from Katarina's lap. Her eyes widened briefly, and she realized how attached she had become to Douglas during these months without Francis, especially during her journey. She wasn't used to having him out of her arms, and had not thought what it would be like for Francis's parents to meet their only grandchild. In Berlin, Douglas was one of four grandchildren her parents showered with affection. Here, as the only grandchild in a wealthy family, Douglas was sure to be the center of attention.

Francis sat beside her, holding her hand tightly. "You look tired—and thin. Is it possible you've lost even more weight?"

Katarina laughed. "I've done nothing but eat during the entire cruise. I am tired, but I'm even more excited. There's so much to see!"

"We'll stay for a couple of days at our penthouse at the Royal Hawaiian Hotel so you can get used to things. Then we'll go on to Kauai."

"That sounds lovely."

"We can do some shopping and sightseeing, and you can walk on the beach and put your toes in the ocean." Francis squeezed Katarina's hand with infectious enthusiasm.

While Gordon and Francis fussed over Douglas, Katarina's eyes were glued to the passing countryside, trying to absorb the exquisiteness of the tropical paradise she was now supposed to call home. Years of shortages and destruction in Berlin made it hard to believe this consuming bright excitement was real. The scene wavered before her like something out of a magazine.

In the hotel lobby, Gordon and Francis stepped away from her briefly to talk to a woman at the desk, taking Douglas with them. As the baby moved out of Katarina's reach, his tiny voice echoed across the marble floors. Katarina ran to comfort her son. But just as she got her hands around him, Francis intervened and lifted Douglas from his grandfather's arms.

"I've just arranged for a tailor to come up to the penthouse," Francis said. He'll help you pick out fabrics for new clothing."

"But you already gave me so much on the boat!" Katarina exclaimed.

Francis laughed. "That's just the beginning, Katarina. You're a Lee now. You have to look like one."

"All right, Francis, but do we have to do this now? I'm so tired from traveling."

"We'll only be here a couple of days," he responded. "We have to make the most of it. The tailor is not coming till the morning."

Douglas fussed again, and Katarina reached for him. Instead, Francis handed the baby back to Gordon. "Grandpa can look after Douglas," he said. "Let me take you for a drink and a tour of the hotel."

"Oh, Francis, I don't know—"

But Gordon had already taken Douglas and headed toward the elevators.

An infectious laugh rose from across the room.

Katarina turned to see a beautiful red-haired woman with piercing green eyes and pale skin. She was tall and slender and wearing elegant white slacks and a lime green halter top that showcased her alabaster shoulders. The woman was holding hands with an older man and waving to someone across the room. Katarina instinctively glanced over her shoulder to see whose attention the woman was trying to get, and in the process she walked right into a young Navy lieutenant. With a gasp she stepped away from him.

"I'm so sorry," he said. "I stepped on your foot. I hope I didn't hurt you."

He put a hand under her elbow to steady her, and she soaked in his pitch black hair, strong broad chin, dark skin, and dancing hazel eyes. His broad shoulders tapered to his fit waist.

She couldn't think what to say, so she merely murmured her own apology for being careless. The man seemed somehow familiar. Katarina blinked her eyes and reminded herself that she had left the land of ghosts. With a gentle smile, the man continued on toward the lovely redhead.

Francis leaned into her. "What was that all about?"

She shook her head. "Nothing. I guess I wasn't watching where I was going, and we bumped into each other."

"Who was that?"

"I told you, just a man I bumped into. I'm hardly likely to introduce myself to a strange man the first day here."

"No, of course not. Let's go walk on the beach," he suggested. "You can tell me what's happening in Berlin."

"I don't want to talk about Berlin," she answered. She forced a smile. "I'm in Hawaii! Why talk about Berlin?"

That seemed to be all the cue Francis needed. As they walked, he pointed out one thing after another, restaurants and theaters and beach attractions and elite shops, all the while assuring her she would have plenty of opportunities to enjoy Honolulu. The penthouse suite at the hotel was available exclusively to the Lee family and their guests, and he promised to bring her often.

Feeling the sand between her toes was exquisite, and Katarina couldn't wait to bring Douglas to play in the sand. The thought that the warmth of the sun was available year round was almost more than she could fathom. But she was tired—and anxious to be with her son.

"Francis, could we go back to the hotel now? I'm worried about Douglas. Your father is lovely, but he is a stranger to the baby."

"Douglas will have to get used to the attention," Francis said. "A whole family is waiting for him. He'll learn soon enough his mother is not the center of the universe."

Katarina felt as if he'd slapped her. "You're right," she said coldly, and started back to the hotel nevertheless.

****

The penthouse was lavish. A glass table piled high with tropical fruit and warm food on lit burners welcomed her. Francis's hand never left Katarina's arm as he showed her around the suite. Four expensively appointed bedrooms and an office opened onto an exquisite sitting and dining area. The artwork on the walls was not run-of-the-mill hotel reproductions, but carefully selected original pieces that captured the ambiance of the islands. As she looked around the extravagant rooms, Katarina knew she truly had escaped Berlin. As Francis's wife, she would never be hungry or cold again.

The rest of the evening, she stayed on the couch by the window, her legs curled under her as she watched life moving below her. She had managed to get her son back for a few moments after dinner, but then Gordon and Francis insisted on putting him to bed. Katarina felt she could hardly object; Francis and Douglas had been separated for weeks already, and she had to admit Douglas seemed to be adjusting to the attention. Mesmerized, Katarina watched the scene out the window, till the horizon cradled the sun in a blazing, glorious sunset.

****

The smell of the sweetness of her skin after her long, luxuriant bath intoxicated Francis. As he watched her get ready for bed, he wanted her more urgently by the moment. Pulling the towel away from her, he touched her slowly, his hand traveling purposefully across her belly and down to her warm, moist spot. With the fingers of his other hand, he traced her facial features, her mouth, her nose, the full circumference of her soft face. She had been far too independent in Berlin, but it would be different here. She was Francis Lee's wife, not a prominent ballerina or the member of a Resistance household.

He took her before she was ready.

****

She listened to the gentle rhythm of his sleep.

Francis could sleep through the end of the world, especially after sex. But even here, during the first night of the new life she had waited to begin, Katarina's mind roamed the darkness inhabited by ghostly shadows.

****

A phone call in the morning demanded that Francis and Gordon return to their plantation sooner than planned. Secretly, Katarina was glad. She hadn't wanted to spend the morning with a strange tailor, feeling pressure to design a wardrobe. Instead, she just wanted to see her new home. This time, she insisted Douglas would sit on her lap as they flew in the small aircraft from one island to the other. They flew over pastures, ranches, and sugar fields that Francis proudly pointed out as their own. Fields of cattle dotted the landscape. Tiny white beaches tucked into mountains seemed to grow from the shoreline. Dense forests scurried up against old, dormant volcanoes, their peaks shrouded in clouds.

A limousine waiting at the airstrip took them directly to the estate. The Lee family home was like a small kingdom, covering a vast area of outer fields, with horses and stables near the main house in the middle of the property. Katarina was enchanted with the verandah that stretched from one end of the house to the other. Cottages occupied by staff formed a ring around the main house. Francis pointed out his mother's garden, which he had spoken of many times in Berlin. It was filled with koi ponds, waterfalls, and seemingly endless varieties of flowers, all lovingly selected and planted by his mother and nurtured daily by the gardeners who lived on the property. Francis promised her she could walk to the beach and watch the whales and dolphins from the shore. It was an absolute paradise, and Katarina gulped in the clean, sweet air.

Francis escorted her into a large hallway, with walls of solid mahogany stretching up fifteen feet. The hallway was brightened by a row of beautiful vases filled with handpicked flowers drenched by the sun streaming through French doors. Servants appeared to handle the luggage. She heard Gordon call them by name, but most of what happened was a blur.

Then several young women emerged from one of the rooms, laughing. Their voices hushed abruptly at the sight of the willowy blond.

"Katarina, these are my daughters," Gordon said, "Kim and Stephanie. And this is their good friend Maria."

Kim and Stephanie murmured hello with unconvincing warmth. They were both quite a bit younger than Francis, just a few years older than Katarina, with the same striking black hair their brother sported. Both of them strongly resembled the life-size portrait of their deceased mother that hung on the wall behind him. Kim eagerly reached for her nephew. Katarina supposed Douglas was already adjusting to the strange surroundings, because he went to Kim without protest.

"Hello, Francis," said the third young woman.

Katarina glanced at her husband, and in that instant she knew this woman had a hold on Francis. Her black hair hung softly around her face, a stray hair brushing across her full red lips. Her voluptuous figure made Katarina suddenly self-conscious about how thin she was.

"Hello, Maria," Francis said. "I'm pleased to

introduce my wife and son."

"He's adorable," Maria said of the baby. She barely glanced at Katarina, before stepping forward to greet Francis more intimately. She kissed him full on the mouth. "Old family friends," Gordon explained quickly.

Francis put a hand on Katarina's shoulder. "Come on, let me show you upstairs," he said. "Kim had a great time decorating for Douglas." He led her up the winding staircase as she watched Kim disappear with her son into another room.

The view from their bedroom was as breathtaking as anything she had seen so far. The back of the house sloped gently down to the beach, where waves danced and glittered in the sunlight. The room was painted in soft hues of blue, pink, and beige, and the canopy bed was layered in pastels. On the private balcony, an enormous crystal ball shot prisms of color across the bedroom walls. As she stood, breathless, absorbing the beauty, Francis stood behind her, his breath tickling the back of her neck.

She turned and faced him. "Francis, this is newly decorated, isn't it? I can't imagine you with these soft colors."

He shrugged and stepped back toward the bed, pulling her with him.

"My room was very masculine. Kim thought this would be more welcoming for a woman." He slipped his hand under her blouse.

"She did a beautiful job," Katarina said.

"We must try out our new bed," he whispered, his hands widening their exploration.

"Francis, it's the middle of the day. Everyone is

downstairs. Douglas is awake."

"Douglas has plenty of people to look after him." Ignoring her protests, he unbuttoned her blouse and unhooked her skirt, letting it fall to the floor. In a moment, her undergarments were out of the way. His mouth covered hers as he slipped a finger inside her. She already felt his hardness against her leg. He pulled her down to the bed with him and undressed quickly.

In her mind, Katarina told herself that Francis was trying to make their reunion memorable. Her body did not respond. Katarina was determined she would learn to love this man, to respond to his touch consistently. She had to. It was a matter of survival. A long sigh escaped her, which he mistook for passion.

Chapter 25

Kauai: June 1948

Katarina was spellbound by the tropical paradise that could not have been further removed from the desolation of Berlin. Francis was devoted to her for the first few weeks. They rode for hours on the purebreds that filled the Lee family stables, and Francis took her for picnics on the beach or by the waterfalls in the mountains. Everything was fresh and intriguing, and the never-ending lushness of the plantation filled her senses as never before. Even before the war, when she had loved Berlin, Katarina had never imagined what it might be like to live in a place like this. Gradually, though, Francis had to return to his responsibilities and left Katarina on her own for increasingly longer periods of time.

When Francis wasn't around, his father turned out to be Katarina's new best friend. She enjoyed Gordon's company and appreciated the lengths to which he went to help Douglas adjust to a new place and a new family. Francis's sisters, however, were problematic from the start. Though they doted on Douglas and clearly adored their brother, it became clear early on that they had no use for Katarina. When Katarina tried to talk to Francis about it, she expected him to take her side. Instead, he merely shrugged and said it was the same with her family. Didn't she worship Anthony? And hadn't she refused to accept Gertrude? His comments stung her, and for a while she clamped her mouth shut.

And then there was Maria.

The old family friend seemed to spend more time at the Lee home than at her own. Ostensibly, she was coming to visit Kim and Stephanie, and they did often linger at the stables together. However, nearly every day Maria seemed to find some reason to seek out Francis, leaning heavily on his arm as she laughed in his ear, or thinking nothing of disappearing with him behind closed doors.

Katarina had had enough. She was in the library, a dark room compared to the rest of the house. The dark mahogany shelves and desks, with large captain's chairs and dark drapes, made the library a distinctly masculine room, yet Katarina enjoyed the room and often went there to read while Douglas napped. She was there when she heard Francis and Maria come into the house together, and from their conversation and laughter through the open library door, Katarina surmised they had been together most of the morning. Breathing heavily, she began to pace the polished wood floor. Finally Francis came in.

"Francis, we need to talk," she demanded.

Barely glancing at her, he began to flip through the mail left for him on the desk. "Francis, I'm talking to you," Katarina said as she leaned against the desk. She covered his hand with hers to stop him from picking up more mail. "I understand your sisters are great friends with Maria, but do you have to spend so much time with her?"

"I don't know what you're talking about," he said,

barely glancing up at her.

"Every time I turn around, she is right behind you. What have you been doing together all morning? I thought you were going to work."

"How I spend my time is none of your business," he snapped. "I am not accountable to you." He removed her hand with a deliberate motion and began sorting mail once again.

"Don't do this, Francis. Don't ignore me." Her violet eyes flashed with anger. "Who is Maria to you?"

"She's a family friend. You know that."

"And you were going to marry her, weren't you? She's the one your family picked out for you, not me."

His look was cold and mocking. "Katarina, I think your imagination is getting the best of you. We're no longer in Berlin. Nobody here is out to get you."

Impulsively, Katarina picked up a crystal paperweight and threw it as hard as she could against the wall behind Francis. It splintered into a thousand pieces. He came around the desk immediately and pushed her down into a chair.

"Don't you ever lose your temper like that again. You will not confront me about where I go or who I spend time with. Do you understand?"

She stood and slapped him faster than either one of them could realize what was happening.

Then she turned and walked out of the room.

Kim and Stephanie stood in the hall, stunned at what they had overheard. Katarina pushed right past them and marched out to the stables. She didn't wait for a groom to saddle her horse; she did it herself. As she led the horse outside, she found Gordon waiting for her. He kissed each of her cheeks.

"Katarina, what's wrong?" Gordon asked. He seemed genuinely concerned, the only person in the household who would be.

"It's nothing," she said, shrugging. "Francis and I just had words, that's all."

Gordon patted the side of the horse's head. "Katarina, he said you had a lover in Berlin. He said you were talking in your sleep."

"Did he tell you I say a lot of things in my sleep?" she responded. "Did he tell you that I beg the ghosts not to rape me any more? That I plead with them not to kill my baby? Did he tell you that I hardly sleep?"

Gordon shook his head. "We only know you have been through unimaginable horror. Francis has never told us the details."

"That's because he doesn't know the details. I do not want to stir up old ghosts if I can help it, though I can't help what I say in my sleep. But I assure you, Francis is the only lover I chose to take in Berlin."

"I'm sorry. I will deal with my son."

"While you're at it, you can tell your old family friend to find her own husband and make her own babies, and leave mine alone!"

Katarina slung herself into the saddle and clicked her tongue. The horse responded with an immediate gallop.

****

The next six months went by slowly. Francis and Katarina did not speak of Maria again. Francis moved his hands over Katarina's slim body in the privacy of their bedroom, and she did her best to respond, and even to initiate. Douglas thrived and was now walking around the plantation, requiring constant supervision that his grandfather and aunts were happy to provide.

Katarina's lifeline was the letters from Berlin, especially Anthony's. Berlin was finally on its way to recovery. In a play for power, the Soviets had blockaded Berlin, cutting off crucial supplies during the winter, but the Americans and English had risen to the occasion with a massive airlift to deliver food, fuel, and essentials during the 1948-1949 winter. Of course, Katarina had followed all this in the news, but she relished Anthony's perspectives.

My dear Katarina,

Well, we did it. Because of a quarter of a million flights into Berlin, we survived. Our bond with the British and Americans is strong. I believe they are beginning to realize we won't give up on ourselves, even when we thought they would give up on us. And not every German is the enemy in their eyes any longer. Some of us really are the good guys!

I still worry about the Soviets. The blockade didn't work, but they are still hungry for power in Europe, and I'm sure they will try again. You were right. It never stops. There are always Hitlers standing there and waiting. The Soviets want us to believe Communism is the way to freedom, but of course it's not. I fear for what is happening in East Germany.

I am enclosing some recent photographs of Alexandra. She is growing into a smart and beautiful girl. We cannot express our gratitude for the lovely clothing and other items you sent for all of us. And the pictures of Douglas delight us most of all.

You do not speak of Francis in your letters. I do hope you are finding a way to make it a good marriage, as you hoped. His father seems like a wonderful man. I received a letter from Gordon inviting me for a visit.

Right now I do not think that is possible, but it was thoughtful of him to ask.

I'd better sign off and get to work on my sermon for Sunday.

Love,

Anthony

The letter fluttered to the ground, and the pictures of Alexandra with it. Katarina did not bother to pick them up.

"Why won't he come?" she murmured. "I need him!"

****

Christmas of 1948 came and went. Francis took Katarina to a New Year's Eve party at the hotel in Honolulu. She turned the head of every man in the ballroom when she entered. Her gown was black taffeta, a simple A-line with silver threaded tapestry woven into the fabric. Katarina slid enough bracelets around one arm to cover most of her scar, and wore her golden hair loose and cascading to cover the lash marks on her shoulders. Around her neck was a cross filled with diamonds, a gift from her family in Germany.

Katarina could not stop Maria and her parents from attending the party, which was hosted by the Lees. Of course old family friends would be there. Gordon introduced Katarina to Maria's parents, and she felt Francis's pride as he cradled her elbow during the introduction. He danced very closely with her that night and talked more than he had in months, giving Katarina a glimmer of hope that things might improve between them. When she saw Maria glaring at them across the ballroom, Katarina merely smiled slyly and snuggled against her husband's chest.

At the end of January, Katarina was becoming more frantic by the day. She had not heard from her family for weeks—not even at Christmas. She followed the news, looking for any reason why they would not be able to send letters, and heard none. And then one day, rummaging through a drawer in the chest in the hallway, looking for some wrapping ribbon, she found the bundle of letters. Weeks, even months, of letters from her family were there, unopened. Even before this recent silence, they had written far more than she ever knew.

Kim and Stephanie had put them there. They claimed that this had always been the family's system for mail that didn't get picked up off the desk in the library, but the only mail in that drawer was Katarina's. She seethed at their cruelty, but Francis seemed unaffected, and even Gordon, her only true ally in the house, distanced himself from the dispute. Katarina withdrew more and more to the room Francis had allowed her to remodel into a dance studio; no one bothered her there.

In her dreams, Katarina was always losing Anthony. Over and over, she watched him fall into a deep hole, but when she tried to reach for his hand, thousands of skeletal hands came up instead. Then she was opening a grave to find him, and she would feel ghosts breathing beside her. She used to wake up screaming for Anthony, but over the months she had learned to catch herself at the point of waking and swallow the scream. It only infuriated Francis when she called for her brother. Instead, she would leave the bed, and in the morning Francis would find her on the balcony, curled up in a fetal position.

Each time he found her, he was less patient as she roused and adjusted to the reality of daylight. The increasing frequency of the dreams during the weeks when she got no mail made her practice dancing furiously, exhausting herself in the hope of sleep without interruption.

This was not working out the way Francis had imagined. Katarina was stunningly beautiful, as always, but she stayed in her own world too much of the time. If she would make one quarter of the effort to connect with his sisters as she did to stay in touch with a family on another continent, everyone would be much happier. Instead, he would find her in the kitchen chatting with the cook and kitchen help, eating and feeding Douglas. He had asked her over and over again not to be so friendly with the staff. When he said it simply wasn't proper, she just stared at him blankly. One time she had actually laughed at him for being too serious. And she did exactly what she wanted to do, just as she had in Berlin. Why couldn't she understand those days were over?

Francis's fury was fueled by his own father's behavior. Gordon rode with Katarina nearly every day, and more than once Francis had found his father and his wife together in the library talking about the family business. He had dismissed Katarina, and she'd left the room rolling her eyes. Then he turned on his father.

"Dad, you've got to stop coddling her. She's never going to adjust to being my wife if you keep treating her like this."

"I don't know what you mean," Gordon answered. "You have a lovely wife and child, and you don't appreciate what you have. She can make anyone's heart melt with her smile, but you give her so little reason to smile."

"Well, you seem to be making up for what you think I'm lacking! You spend far too much time with Katarina."

"We share a love of horses, and she's interested in learning the family business, which is more than I can say about my daughters."

"She has no reason to learn the family business!" Francis thundered. "I insist that you stay away from Katarina!"

Gordon's eyes narrowed. "You, my son, are sadly mistaken if you think you can speak to me in such a manner without recriminations. All this still belongs to me. I can skip a generation and leave it all to Douglas."

"I'm warning you, Dad. Leave my wife alone."

"Francis, do you think I don't know about your escapades with Maria in that empty cottage? You can go to hell if you think I'm going to stand by and watch Katarina become more unhappy every day. She'll leave and take my grandson with her, and I do not intend to let that happen."

Gordon abruptly clutched his chest, unable to speak, as he stumbled to the floor.

"Dad! Someone call Dr. Stuart!"

****

Katarina sat next to Gordon's bed in the rocking chair all night. He'd had a mild heart attack, but he would recover soon. When he opened his eyes, she took his hand.

His voice was a whisper. "Katarina, if you were lying in this bed, what would be your last wish?"

"Shhh. Nobody needs to make a last wish," she said.

"But what is your wish, Katarina? What do you want most of all?" She smiled. "I want to see Anthony."

Gordon drifted back to sleep. When Dr. Stuart came to check on the patient in the morning, he told Katarina to get some rest herself. Reluctantly, she went to her own bedroom to change. Francis was just getting dressed.

"Francis," Katarina said, "I saw you look in on your father during the night. Why would you not want to stay in the room with him?"

"He was being well looked after," he answered flatly as he buttoned his shirt.

"He could have been dying."

"But he wasn't."

"But he could have been. Your sisters stood there telling me I had my tentacles around their father, and you said nothing."

Francis's eyes were dark with fury, causing Katarina to suck in her breath. "Katarina, your heart is unnaturally cruel," he accused. "You love the adulation from my father, and you use it to divide the family."

Katarina expelled her breath, exasperated. "Stop this! You're just being foolish now. Don't blame your father for everything that's wrong between us. My family welcomed you with open arms, so don't use that as an excuse for the way your sisters treat me. You never defend me with them—and you flaunt your old lover in my face constantly!"

Francis slid his wallet into his trousers and ran a comb through his hair. "You're making a mistake," he said.

"I won't take the blame for what happened to your father or what has happened to us! You'll lose any feelings I have for you, and your father's as well."

Francis grabbed her arm and threw her on the bed. "You're no angel, dear wife. My father knows that. You're fooling yourself if you think he cares about you. He just doesn't want to lose his grandson."

He slammed the door behind him.

****

Three months later, Gordon was his old self. In order to keep peace in the household, Katarina stopped her outings with Gordon, unless someone else was available to go along. She didn't see Gordon for days at a time, spending most of her time with Douglas on the beach or in the carefully tended gardens. Katarina still shared Francis's bed and accommodated his desires, but it was not the same between them.

One morning she awoke later than usual. The house seemed dark, the sky filled with dark clouds and a howling wind. Katarina had been up half the night with a mare that had gone into a difficult labor. There had been no time to send for a veterinarian. As a girl, Katarina had assisted her father often enough to know what to do. The newborn was in a breach position, and she had reached in to turn it. Now she wanted to know how both mother and baby were doing. She dressed quickly, and went down to the stables.

Maria was there, crying and pushing away from Francis's embrace outside one of the stalls. She threw an engagement ring at him.

"I should have given this back to you a long time ago," she cried. "I truly believed you would come to your senses and I would be wearing it again. Why didn't you just leave her in Berlin?"

"It's not that simple, Maria," Francis said.

"I know. There's Douglas. You don't want to lose him. But when you came back and wanted to make love to me, I believed you would divorce her. I've waited for over a year."

"You knew my situation," Francis said. "You're the one who chose to wait."

"Leave her!"

Katarina couldn't stand to hear more. She stepped into the stables and made her presence known.

Maria glared at her, daring her to say anything.

"Maria, I want you off our property right now. Don't come back. You are out of my husband's life once and for all."

Maria looked at Francis. "Tell your wife that won't happen," she said. "Are you going to tell my parents that I'm not welcome here? Are you really willing to do that?"

Katarina stared at her husband, waiting for him to step up.

He was silent.

Maria advanced toward Katarina, screaming, "How dare you try to turn him against me, you bitch! Go back to the gutter he found you in."

Katarina looked to Francis once again, but once again he was silent. Her life changed forever at that moment.

The dark skies gave way to cracking thunder. Katarina turned and ran out of the stables. She ran to the beach and pounded against the sand, oblivious to the storm raging around her. The rain was coming down so hard she might as well have been in the ocean.

Soaked, she fell to her knees, screaming.

A hand touched her shoulder. Francis tried to pull her to her feet, but she shoved him away. "Don't ever touch me again!"

He pushed the wet blonde hair from her face as the rain beat down on them. Their foreheads touched as he asked her, "Did you ever love me?"

Katarina nodded. "Yes, I did, in my own way."

"Katarina, there is nothing but friendship between Maria and me. I have loved you from the moment you walked into my office in Berlin."

"It's too late, Francis. I heard what you said to her back there. And I heard what you did not say."

"This is insane, Katarina. Let's go back to the house and talk about this." Once again he tried to help her stand, but she resisted.

As she rose to her feet under her own steam, she murmured, "Oh, my God." Blood soaked into the sand beneath her feet. She looked at Francis. "I'm losing the baby."

"What baby?" he screamed into the wind.

"I'm eight weeks pregnant. I was going to tell you today." She lost consciousness as he caught her in his arms.

When she woke, Francis was sitting next to the bed, dark circles under his eyes. She had roused momentarily a few times, once to find his head lying on her hand, with the wetness of his tears.

"Francis, the baby?" she asked now through parched lips.

He shook his head. "You were farther along than you thought, twelve weeks. It was a little girl."

Katarina turned her head away as the tears began to

flow. "Where is she?"

"We buried her, Katarina."

"Buried her? How long—"

"Two days. You've been unconscious most of the time."

"Did you name her?"

"Father Murphy baptized her Anna Christine Lee."

She was sobbing now. "Thank you."

Outside the sky was a bright blue. Suddenly the room was stifling her. "Please, could you let in some fresh air?"

Francis walked over and opened the balcony doors. "Katarina, I'm glad you're better. But I believe the earth could be melting under your feet and the only person you would want to help you is your brother."

"What do you mean?" she asked feebly.

"I mean, even while you were half unconscious after losing our baby, the only person you called out for was Anthony."

Katarina turned over on her side, turning her back on Francis. "I'm tired, Francis." She drifted back to sleep, and Francis left.

****

Katarina spent days holed up in her room. Gordon brought Douglas in from time to time, but even her son didn't cheer her up. From the balcony, she watched the birds soar over the ocean and wished she were one of them. As she felt stronger, she began slipping out of the house early in the mornings to walk on the beach or visit the stables. She loved the soft nose and big eyes of her mare. She was returning from the stables early one morning when she saw Francis sitting at the far end of the garden.

"Francis, isn't this a little early for you?" she asked.

"How would you know?" he retorted. "You're always out of the house at the break of dawn. Come in the house and have breakfast with me." He tried to reach for her hand, but she pulled back. She couldn't bear to have him touch her, not even to hold her hand.

"No, I'm going down to the beach," she said. "I can't breathe in that house. I feel like a prisoner. And yesterday I looked out and saw Maria holding Douglas in the back yard. What was she doing with my son, Francis?"

"Katarina, I have not spoken to her since that day at the stables. I promise that's the truth. But I can't put a stop to the friendship she has with my sisters. It's unrealistic to ask that."

"Then let's move," she said simply. "We can build our own house, start fresh. Yes, that's what we can do."

Francis looked at her like she had lost her mind. "This is my home, Katarina. I'm not going to leave."

"Fine. I gave you a chance. You didn't take it." She turned to go down to the beach.

"Katarina, stop this! You have all the freedom you want. Have I asked you for anything these last few weeks? You live in your own little world, and I've left you alone there. You're turning away not just from me but from your own son. When was the last time you spent any time with Douglas?"

He had pushed her last button. "Leave me alone!" she screamed.

Francis grabbed her wrist. "I will leave you alone for now. But I will not be patient indefinitely. You are my wife. Don't even think of leaving. I can send you back to Germany at any time."

"Now look who is being cruel!"

They glared at each other.

Finally Katarina spoke. "If you send me away, I will take Douglas. Your father will lose his precious male heir."

He released her wrist and said quietly, "Go to hell, Katarina."

In less than a whisper, she replied, "I have been to hell and seen it. I don't have to go there," and as he left she clenched her fist. Still she wanted him to love her again, wanted him to look at her the way he looked at Maria.

Katarina and Francis were civil to each other over the next few months during the daytime hours, especially if anyone else was around. They had breakfast together, and dinner with the family. For Gordon's sake, she produced a bright smile whenever he was in the room. But she knew Francis was going off in the night to be with Maria, and she didn't care.

Letters flowed freely from her family now, unimpeded by Kim and Stephanie. When she wrote, she told them nothing of the disintegration of her marriage, but filled the letters with tales of the family business and the tropical setting. When Anthony wrote, she read his letters until she knew them by heart.

One morning she stood looking in the mirror after a ragged, sleepless night. She had gone into the bathroom to shower; perspiration had soaked through her nightgown. When she looked into the mirror, she peered into her own eyes, the lines of her own face, and saw someone she no longer recognized.

Francis rushed into the bathroom when he heard

the glass shatter. Katarina was staring blankly into the cracked mirror. She whispered, "I hate who I am. I don't know who I am any more. How could you ever have loved me?"

She let him gather her into his arms and lead her to the bed. She did not protest a few minutes later when he began to make love to her. For a few moments, the familiarity comforted her.

Later, they did not speak of what had happened as they sat in the garden together. He told her over and over that he loved her, that he felt for the first time in a long time they could recover their marriage, that he wished for them to return to life as it had been for them earlier.

****

Katarina's lips parted as she looked up. Could it be true? His hair was wind blown, his face looked gaunt. His collar was open, and the cross at his neck glinted in the sun. She stood, not knowing if her legs would carry her.

"My God, my God!" Katarina ran into the open arms of her brother, Father Anthony Von Rahmel. She laid her hand against the side of her face and asked, "How?"

Anthony turned to Gordon, standing beside him. "Your father-in-law sent the necessary paperwork and tickets. He convinced me the time had come."

The smile that cracked her face was the first genuine one since her early months on the island.

Francis watched as his wife and her brother walked arm in arm into the house.

With a sigh he turned to his father.

"Dad, how could you? I lose all control and any

hope with Anthony in the picture."

"I disagree, son. He is your only hope."

Chapter 26

Kauai: August 1949

The transformation in Katarina was immediate.

Her face softened, her voice mellowed, and for the first time since arriving at the Lee plantation, she seemed genuinely relaxed. But Francis's fury at his father's interference roiled for days as he watched Katarina revel in her brother's presence. As Francis watched the two of them walk through the gardens at the end of the first week, he said to his father, "This will be the last time you interfere with my marriage."

Gordon looked unperturbed as he poured himself more orange juice. He had hoped to enjoy his breakfast.

"Did you think I was going to stand by and watch her fall to pieces?" he asked. "Your marriage is falling apart. Your wife is consummately unhappy. I believe that man can help her, and she will settle in and stay."

"Stop it, Dad. Do you honestly think I would let her get custody of Douglas if she left? We know every judge on these islands. All we have to do is mention Grigory."

"Katarina told me nothing happened with this Grigory fellow, that she was just talking in her sleep." Gordon stabbed a piece of sausage.

"And you believed her, of course."

"Why shouldn't I?"

"Because I am your son, and I'm telling you I believe something happened."

Gordon chewed thoughtfully before speaking. "And what will you tell the judge about Maria?"

"Nothing. I'll have Katarina declared insane. She's not leaving, and she's not taking Douglas."

"You can't keep her in a cage, Francis. I know next to nothing of what's she been through, but you've seen her official files. You know what horrors she lived with. She was in a concentration camp, for God's sake. Freedom is everything to her. You have to work harder on your marriage."

"I was," Francis retorted, "until you brought Anthony here. When her brother is around, Katarina doesn't care about anyone or anything else."

****

Katarina sat cross-legged on the middle of Anthony's bed, watching him rummage through the few items of clothing he'd brought with him.

"We have to get you some new clothes," she pronounced. "You can't go around looking like a priest all the time."

He laughed. "But I am a priest, Katarina."

"Well, then, you don't have to look like a destitute German priest. Our Father Murphy wears colorful shirts and shorts. Nobody here wears black the way you do unless someone has died. Trust me."

"I don't need a new wardrobe."

"You're on vacation in Hawaii and you've been walking around in black wool for days. Today that changes."

"Whatever you say." He gave up. What was the harm in a couple of shirts?

Katarina jumped off the bed. "I'll ask the cook to pack a picnic basket. We'll have lunch on the beach."

Francis was waiting for her at the bottom of the stairs and pulled her into the library.

"You're hurting my arm, Francis," she said stiffly. "What do you want?"

His eyes bored into her. "I want you to understand that nothing is changing just because Anthony is here. I will not allow him to interfere in your life the way he did in Berlin."

"My brother is hardly likely to ask me to carry out an undercover mission in Honolulu," Katarina retorted.

"You are my wife, Katarina. Just remember that. You owe me your loyalty, not him."

She pulled her arm out of his grasp. "I don't owe you anything. I've paid my dues." As she turned and stalked out of the room, he slammed his fist on the desk and cursed.

****

The wind billowed the blanket as they spread it in the sand. Katarina demanded that Anthony remove his black socks and clunky shoes. She was dressed in white shorts and a lime green short-sleeved shirt that showed off her long, tanned limbs. As she arranged the fried chicken and pineapple, Anthony held the squirming two-year-old Douglas and stared slack-jawed at the dolphins. Douglas squealed in delight.

"God has done marvels on this planet, hasn't he, Katarina?"

"Well, I guess if you have to thank someone, it might as well be him."

"Katarina, I had hoped that in this new place your faith would return."

She shrugged. "I like Father Murphy, but moving to Hawaii didn't erase everything that happened in Germany."

Anthony stroked Douglas's head. "Gordon told me that you lost the baby and how sick you were."

With a sigh, Katarina said, "I suppose he also told you that Francis and I are not exactly getting along."

"He's twenty years older than you and he likes things his own way. You knew that when you married him. But he loves you." Anthony set Douglas down on the blanket, and Katarina began pulling chicken off the bone for her son.

"Anthony, please. He loves me when he wants to."

"I don't believe that. I see it in his eyes."

"Then we are looking at different eyes. My God, Anthony, he's having an affair with the woman he was engaged to before he went to Germany. I don't make him happy. Why should I pretend he makes me happy?"

"But look at all he's given you!" Anthony gestured to the beach and the house up the hill. "He brought you here because he wanted you here."

Katarina shook her head. "We both know he brought me here because I am the mother of his son, and around here, sons are everything." She blew out her breath and stretched her legs out in front of her on the blanket. "I'm in shackles, Anthony. All this wide open space around me, yet I feel like I can hardly move."

"I don't know what to say, Katarina. I came all these miles hoping to find you happy, hoping to see the joy missing from your letters."

She smiled. "You're here now. That's my joy." She pushed the chicken toward him. "Eat up. We're going into town to get you some clothes."

"But how will we get there?"

A grin cracked her face in half. "I have a driver's license now. And the Lee family has charge accounts all over town."

****

They returned with their arms full of packages. Francis was in the living room when they tumbled into the house. He was usually in the fields at this time of day, so Katarina was startled to find him sitting there.

"Katarina," Francis said sharply, "this is the third day in a row you failed to tell me where you were going. We discussed this just this morning."

She was momentarily without words.

Anthony came to the rescue. "Aren't you overreacting, Francis?" he asked. "Katarina is not a child. We just did a little shopping."

Francis pulled himself to his full stature. "I don't see how this concerns you, Anthony." He glared at Katarina. "I'll expect you on the terrace in one hour for drinks. Father has invited a few people for an informal dinner party. Father Murphy will be there."

Katarina caved inside. She didn't want to share Anthony with anyone, much less a room full of the Lees' friends. But Anthony responded brightly.

"I look forward to it," Anthony said. "Katarina has already told me how much she likes Father Murphy."

It was not the small dinner party Katarina had hoped for. There were twenty couples attending, along with all the Lees. Katarina dressed in a flowing turquoise pantsuit with large orchids painted on the fabric and put a flower in her hair. She insisted Anthony shed his clerical clothing and dress like a native in some of the clothing they'd purchased that day. He was clearly uncomfortable in the tourist role but cut a striking figure, nevertheless. Female heads turned all around the room as drinks were poured.

Katarina dutifully stayed at Francis's side.

After meeting Anthony, Father Murphy sidled over to Francis and Katarina.

"Your brother makes a fine figure of a man, doesn't he, Katarina?" the priest said.

Katarina smiled. "The women here seem to think so."

"He seems to draw people to him. I suppose he's always been that way?"

"He particularly draws women," Katarina said. "Some people would say he has no business being a priest."

"Surely you're not serious." The priest seemed genuinely shocked.

"Relax, Father. Anthony has loved God since he was ten years old. No woman would ever take him away from the priesthood. He told me once that I envy him because he loves God and I don't. You don't have to worry about Anthony and his God."

She stopped abruptly, realizing how bitter she sounded. Both Francis and Father Murphy were staring at her.

"I think dinner will be served soon," Francis said awkwardly.

****

Francis was up early the next morning, hoping for a long ride before attending to plantation business. He was startled to find Anthony waiting for him at the stables.

"I was hoping I could join you," Anthony said.

Francis nodded. "Certainly." He supposed there was no point in avoiding this conversation. He selected a horse for Anthony, and the groomsmen saddled the animals. They began a slow trot across the plantation.

"Francis," Anthony said, "I haven't quite adjusted to the time change, so I'm sleeping at odd hours. I was out on the balcony about four this morning and was surprised to see Katarina curled up, crying."

"The dreams," Francis explained. "She thinks someone is following her."

"Still? I'd hoped the move here would change all that."

"Well, it hasn't, and she refuses to see a therapist. She went to a few sessions, and then she stopped and wouldn't go back."

"I'm sorry to hear that."

"The dreams don't happen every night," Francis said. "Sometimes weeks will go by and she sleeps soundly. Then it starts up again. She can't find peace, and I certainly can't give it to her. She can't seem to leave the past behind."

"She's always been very sensitive," Anthony observed.

Francis laughed loudly. "Please, Anthony. Your sister has nerves of steel when she wants them. She stands up to me every chance she gets. God help anyone who stands in her way when she wants something." He felt suddenly sad for Anthony. The priest was in a battle with his own soul for involving his family, especially his sister, and he was taking all the blame on his own shoulders.

****

Francis gave them about two hours' warning that

the entire family would be flying to Oahu for the King Kamehameha Day Parade and Holoku Ball. Katarina was grateful she had gone overboard in shopping for Anthony.

Katarina was thrilled to be on Oahu. Francis so seldom wanted to leave Kauai. He seemed content with a life that revolved around the plantation and occasional dinner parties. He had taken her to Oahu only three times since her arrival in Hawaii more than a year ago, and both times were day trips—essentially for a business lunch that gave Katarina an excuse to do a bit of shopping. Her delight at having three days on the island was evident.

"This is freedom!" she said to Anthony as they walked down the sidewalk in a major shopping area. "When I come here, I feel alive."

Anthony had been waiting for a moment like this. "You are free, Katarina," he said simply. "No one is following you any more."

"You think it's all been my imagination," she responded. "I would have thought that episode with Frederick's brother would have convinced you."

"It did! That's why I'm trying to tell you. Frederick's brother turned up dead in the river a few weeks ago."

Katarina stopped in her tracks and stared at her brother. "Grigory?" she asked, her voice barely audible.

Anthony shrugged. "He doesn't tell me specifics. But I know he never stopped looking after that night."

"He did that for me?"

"He has always loved you," Anthony said softly. "It broke his heart when you married Francis."

"He never said—" She choked on her own words

as tears slid down her face. "Would it have changed anything?" Anthony asked softly.

Katarina shook her head. No, she would not have done anything differently. She had wanted out of Berlin so badly, and Grigory could not have given her that. "It's really over now, isn't it?"

Anthony wrapped his arms around Katarina. "You don't have to run any more, Katarina. You can let go and be happy."

"But you've seen what Francis is like now," she responded. "I'm happy to be here on Oahu, but he didn't ask me if I wanted to come. He just ordered both of us to be ready on time."

Anthony agreed as they resumed walking. "Yes, I've had a glimpse of what things are like for you. But still, at some level, I believe he cares for you."

"You warned me not to marry a man I didn't love."

"I was wrong to try to tell you what to do, Katarina. As you always remind me, you're a big girl and you make your own choices."

"And now I must live with them—is that what you're saying?"

"No! Please don't misunderstand. I'm just reminding you that you still make your own choices."

Their steps had taken them back to the Royal Hawaiian Hotel. The ball would begin in a few hours.

****

All heads turned when Katarina entered the ballroom between her brother and her husband, both striking men in their own right. She wore a bright, form-fitting red dress with a slit well up one side, exposing her thigh. Her tanned legs were free of stockings, her feet tucked into soft red sandals. The men were in tuxedos, Anthony looking distinguished and un-priestlike.

Katarina caught her breath when she saw the U.S. Navy uniform across the room. The beautiful redheaded woman on the man's arm was the same one who had waved at him across the hotel lobby more than a year ago. To Katarina's surprise, Gordon took Katarina by the hand and led her to this very couple.

"Lydia," Gordon said brightly, "how lovely to see you. I haven't seen your father in such a long time. Tell him we need to play golf."

"I'll do that," the redhead responded. "And who is this stunning woman at your side?"

"This is my daughter-in-law, Katarina Lee."

"I'd heard Francis had married."

"I don't believe I know your friend," Gordon hinted, nodded toward the Naval officer.

"This is John Malloy," Lydia explained. "He's a dear friend, a former lover, actually."

Katarina sucked in her breath; even Gordon seemed startled.

Lydia laughed. "Don't look so surprised. I'm just stating the truth. I followed John around the world, but it didn't work out. However, he introduced me to my husband, George, which is very much working out. We just had our first child."

The handsome John extended his hand to Gordon. "I'm pleased to meet you both."

The orchestra struck into a song, and couples began to drift to the dance floor. Lydia turned to her friend. "John, why don't you dance with Katarina while I go say hello to her husband—and find my own."

"I'd be delighted." John Malloy offered an open

palm, and Katarina found herself laying her hand in his.

The young officer was a smooth, experienced dancer. He held her close with a hand firmly placed at her lower back. Their legs moved together in such synchronized motion that images of the ballet flitted through her mind.

"So where are you from?" Katarina asked out of politeness. "Iowa. I'm the all-American boy."

"Then you must have had a sweetheart."

"I did, but she didn't want to wait until after the war to marry."

"And Lydia?"

"Let's just say her feelings for me were never mutual."

"I'm sorry for her sake," Katarina said. Her heart was beating too fast.

"I've met you before," he said into her ear. "In time I'll figure out where."

Katarina blushed. "I bumped into you in the hotel lobby last year."

"Surely I would remember meeting you."

"No, I mean I literally bumped into you."

He shook his head. "No, that's not it. I'm sure I've seen you somewhere, in another setting. It will come to me."

He spun her around—and she was staring right into Francis's face.

"Do you mind if I cut in for a dance with my wife?" Francis asked, firmly taking control of his wife's body.

John stepped away and bowed slightly. "Delighted to meet you, Mrs. Lee."

"Likewise."

Francis skillfully danced her away. She felt John's eyes follow her but resisted the impulse to raise her eyes to meet his. Instead she looked blankly over Francis's shoulder at nothing in particular.

Katarina soon broke off the dance and moved toward a table to sit down. "How dare you?" she said. "You've embarrassed me beyond words."

"It was a mistake to dance with that man."

"It was just a dance, Francis! This is a ball, after all."

"If you want to dance, dance with me."

"Stop treating me like one of your stupid cows." To Katarina's relief, she saw Anthony approaching them.

"Everything okay?" Anthony asked, looking from Francis to Katarina.

"Just fine," Francis was quick to respond.

Katarina rolled her eyes. "Oh, when will this nightmare end? What is Maria doing here?"

"It's a public place, and a holiday," Francis said matter-of-factly. "Why shouldn't Maria be here?"

Katarina glared at her husband.

Meanwhile, her brother moved smoothly to intercept Maria.

"We haven't met," he said congenially, "but I would love to have this dance. My name is Anthony." With his hand on her elbow, he turned her around and led her to the dance floor.

Katarina sat with an elbow on the table and leaned her head in her hand. "Great. Now my brother the priest is dancing with your lover."

"I've told you a dozen times, she means nothing to me."

"Does she know that?" Katarina challenged. "Somehow I don't think that's the view she has of things."

"Perhaps your brother the holy man will set her straight."

Chapter 27

Honolulu: August 1949

A tap on his shoulder caused Anthony to turn away from the luscious dessert on the plate before him. He had momentarily found himself alone at the Lee table. He looked up to see a young naval lieutenant.

"Excuse me, I'm John Malloy. I'm looking for the young woman who was sitting with you a few minutes ago."

"I believe she is dancing with her husband," Anthony answered.

"I'm afraid I may have caused offense earlier," Malloy said. "I was dancing with Mrs. Lee, and her husband seemed unhappy about it. I thought perhaps I ought to apologize."

"I'm sure they'll be back in a few minutes, if you'd care to sit down and wait." Anthony gestured to a chair. "I'm Father Anthony Von Rahmel."

"A priest! I didn't realize. I come from a Catholic family. My ancestors came mostly from County Cork in Ireland. We seem to have a lot of priests and nuns in our family, and my mother assured me they were saying Mass for me daily during the war. I guess it worked— I'm still here."

Anthony was relaxed, enjoying the young man's conversation.

"Von Rahmel..." Malloy mused. "The name rings a bell. Did I detect a German accent?"

"I live in Berlin," Anthony said. "I'm here visiting my sister—Mrs. Lee."

"Oh! That's it."

"That's what?"

"Katarina Lee was Katarina Von Rahmel."

"Why, yes, she was," Anthony said, his curiosity piqued. "How do you know her name?"

"She was a dancer, was she not?"

"You sound as if you spent some time in Berlin," Anthony observed.

"I did," Malloy answered. "I believe I saw her perform."

"She would be delighted to hear you say that. She has no performance venue since she moved here."

Gordon approached the table. "Lieutenant Malloy, I see you have met my new friend Anthony."

John shook hands with Gordon. "Yes, Father Von Rahmel."

Gordon laughed. "We were trying to disguise him as a civilian tonight, but apparently he broke his own cover."

"I was hoping to speak to your son and daughter-in-law," John said hopefully, glancing around.

"I'm afraid you've missed Katarina," Gordon said. "Francis put her in a car and sent her back to the hotel."

"But Francis is still here?" Anthony asked, puzzled. He answered his own question when he spotted Francis in a far corner of the room in an animated conversation with Maria. During his own dance with her, Anthony had identified himself and tried to warn Maria to leave Francis alone, but it seemed his effort had been futile.

"This is not my son's proudest moment," Gordon said softly.

****

Back at the penthouse a short time later, Anthony found Katarina on a plush sofa. She had changed from her gown into a casual robe.

"What happened?" Anthony asked. "Why didn't you tell me you were leaving? I would have come back with you."

"It was Francis's decision for me to leave," she said simply.

"Oh."

"I am going to be happy, Anthony, one way or another."

He spoke cautiously. "I certainly want you to be happy, Katarina."

"Then you won't be hard on me about decisions I make for the future."

"What are you talking about, Katarina?"

Katarina rose and began to pace. "You saw her. You danced with her! She's a gorgeous woman, Anthony, and my husband thinks nothing of flaunting her in my face."

"I tried to reason with her," Anthony said. "She is a determined young woman."

"Something has to change."

"Don't make any rash decisions, Katarina."

"But I will make a decision," she answered curtly, "and soon."

****

Back on the family plantation, routine returned. Francis was busy with crops and orders and staffing.

308

Katarina and Anthony walked the beach and gardens and indulged in long conversations and tickle-giggle fests with Douglas. Anthony communicated with his bishop and extended his stay in Hawaii; Katarina seemed too fragile for him to leave right now.

A few weeks later, after a quiet lunch in the garden, Katarina said simply to her brother, "I'm leaving Francis. I'm taking Douglas and leaving. I just have to choose the right time."

"Katarina, please," Anthony pleaded. "I'm a priest. I can't condone leaving your marriage."

"Then you condone his behavior with Maria?"

"I'll talk to him again."

She laughed aloud. "He doesn't want to listen to you, Anthony. He hates that you're here at all. Don't delude yourself."

"But marriage is sacred and holy. You made promises to each other."

"I'm your sister, Anthony. I'm going to do this. Are you going to help me or not?"

****

A break came a few days later when Gordon encouraged Anthony and Katarina to go to Honolulu for a few days. Gordon was anxious for his guest to enjoy Hawaii as much as possible. A few days in the penthouse without any social obligations would allow Anthony an experience he would never forget. Under the circumstances, Francis could hardly protest. And under the circumstances, there was nothing unusual about Katarina packing a few things for herself and Douglas.

Katarina could hardly believe her good luck. She packed carefully, knowing she could take only so much without raising suspicion. In between her skirts and blouses, though, she tucked in a few key pieces of jewelry she had acquired during her marriage.

On the first night in Honolulu, Katarina put Douglas to bed while Anthony ordered dinner from room service.

"I'm not going back, Anthony," she said as they settled down to eat.

"Are you sure this is what you want?" he asked, pouring wine into her glass.

"I will not live my life in a prison," she answered adamantly. Her fingers clenched the stem of the wineglass so tightly that it snapped. Blood instantly stained the pink tablecloth.

Anthony jumped up and wrapped a napkin around her finger. The cut seemed fairly deep.

"You may want to see a doctor," he said. "The hotel must have someone on call."

She shook her head. "I've suffered much worse without the benefit of medical intervention."

Anthony sighed. "He'll come looking for you; you know that. Finally, you have no one chasing you, and you're going to start all over."

"This is different. I have a chance to be truly free."

"He's not going to give up that easily. Despite the way he treats you, he doesn't want you to leave."

"That's just because it will be embarrassing for him, and he'll lose Douglas."

"You can't stay here long. This is the first place he'll look if you don't go home on schedule."

"In a few days I'll phone Gordon and tell him we decided to stay longer," she said. "I brought jewelry. You may be a priest, but you are worldly enough to find a place to convert it to cash. Then we can move."

"I don't know anything about Honolulu!" he protested.

She smiled slyly. "Father Anthony, you've done a lot of things you didn't know anything about."

Katarina hadn't figured on Francis's impatience. Naively she had assumed she had several days to make a plan—until the day Francis expected her to return home. But they had been in Honolulu only two days when Francis confronted her in an elevator.

"You and I are going to chat," he said.

A chill ran down her back as Francis gripped her elbow and ushered her toward the hotel bar. He ordered two scotch-and-sodas and leaned back in the chair to take a long look at her.

She started to speak, but he interrupted her before she got a word out. "I will do the talking, Katarina."

"Damn it, Francis. Leave me alone. I want a divorce."

"I said I would do the talking."

"You don't love me. Just let me go."

"Shut up, Katarina."

She stood up to leave, but he grabbed her wrist and twisted till she sat down again.

"When I am through with you, you will never see your son again."

She couldn't let him see her shake. "I will bring your lovely mistress to court," she said through clenched teeth.

"Katarina, I always get what I want. Your brother will not be here forever. When he's gone, you will see you are truly alone, and perhaps you will come to your senses."

He stood to leave. "If I have to, I will have you declared mentally incompetent, but in any case you will never see Douglas again. I also have the power to send you back to Berlin any time I want." He stopped. Why was he doing this, he wondered. He just wanted her to come home, say she loved him, wanted him. Why was this so difficult? "I'll give you a few days to see the light. I have business to look after, but I assure you I will know every move you make."

She waited until he left before she downed her scotch in one swallow.

Chapter 28

Honolulu: September 1949

Katarina had made up her mind and hardened her heart. Anthony could see arguing with her was pointless. Everything in his being told him marriage was sacred, and he wanted to believe there was still hope that Francis could be reasonable and make an effort to restore his relationship with his wife. But even if Francis relented, Katarina would not. Anthony knew that now.

Anthony cared for Douglas while the little boy's mother worked. If Katarina was going to have a life of her own, away from Francis, she had to support herself somehow. Dancing was her only skill, and the months of working out in the studio at the Lee plantation had paid off. She could still dance, perhaps not with the glimmering artistry of her pre-imprisonment performances, but still with shine and beauty. Once she had told the hotel manager who she really was—other than Francis Lee's foreign wife—he was anxious to bill her as a star attraction. Billboards all over the island boasted of Munich's premier ballerina now appearing on Oahu at the Royal Hawaiian Hotel. Tonight was her opening night, and Anthony had butterflies in his own stomach. He knew his sister would perform flawlessly. He also knew she was still under Francis's watchful eye; every time Anthony saw a stranger look their way, he wondered if the stranger was on Francis's payroll. He had managed to sell a few pieces of the jewelry, but Katarina still needed a substantial sum before she could break away once and for all. She needed this job, even if it was right under Francis's nose. So far Francis had left them alone, but they both knew that could change in an instant.

Uncle and nephew were taking a walk while Katarina practiced when a car pulled up to the curb and Lydia stepped out.

"Father, I'm delighted to see you. I tried to reach you at the plantation and thought perhaps you had returned to Germany. I only just found out you were right here on Oahu." She hooked an arm through his. "May I join your walk?"

"If you don't mind going at the speed of a two-year-old," Anthony answered.

Douglas was quite absorbed in ferreting out just the right pebbles to pick up. "Father, I confess I had a reason for tracking you down."

He looked at her with raised eyebrows.

"Don't worry. It's all completely appropriate," she said, laughing slightly. "Some of our business representatives are planning a trip to Berlin. We're interested in expanding our holdings. We're convinced Germany is headed for prosperous times, and we want to be in on the ground floor."

"I'm not sure what you have in mind. I'm a priest, after all, not a business man."

"But your family has holdings. We think your factories may be just what we need."

"Some of them are in the Eastern sector," he

explained. "I'm not sure how useful those would be."

"And the ones in the West?"

"They do not operate at anywhere near pre-war levels."

"Then perhaps there is room for an agreement after all." They were passing a restaurant. Lydia took a deep breath of the cooking smells. "I'm famished. How about if we go inside? Wouldn't Douglas like a hamburger?"

Anthony laughed. "The good old American hamburger and fries."

"Exactly."

Over lunch Anthony asked more specific questions about Lydia's business needs and agreed it would be worthwhile to have her business team visit the Von Rahmel factories and talk with Jona and Hans. He offered to make arrangements as soon as he returned to Berlin, which he expected would be soon.

What he failed to tell anyone was that he was ordered to Paris; he would be leaving Berlin. He felt that even for him the fight was over. Berlin would be a new place, Germany would survive, and he needed a new beginning.

"May I be frank?" Lydia asked as she encouraged Douglas to eat more of his burger.

"By all means."

"I wasn't sure when you would return home, because there seems to be trouble in paradise. When I called the Lee house looking for you, Francis's sister told me in great detail what's going on between him and Katarina. I know you want to help as much as you can before you have to go back to your own life."

"Yes, of course."

"Then tell your sister to be careful. Francis has tremendous influence all over the islands. She will have to reckon with him, whether she wants to or not. Frankly, I'm shocked she had the courage to cross him and take his son with her even this far."

"You will never know the depth of her courage," Anthony said simply. They strolled back to Lydia's car, and she drove them back to the hotel.

As Anthony and Douglas got out of the car, she said, "Father, I'll be here tonight if you care to talk more. My husband and I are bringing John Malloy and his date here to see a new dancer. She is supposed to be quite spectacular."

Anthony couldn't help but laugh. "What's so funny?" Lydia demanded.

He shook his head. "Nothing. Tell me tomorrow what you think of this new dancer. If you're free, I'd like to go back for another American hamburger."

"I'll see you in the lobby at noon," she said. "My young cousin is visiting. I'll bring her along to look after Douglas."

When the curtain went up that night, Lydia's mouth dropped open. Beside her, John Malloy's jaw did the same. He was spellbound as they announced the dancer's name and gave a short history of her career. When the orchestra struck its first chord and she began to move, the audience was mesmerized. Lydia glanced at John's date, a petite Navy nurse, wishing he would pay half as much attention to the woman beside him as he did to the one on the stage.

John excused himself immediately after the performance and told the others he would meet them outside the hotel. Then he made his way backstage;

smiling his way past anyone who wondered what he was doing there. In the doorway to her dressing room, he watched her brushing her beautiful silken hair.

Katarina turned when she heard him clear his throat. Her eyes widened. "Why, you're the gentleman who danced with me."

He grinned. "Now I remember where I first saw you. In Berlin. You were dancing for the American officers and their wives."

Katarina was amused at how nervous he was as he shifted back and forth on his feet. He was even more stunning in a black tux than he had been in his naval white dress uniform.

"I can't stay," he said. "I'm with friends. But I would love to take you to dinner another night."

She leaned her head to one side to take him in. "You met my husband," she said.

"It's just dinner. That's all I'm asking."

Katarina slowly nodded. "I'd be delighted."

"Tomorrow night? I'll pick you up after your performance."

Going out with this young man could get them both in trouble. Katarina knew that. Yet there was something irresistible about him.

The other intractable truth was that Anthony would not approve.

****

She was right.

"Katarina, I came here to help you through some emotional problems and help you put your marriage back together," he said. "Suddenly, I've helped you leave your husband, and now you want to see another man. You're still married, Katarina."

"Excommunicate me if you must, Anthony, but I am not going back to Francis. I've got a job, and as soon as I get a paycheck Douglas and I will move and make a new life. Why shouldn't I go to dinner with a lovely young man?"

The audience loved her again the second night. John was in the audience once again, this time alone. They had dinner that night, and again the next night, and on the day after that, they took a long walk on the beach before her rehearsal began. Katarina and John saw each other every day for a week and spoke on the phone several times each day, as well. They talked incessantly, like old friends, and Katarina's heart beat faster just thinking of John Malloy. Yet he never touched her. Francis left seething messages with the hotel desk, which Katarina ignored. After only a week with John, Francis had faded considerably into unreality.

In their second week together, John suggested a drive. When they reached Lookout Point in the middle of the island, John pulled the car to the side of the road and turned off the motor. He turned to face her.

"I would really like to kiss you, Katarina," he said softly but firmly.

She wanted him to kiss her, too. But was it too soon, when she still had Francis breathing down her neck? Sooner or later she would have to deal with the messages he was leaving or meet him face to face.

"John," she said, turning away, "I wish I had met you at a different time in my life. Right now, I'll only bring you trouble."

His eyes were fixed on her face. With one finger he turned her face back toward his.

"You could never bring me trouble. I know it's complicated. I know you're married and have a little boy. But I can't believe you plan to go back to Francis. If I did, I'd back off immediately."

She shook her head. "No, I'm not going back."

"Honesty is all I ask for." He took her in his arms and kissed her long and softly, and she willingly pressed her body against his. "I love you, Katarina."

Abruptly, Katarina pushed away. "No! It's too soon for that."

"Love chooses its own time, Katarina."

"Come back in a year. Perhaps my life will be less complicated then."

He shook his head. "It's too late to put me off. I'm completely smitten. I'll help you get a divorce. Then we can marry."

Involuntarily, she laughed. His face fell.

"I'm sorry, John," she said when she regained composure. "I know you're serious. I've loved every minute we've spent together, but marriage? There's so much you don't know about me, and if you knew the truth—"

"It wouldn't change a thing. I know myself well enough to know that when I'm sure of something, I go after it. And I'm sure of you."

His eyes did not waver.

"All right," she finally said. "Let's see where this goes. It won't be easy to divorce Francis, and your nice Catholic family won't be thrilled you want to marry a divorced woman with a child. We could never get married in the church, you know."

He touched her nose with his finger. "They will be happy to know your brother is a priest. That will go a long way with them."

She sighed and smiled. "Okay, you win."

He leaned in and kissed her over and over.

When she returned to the hotel, the spell was broken. Anthony was pacing around the penthouse, and instantly she knew why.

"Francis was here," she said flatly.

"He tried to take Douglas," Anthony said, cutting to the chase. "We got into a bad argument. This is not a good time for you to be starting up another romance. Francis has his spies, you know, so he's fully aware of how you're spending your free time."

"How I spend my time is my business, Anthony."

Anthony groaned. "Katarina, why couldn't you just wait a little longer?"

"I can't be a prisoner!" she shrieked.

"He'll be back, Katarina."

The pounding at the door made them both jump. "Katarina, open this door immediately. The penthouse belongs to my family, and I have a key. There's no point in trying to keep me out."

When she opened the door, Francis pushed her with such force she nearly fell.

From across the room, Douglas started to whimper.

Anthony sprang to the door and let out a swing, smashing his fist into Francis's jaw.

"I warned you an hour ago," Anthony said. "I will not tolerate the way you are treating my sister."

"She is my wife," Francis said as he wiped blood from his face.

"Then treat her like one," Anthony retorted.

Francis stabbed a finger in the air toward Katarina. "Did you know she went to a lawyer? I will escort you to hell, Katarina, and leave you there where you belong. But my son is coming home with me."

By now Douglas was wailing. Francis strode across the room and picked him up, which only made the child cry louder.

"What have you done to him?" Francis demanded. "Why is he afraid of his own father?"

"Francis," Katarina cried, "don't do this! Just give me a divorce. You can marry Maria. That's what you want."

"Don't tell me what I want!" He shoved the boy into Katarina's arms. "Calm him down," he said. "I'll give you a few minutes to pack his things while I make arrangements for the plane. My son is going home today." Francis stormed out. He stopped in the middle of the hallway. For the first time since he could remember, tears came to his eyes. All he wanted was her. Why did he treat he like that? What was wrong with him? He only wanted her, always had.

Lydia came through the door before Anthony could close it behind Francis. "It appears I came at a bad time," Lydia said calmly.

Douglas clutched his mother's neck, but his wailing had subsided.

"Father Anthony," Lydia said, "perhaps you could take Douglas to another room. I'd like to talk to your sister."

Douglas willingly went to Anthony's arms, and the priest withdrew, leaving Katarina and Lydia alone.

"Mrs. Lee, I realize I hardly know you," Lydia began, "but I happen to be quite fond of my old friend John Malloy. I came here to tell you it's a bad time for you to start anything with John. I can see now that going back to your husband is not an option, but I would still like for you to stay away from John until your divorce is final."

"He wants to marry me!" Katarina protested.

"I know that's what he thinks he wants," Lydia responded, "but I can't stand the thought of his getting hurt."

"Why would you think I'd want to hurt him?"

"I'm sure you don't want to hurt him, but I don't like the thought of having him in Francis's path."

"I don't either," Katarina said, as she sagged into a chair and put her head in her hands. "I told him I would only bring trouble, but he doesn't care."

Lydia nodded. "I know how stubborn he can be." She paused. "Look, you can't stay here."

"I know. As soon as I get a paycheck, we'll move."

"No, you need to move tonight. Now. Francis will be back tonight."

"But where will I go?" Katarina cried. "I have no money of my own yet."

"I have a place," Lydia said. "We'll go right now."

"But Francis—"

"Leave Francis to me. We've been doing business with his family for two decades, but I can change that whenever I want. He won't want to have to explain that to his father."

A voice came from the still-open door. "I agree, it's time for you to leave." They turned to see John standing there. "I saw a limousine pulling away with Francis in it," he said. "I had to see if you were all right."

"We're just leaving," Lydia said. She gestured to a closed bedroom door. "Go get Anthony. Tell him to start packing."

John complied, and in a moment Anthony returned.

"I didn't want to leave you like this," Anthony said, rubbing his forehead.

"What are you talking about?" Katarina asked. "We're going together."

Anthony swallowed hard "Katarina, I got a message from Rome. I have to leave in three days. The Vatican wants to have 'a talk' with me, as they so kindly put it. Most likely it will deal with moving me elsewhere, away from Berlin."

"You can't desert me now!" Katarina protested.

"I don't have a choice. I took a vow of obedience, and I have pushed up against the limits by staying in Hawaii this long."

Frantic, Katarina turned to Lydia. "Please tell him he can't leave!"

Lydia put an arm around Katarina's shoulder. "We'll take care of you. I'm not going to let Francis hurt you. I'll take you and Douglas with me now, and John and Anthony can finish packing and come later."

****

They came around the north side of the island and pulled up to a white cottage trimmed in blue. Katarina carried Douglas into a great room with large windows that overlooked the ocean. On top of a grand piano was a fresh bouquet of flowers. At one end of the great room was a dining nook and at the other end a small bar. To the right was a bedroom and a large bathroom. The loft was made into a second bedroom. The cottage had a wraparound verandah shaded by palm trees. French doors led directly out to the beach.

Lydia took Douglas from Katarina's arms. "I'll

settle Douglas in the bedroom while you try to relax."

"Thank you. Do you mind if I pour myself a drink?"

"Help yourself."

Katarina crossed to the bar as Lydia disappeared with Douglas. She gulped scotch, and when Lydia returned, Katarina pretended to be pouring her first drink. She had long hated the smell of any kind of whisky, but she needed a drink, and it was handy.

A few minutes later, they heard another car pull up and watched as Anthony and John carried in suitcases.

Lydia showed Katarina around the well-stocked kitchen. "George and I come here to get away sometimes. I think you'll find everything you need. I'll watch Douglas for you when you're working, for now. The rest we'll figure out as we go along."

"This is incredibly generous of you," Katarina said. "I'm virtually a stranger, but you are helping me."

"You're in danger," Lydia said simply. "How can I turn away?"

Anthony spoke up. "Are you sure Francis won't come here?"

"Francis doesn't know about this place," Lydia assured them.

"But if he's been watching Katarina—"

"I will make sure to let Francis know he has to leave Katarina alone or explain the loss of a profitable business arrangement to his father. Believe me, I can handle Francis Lee. I've known him all my life."

John stepped over to Katarina and wrapped her in his arms. "I wish you could stay," she said.

He kissed the top of her head. "Me too. But I'm shipping out on a short mission in a few hours. I'm just glad Lydia will be looking after you."

"You're leaving?" Katarina said, blanching. "How long will you be gone?"

"Just a week. It's a short trip." He leaned down to kiss her deeply, then led her by the hand to the door.

Katarina and Anthony stood in the middle of the great room as John and Lydia left. For a long time, they just looked at each other, then moved to stare out the window. She saw only darkness and heard the howling wind and the waves crashing on the beach.

"What a mess I've made," Katarina said. "How am I going to sort it all out when you're leaving me in three days?"

"You have Lydia now, and John. You won't be alone."

"But I hardy know Lydia, and I don't know how things will work out with John." Anthony rubbed her shoulders. "You'll have to be honest with John, Katarina. How much have you told him about your past? About Alexandra?"

She shook her head. "Practically nothing. And he doesn't care. He loves me just as I am."

"You'll have to tell him," Anthony prodded. "To really understand you, he has to know."

"Isn't it enough that he loves me?" Katarina asked, turning to face her brother. "Why do I have to keep reliving the past?"

"He has a right to know," Anthony insisted. "You have to tell him."

"Why? So he can be haunted by the images of children being thrown alive into pits and then set on fire? So he can know about the men? So the Nazi ghosts can chase him, as well?"

"Katarina, you can't control what happened in the past, but you can control the future. You survived against all odds. Don't let evil win now."

Katarina wiped her tears as she felt hysteria burgeon within her. She swallowed it immediately.

On the third day, Katarina and Lydia took Anthony to the airport. Lydia held Douglas while Katarina pressed her face to the terminal window, watching Anthony's plane rumble down the runway and lift off.

Flying from the other direction, John returned from his mission early. He drove out to the beach cottage immediately—and got there before Katarina did. He was waiting for her on the front step. She squealed with delight and fell into his arms while Lydia unlocked the front door. Katarina would not be alone on her first night without Anthony after all. Looking up, Katarina caught Lydia's eye.

"I think I'd like to have Douglas at my house overnight," Lydia said. "My son will be delighted to have someone to play with."

They waited until the car was out of sight before John gestured toward the bedroom. They were wildly pulling at one another's clothing, leaving a trail behind them.

He lay beside her after making love, pushing the hair from her face and studying her expression. "When you divorce, we'll marry right away."

She smiled. Any doubts she'd had a few days ago had dissipated. This was the man she wanted to spend the rest of her life with. He loved her for who she was at that moment in time, and she responded to him without wanting anything from him but love.

They made love again. His mouth was on every

inch of her, and it seemed so right.

No agenda, no reason to be together, just love, with hearts beating wildly for each other. He traced the scars on her back with one finger as they sat with a blanket around them.

"Can you talk about where the scars came from?" he asked softly.

Katarina took a deep breath and began talking. She told him about Frederick—but did not tell him the baby had survived, saying instead simply that the baby was dead to her. She told him she had been in a Nazi prison—but did not tell him she had submitted to the guards there to preserve the life of her child. She told him she had worked in the Resistance—but did not tell him she had slept with a soldier to keep Anthony safe in an attic. She told him she had married Francis for all the wrong reasons—but she did not say she had seduced him to make him marry her so she could get out of Berlin.

They talked for hours, but she guarded more than she told.

Chapter 29

Oahu: November 1949

Lydia had made her threat clear. Francis steered clear of Katarina when she came to the hotel to dance, and he couldn't get anywhere near his son. He decided to focus on Lieutenant John Malloy. Wherever John was, Katarina was sure to be. After calling in some favors at the naval base, he determined that John Malloy was spending the evening at a bar with friends.

Francis stormed into the bar. To his disappointment, he saw only Lydia, George, and John. No Katarina. Nevertheless he sauntered to their table and suggested that he and Lieutenant Malloy should have a private conversation. John picked up his drink and moved to another table, gesturing that Francis should sit down with him. Francis ordered a scotch.

"So you think you love her, Lieutenant," he said caustically.

John pushed his own drink away, determined not to let anything impair his judgment. Obviously Francis had started drinking long before arriving at the bar. John said nothing to Francis.

Francis's eyebrows rose. "Hypnotized by her brilliance, are you?" He leaned in closer and swirled his drink.

Still John said nothing.

"Let me tell you a secret. Don't hold your breath. I have no intention of divorcing her. She is a spice that will devour you. She'll taste like the sweetest honey that ever crossed her lips; then all of a sudden you'll realize those kisses will kill you. The honey goes into your blood, and it will poison you. You will die with a broken heart. That's what you have to look forward to."

"I don't believe that," John said simply. "The difference between you and me is that I do not want to own her. Katarina is her own spirit."

Francis threw back his drunken head and laughed. "Remember that when she goes running back to her brothers, or to some other man who tries to rescue her. She doesn't know how to make a move without consulting her precious Anthony."

"I think this conversation is over," John said. "You'll be hearing from Katarina's lawyer before too long, I'm sure."

With that, John stood up and returned to the table where he had left George and Lydia, refusing to turn his head and look again at Francis's seething face.

****

The Cottage: December 1949

Katarina tied her hair behind her neck. Douglas was napping. He was a sound sleeper and not likely to wake up for at least another half an hour, but she didn't want to leave him for more than a few minutes. Nevertheless, she was anxious for a swim, some way to dispel the physical tension mounting in her body. She locked the cottage and ran down to the beach. She would be gone no more than ten minutes.

As she started back toward the house, her energy spent after a vigorous but abbreviated swim in cold water, her eyes widened, and she screamed. Her feet carried her faster than she could ever imagine they could move. She reached the house just in time to see Douglas being placed in the family limousine. With his little arms around Francis's neck, Douglas saw his mother and called out to her. Francis set him in the car and left him there, slamming the door and turning to face Katarina. Despite the warmth of the sun, she shivered as she stood before him.

"Don't bother trying to call anyone," he said, his voice steely. "I cut the phone line. If you love your son as you say you do, you will come back and we will be a family."

Katarina said nothing as she felt herself slipping away into desperation.

Francis reached out and gripped her chin, forcing her to look at him. "Come home with me now, and this will all be over."

She stepped back from his reach. "I will have my son back without coming back to you. You'll hear from my lawyer. You can't take a child from his mother, no matter who you are."

He lurched forward and grabbed her long ponytail. Pulling her close, he kissed her, hard.

When he let go, she backed away from him, trembling and wiping the kiss from her lips. He pulled her close again, touching her in familiar ways. He touched her breasts as they heaved and slowly moved a hand down across her belly. Frozen for a moment, she could hardly believe he dared to do this.

She pushed him away. "You will never have me again! Just give me back my son!"

Francis laughed and shook his head. He joined

Douglas in the back of the limo and signaled the driver.

Katarina collapsed on the steps as she watched her son disappear.

The next morning when Lydia realized something was wrong with the phone, she drove out to the cottage and found Katarina in a heap on the floor, surrounded by empty wine bottles. Lydia helped her to the bathroom, where Katarina became violently ill.

When Katarina finally emerged from a long shower, Lydia handed her a mug of fresh coffee. The steam swirling around her face pinked up her cheeks and an otherwise colorless face. Lydia smoothed Katarina's tangled hair from her face, waiting for Katarina to explain what happened.

"Get dressed," Lydia said, when she knew the whole story. "We're going to the lawyer's office now."

Katarina looked up at Lydia. "I feel like such a fool. What will I tell John?"

"He loves you. That's all that matters."

"Why are you helping me?" Katarina asked. "You wanted me to stay away from John."

"I've seen more of Francis than I can ignore," was the quick response.

Within an hour, Katarina's lawyer was making furious threats on the phone to Francis's lawyers but getting no result. The final answer was that Katarina could return to her husband and son. Nothing prevented her from doing so. Her own lawyer concluded they would have to fight for custody after the divorce was final, but there was little he could do before that.

Katarina made it through the days by keeping busy. John spent as much time as he could with her. When they were together, they made love greedily. He made her forget what was going on in the present, and sometimes even the past. She rarely woke with the old nightmares if John was lying beside her. When he was not there, she held his pillow, inhaling his scent to keep him near. Whenever possible, he attended her performances. Katarina danced, and she made love, and she savored her freedom. Gordon once sent a recent photograph of her son via Lydia, but no note. Anthony wrote less frequently now, and when she read his letters, Katarina could sense he didn't know what to say to her.

She was a married woman madly in love—and living with—another man. Longing for Douglas made her heart feel it would burst, but she could not give up John.

****

Kauai: May 1950

Francis hung up the phone after talking to Lydia. She had pleaded with him to stop trying to control Katarina. This nonsense had been going on for six months. Couldn't he see that Katarina was not coming back to him? Did he really believe it was in his son's best interest to keep his mother away from him? They had known each other since they were children, she said, and she was certain he had not lost all vestige of kindness, so why was he doing this to Katarina?

"She isn't being honest with any of you," he'd told Lydia. He'd wanted to tell her to ask Katarina about Alexandra, but he held back. That was his secret weapon for court, when it was time to show she was an unfit mother.

He turned and looked at the woman in his bed. "Maria, I think it's time for you to go. I don't need the servants talking."

Maria laughed. "You don't think they know how many nights I spend with you?" She let the bedding drop away, exposing her bare breasts. "You'll take her back, if she comes back, won't you?"

Francis threw back the blankets on his side of the bed and swung his feet to the floor. "Maria, I've never lied to you. Yes, I would."

"She won't come back," Maria said as he disappeared into the bathroom.

****

Oahu: July 1950

Katarina sat in the doctor's office, stunned. The nausea was not her nerves after all. She had been so careful this time. Now what would she do? How was she going to explain this pregnancy? Three and a half months, and she didn't even show. She'd been so distraught in recent weeks that she'd eaten little and had actually lost weight instead of gaining.

She walked for a long time on the beach before it came to her. This was her ace. Francis would have to let her go now and give her a divorce. He would never stand for being married to her now that she was bearing another man's child.

That evening she called Francis and asked to meet with him. He coldly said he would send the plane for her, so she should be at the airport in the morning. John was gone on a long assignment and had left his car for Katarina to use. She hardly slept that night, but instead of fear keeping her awake, it was excitement. This was sure to work! In the morning she drove to the airport and looked for the Lees' plane.

On Kauai, the family limousine was waiting for her

and whisked her back to the plantation. She looked long and hard at the house as the wind plastered her skirt against her legs. Somewhere in that house was her son, six months older than the last time she'd seen him. Katarina had not tried to negotiate with Francis to see Douglas on this visit, but still she hoped for at least a glimpse of him.

The front door opened, and Francis appeared. "Let's go inside so you can tell me what was so urgent that you actually found your way back here." He led her to the library and took his seat in the leather chair behind the desk.

Katarina noticed how tired he looked, for the first time seeing the sadness in his eyes, and she realized she had done this to him, caused him sorrow. She was responsible for this, not him. She wanted at that moment to reach out, but he would take it as an indication she wanted to stay. The words did not come. She sat across from him and crossed her legs. She had practiced this conversation in her head for half the night, but suddenly she didn't know where to begin.

"I guess you need something," Francis said. "Somehow I don't think you came to tell me you love me."

She clenched her teeth, freshly determined to get this over with as quickly as possible. "I want my divorce. You can keep Douglas and let me have visitation rights."

His face immediately darkened. "You're a cold, selfish bitch. To be free is so important to you that you would discard another child. After what you did to Alexandra, I should have known you would be capable of this."

"Just give me the divorce," she pleaded.

"No."

"I'm pregnant, Francis. I'm carrying another man's child. How would that look in front of your high society friends?"

"You're lying," he said.

"No, I'm not. Would you like the name of my doctor?"

"That won't be necessary. Does the lieutenant know?"

She shook her head. "He's away on assignment. I only found out yesterday. You can't possibly want me now." If he took her back now, he would be taking John's child as well, and she could not imagine he would tolerate that.

"You underestimate me, my dear wife," Francis said softly. "It won't be as simple as that."

She waited.

"I'll let you choose your freedom," he said, his face dark and brooding. "You can have your divorce under these conditions: You will stay here through the rest of your pregnancy. You will not let John know about the baby. You will deliver the baby here, and sign the adoption papers giving that man's baby away."

"Francis, no!"

He continued coolly. "Once you have signed the adoption papers, I will sign the divorce papers."

"You criticize me for giving up Alexandra, and now you're asking me to give up this baby?" She could hardly believe even Francis could be this cruel.

"Your other option is to tell John Malloy that your relationship is over. Come back here, and you and I will raise the baby as our own."

"That's mad, Francis! You can't be serious." Katarina lurched to her feet.

"Of course I can, and I am. It's your choice."

Her hand came to her mouth as she stifled a scream before picking up a vase and throwing it at the wall behind him.

Amused, Francis sprang from his chair, knocking it over, and strode across the room and locked the door. Katarina backed toward the wall, knowing what Francis planned to do next. A few seconds later, he had her pressed against the bookshelves, gripping her arms in his hands.

"Let go of me, you bastard." She struggled against his strength.

He just grinned. "You are still my wife. Can you honestly say your lover has satisfied you? He's a pathetic, lovesick fool who doesn't know what to do with a woman."

He bent to kiss her, and she bit his lip. In response, he shoved her to the floor and sprawled on top of her. Leering at her, he put a hand under her skirt and brought his mouth down on her again as his hand moved against her skin.

When he was finished, he left her there "to consider her options."

She had only one option. She had to get out—permanently, even if it could not be immediately. As she flew back to Oahu that night—without seeing Douglas—she knew she couldn't possibly live with Francis again, much less bring another child under his tyranny, a child he was sure to hate. But what would she say to John? He would be home in a week, and he would never stand for Francis's terms. After giving up

Alexandra, she was now giving up Douglas, too, leaving children behind like crumbs on a path.

Back at the cottage, she packed her things and gave immediate notice at the hotel.

She anguished over what she would say to John. Obviously she could not tell him she was pregnant; but what pretense could she give for moving back to Francis's home for the next five and half months? More sleepless nights passed as she tried out one scenario after another.

And then one night John called. His orders had changed. He would not be home for six months yet, and would probably not be able to call, but he promised to write often. She heard the despair in his voice, how much he missed her, how he would have said a real goodbye if he'd known he would be gone so long. Stifling her relief, Katarina promised she would wait for John and they would be together forever. He would never have to know about the baby. He wouldn't have to know she was living with Francis.

Perking up, she told him she was pretty sure she would have her divorce by the time he got back, and they could marry right away.

The next day she arranged to have her mail forwarded to a post office box in Kauai. She thanked Lydia for everything and simply said she was going away while John was gone, not telling a soul where she was going. Then she called Francis and told him to send the plane.

****

As she stood in the library again, she said, "I will put the baby up for adoption, and John will never know. I want the divorce papers signed the moment I hand over the baby. And you will not touch me while I am here. Do you agree to that?"

Francis's voice was strangled with emotion. "How many children are you going to leave behind? Alexandra? Douglas? This bastard baby? Don't your children mean anything to you?"

"You are the one who specified the terms, Francis. You gave me no more choice than the Nazi guards."

"How dare you compare me to those animals!"

"No one is going to control me ever again," she said through clenched teeth. "You win, Francis. But after this, I am free."

She pivoted on one foot, left the room, and climbed the stairs to see her son. She stroked her own belly on the way up the stairs. This was the first baby conceived with love and no ulterior motive. Both parents would have loved this baby. Alexandra and Douglas both entered the world under difficult circumstances, but this baby would have been different.

But it was not to be. She just had to get through the next five and half months.

Chapter 30

Kauai: May 1950

The weeks went by in a void. In spite of her ever-expanding abdomen, the rest of Katarina seemed to waste away. Her face grew haggard, and her hair lost its luster. At some point in every day, Katarina found herself in tears. She just wanted the pregnancy to end so she could escape from this place and its heartache. But every day closer to the birth also carried her closer to permanent separation from Douglas.

Katarina shared Francis's bedroom under her terms, but most nights he did not come to bed until very late. She knew where he'd been—with Maria, of course—but she didn't care. In fact, she was glad. The more satisfied Maria kept him, the less likely he was to break his promise not to touch her. Her dismal sleeping patterns returned, and Francis found her at odd times in odd places.

"Come into the house, Katarina," he said one night at the end of the first month, when he found her once again in the garden at two in the morning. "You've been out here every night for the last two weeks."

She knew he was coming from Maria's. "Please just let me leave. Let me take Douglas and this baby and leave. I won't ask you for anything."

He sat next to her on the bench, causing her to

shrink away visibly. "You made your choice, Katarina. I told you we could raise this child together. There's no need to lose either Douglas or the baby."

"Your compulsion to control is sickening!" She raised herself off the bench. "Why would you want this child? Why would you want me when you know I don't love you—and you love Maria?"

"I've told you many times, Maria is nothing. Didn't you ever love me, even for a moment?"

Katarina's bottom lip quivered. "I thought I might, at one time. I certainly never wanted to hurt you."

"Yet here we are."

"You suffocate me, Francis! Why can't you understand that? I'm not a trophy for you to display at your pleasure. Besides, your son is what really mattered to you. If I'd given you a daughter, we might not even be here now."

He stood, enraged. "How dare you say such a thing about me! You used your pregnancy to marry me and find a way out of Berlin. I loved you, so I didn't care. But I don't think you've ever loved anyone, not even your own children."

"That's not true!" she cried. "I do love Douglas. Please don't force me to give up my children for my freedom! If you've ever loved me, you won't do this."

"Don't give me ultimatums, Katarina," Francis said coldly. "You're in no position to do that."

Katarina sighed heavily. "Then let me leave, alone. You keep Douglas. Just let me leave with the baby."

"No deals. I gave you the terms, and you agreed."

"You bastard!" she screamed.

He walked off without looking back.

****

Letters from John came regularly. Katarina knew Francis had made sure she could not leave the island by boat or by plane. Since she was captive, he seemed not to mind if she took a car into town every now and then under the pretense of shopping. Usually she came back with clothing or toys for Douglas, and in her purse letters from the post office box. She savored every one, and wrote back fastidiously, spinning a web through the weeks about progress toward a divorce. The lawyers had drawn up the papers, she wrote. She and Francis had come to terms, she wrote. It would be final before John came home, she promised. Eventually she told him she was spending some time at Francis's home as one of the conditions of the divorce, but she swore her love for John. In the end she poured out her grief that Francis would probably never let her see Douglas again once they divorced.

The time came sooner than she expected, almost three weeks early. Katarina was picking at a breakfast of sweet muffins and eggs on the terrace when time seemed to stop and the pain took her breath away. Her water broke only a few minutes after the first contraction, and Katarina felt herself sliding out of the chair as she called feebly for help.

She heard voices and saw faces swimming above her, all jumbled together. Then she felt Francis lifting her and carrying her into the house and telling someone to call for Doctor Anderson. The next few hours were a blur, till finally she heard a baby's shrill cry. As the doctor held the baby up, Katarina reached for the child. The doctor placed the baby girl in her arms, and Katarina pressed her hot cheek against the little girl's as she murmured, "Your name is Rosemary, after your father's mother. That's what I want on your birth certificate."

When the doctor had finished, Francis motioned for the nurse to leave, as well, and moved closer to the bed. He could hear Katarina's murmurings.

"Sweet Rosemary, how warm your cheek is. Your little body is so plump." She rubbed the soft strawberry blonde hair as she glanced up at Francis. "I don't remember Alexandra's baby hair, or even Douglas's." Tears sprang out of her eyes. "Please, Francis, I beg you. Don't make me send her away."

He allowed her two days with the baby. Katarina knew he hoped she would change her mind about leaving if she felt close enough to the baby. She was not changing her mind, but she was determined to savor every tearful moment with Rosemary. She tried desperately not to think about her first daughter and the horrors surrounding her birth. She blocked out memories of Douglas's arrival. But instead of feeling stronger as the time passed, Katarina's temperature began to climb. She was bleeding too heavily, and she had to surrender the baby to someone else's arms as she slid into near unconsciousness. She barely heard Francis bark the order to send for the doctor again.

When she finally roused, she knew that days had passed. Only a nurse sat by the side of her bed. There had been times she would open her eyes and Francis was holding her hand, wiping her forehead with a cool cloth.

Sometimes she thought she had heard him saying he loved her more than life itself, and she saw the slow tears fall from his eyes. She could feel his tears on her hand as he held it, and at one point her hand rested on his head before she drifted back into sleep.

"My baby," Katarina muttered now. "Please bring me my baby."

The nurse shook her head. "I'm sorry."

Katarina turned her head and closed her eyes. Rosemary was gone forever, and she hadn't even been able to say goodbye. When Francis entered the room, she pushed herself up on her elbows and glared at him. "How could you? How could you do this to me?"

Francis simply laid some papers on the table next to the bed. "I've already signed," he said. "Just sign the papers, and you are free when you are well enough to go."

She had seen the unsigned papers earlier and knew they specified that she would never seek custody or make contact with Douglas again.

Katarina had to ask. "What happened to Rosemary?"

"She went to a good family. Don't worry about her."

"Can't I know where she is?"

"For what purpose, Katarina? You're not going to tell John, I'm sure." He left the room, and she signed the papers.

Two days later, she was determined to get out of that house. Doctor Anderson advised a few weeks of recovery after the crisis she'd been through, but Katarina couldn't stand to be under Francis's roof a minute longer than necessary. She called Lydia and arranged to return to the beach house. Her friend would only know that she had been ill. John would be home soon, and Katarina intended to be waiting for him right where he had left her.

Francis took her to the airport himself. She gave Douglas a huge hug and told him she loved him, but she didn't look back even when she heard him crying for her. She now saw she was no different from Helena. At the last second, Francis caught her hand.

"It's not too late," he said. "I haven't sent the papers to the lawyer yet. I will hold them until you get on the plane. You can still change your mind."

She looked into his tear-filled eyes; he was heartbroken. She didn't want to do this to him, and just for a moment her heart melted. Maybe it would be better to stay. But then she pulled her hand away. She heard Douglas calling to her and crying, and she shut the sounds out as she turned and walked toward the plane.

Francis felt as though someone had hit him in the stomach. He had never known such pain could exist in losing someone, but he still had his son… He kissed the boy's cheek and watched her leave.

Katarina boarded the airplane. John was her new life—her only life, the only freedom she had known since childhood, before the Nazis rose to power. John would never know.

Freedom. Life.

Love at last.

Epilogue

After my parents married, they lived in California, a long way from Hawaii. A lifetime away. My mother's lifetime. I'd like to say it was happily ever after, but that would be another lie. They'd married quickly and idealistically, after all, and that only goes so far when someone has the sort of life my mother had.

This is a book of fiction based on a true story. I tried to keep as much of the truth in it as I could find, although some dates and names have been changed at the request of persons involved.

When I finished writing about my mother's life, I kept the manuscript in a box till I married my husband, Loyd. When he saw it, he encouraged me to get it into the computer, and together we worked on the editing— he was my comma king. Many people have encouraged me and helped get this story published: Ed; Sarah; Rod; Angela; Pollingers; Brights; Neals; Littletons; Travis, my computer king; Verna, who tried hard to get it out at the start to all the agents; Camilla Wray, an exceptional agent, who gave me the best advice and encouragement and told me to keep getting it out there. Thanks to them and a lot of prayers to my God, I have learned never to give up. I just had to wait till it was my time.

I hope someday I will be able to tell more of Katarina's story, about her children, and her work that continued all over Europe with Grigory in her relentless wish to find those who had hurt her. In the second half of her life, what did she become? And how did her children fare? How did they learn of her, those too young to remember her at all and those old enough but left behind? Did they ever find one another? The secrets, lies, and loves of Katarina Von Rahmel Malloy—did she ever find peace? Ever let go of the memories and nightmares?

A word from the author...

I have spent most of my life between Europe and the United States. Born in California, my early years were as a Navy brat there and in Hawaii, followed by private school in Europe. Being a flight attendant for thirty-four years gave me the opportunity to do research and to speak with people to produce this book.

My college and work years were centered on the East Coast till I moved with my husband to the Hill Country of Texas, where I now live with nature, ranches, and assorted animals, including wonderful horses and rescued dogs and cats.

Thank you for purchasing
this publication of The Wild Rose Press, Inc.

If you enjoyed the story, we would appreciate your
letting others know by leaving a review.

For other wonderful stories,
please visit our on-line bookstore at
www.thewildrosepress.com.

For questions or more information
contact us at
info@thewildrosepress.com.

The Wild Rose Press, Inc.
www.thewildrosepress.com

Stay current with The Wild Rose Press, Inc.

Like us on Facebook

https://www.facebook.com/TheWildRosePress

And Follow us on Twitter
https://twitter.com/WildRosePress